The Arrangement

by Felice Stevens

The Arrangement
July 2016

Copyright © 2016 by Felice Stevens
Print Edition

Cover Art by: Reese Dante
www.reesedante.com
Cover Photography by Alejandro Caspe
Edited by Keren Reed
Copyediting and Proofreading services provided by Flat Earth Editing
www.flatearthediting.com

All rights reserved

No part of this book may be reproduced or transmitted in any form or by any means, electronic or mechanical, including photocopying, recording, or by any information storage and retrieval system, without written permission from Felice Stevens at www.felicestevens.com.

Published in the United States of America

This is a work of fiction. Any resemblance to persons living or dead is entirely coincidental.

Carter Haywood lives for the weekends, specifically the one weekend every month when he escapes real life, with all the pressures of work and caring for his special-needs brother, to do whatever he wants, with whomever he wants. Sex is only a release; he's not looking for love, a relationship, or even a second night with the same man, until he walks into a bar and finds someone who makes leaving it all behind impossible. After one incredibly passionate encounter, he breaks his rule and goes back. He needs to see this man again. And again.

Damaged goods. That's all Reed Kincaide sees and hears when he looks in the mirror. Anxiety and ADHD define his life, and he's learned to keep people at a distance, never letting them get close enough to know who he really is. When Carter proposes a monthly weekend of sex without strings, it's the ideal arrangement for him. Or so he thinks. Every month, leaving Carter proves to be more and more difficult. It's not only the intensely hot sex they have in their hotel suite; Reed wonders about the secret life Carter refuses to share. As months pass and they grow closer Reed finds himself falling for Carter, but he needs more than hurried hugs and farewell kisses. He wants it all.

Letting Reed into his carefully constructed family life could upset Carter's whole world, but it might be the risk he's finally willing to take if it means keeping Reed. Once bodies are engaged, the heart is sure to follow, and Carter and Reed discover that holding on to each other is the first step in letting go of the past.

Dedication

To my children who keep me in check, every day

Acknowledgments

Thank you to my editor, Keren Reed for all her hard work. To Hope and Jessica from Flat Earth Editing, you guys are great, even if you do make me put glasses on the table and not on the floor. To Dianne Thies, thank you for being there and obsessing with me. Thanks to Carroll Poe and S.c. Wynne for keeping me sane, sort of. And to the readers, especially those in my reader group, Felice's Fierce Fans, you guys continue to inspire me. Especially with your pictures of Carter Dane.

Subscribe to my newsletter and receive exclusive content, chances at giveaways and sneak peeks at works in progress and what's coming up in the months ahead! No spam, ever!
bit.ly/FeliceNewsletter

Chapter One

"COME ON, JACKSON, you know it's only for a few days. I'll be back late Sunday night."

Carter Haywood kneeled on the front stoop of the house he shared with his ten-year-old half-brother and forced a smile. As he did every month, Carter wrestled with his guilt and wondered if he was being selfish by leaving for the weekend. He loved his little brother dearly, and where most of his acquaintances spent their nights and weekends either hooking up at bars if they were single or being all domesticated and cute if they were married, Carter went straight home and did homework, worked on therapy exercises, and before he fell asleep, jerked off to nameless, sometimes even faceless guys whose profiles he saw online.

With certainty, Carter knew if he didn't get away on these monthly jaunts, the pressure of not only his job, but being the sole caretaker of a child with special needs would consume him, and he might end up resentful and angry. Carter had precious little time to call his own. Not to mention it was the only opportunity he had carved out for actual physical sex with a person instead of his hand. And tonight would have to be the only night this weekend for fun and games, as he had a charity function on Saturday night that as a board member, he had to attend. Alone.

Sex with whatever man he'd find this weekend was the furthest thing from Carter's mind at the moment, with Jackson's soulful gray eyes gazing up at him, glittering with unshed tears. Carter felt like an absolute shit and was about to say *fuck it*, and stay, when Helen, knowing how he tortured himself every month, took control and said in her most cheerful voice, "Jackson will have the best time this weekend. After therapy tomorrow we're going to go to the Hall of Science, right?" With genuine fondness, she placed her hands on Jacks's shoulders and gave him a gentle squeeze.

In a flash, Jackson's mood shifted, and his face lit up. "Yes."

Carter relaxed at his brother's spoken word. From the start, Jackson had been heartbreakingly silent, only occasionally verbalizing in school and at home. Recently, the paraprofessional who sat with Jacks during school reported he'd begun to participate in classroom discussion, and it gave Carter a little more positive reinforcement that all the therapy and help he'd given Jacks worked. And their neighbor Helen, a retired special education teacher, was probably the one person in the world he trusted to leave Jackson with.

"Go on, Carter. You know we'll be fine." Her reassuring smile took the edge off the constant worry that gnawed at him that no matter how much he did—the different therapies, the psychiatrist, the medications—it was never enough. That he wasn't equipped to handle a child with problems. The last thing he wanted to do was fail his brother; all they had was each other.

"I'll bring you back a present, Jacks. A surprise."

Carter wasn't certain Jackson always understood him, but by his bright smile and unexpected hug, he knew he'd been given the green light to leave. Swallowing down his emotions, he passed his hand over his eyes in an attempt to brush away the wetness and was met with Helen's tender look.

"I'll call you tonight and send you a video as usual. Maybe we'll make cookies; how about that, Jacks?" She deliberately turned them both away to head back inside the house as Carter juggled his garment bag and small overnight case and hurried down the steps to the black car idling at the curb. Traffic into the city on any night was a bitch, but on a Friday night it could actually take an hour from his house in Brooklyn to the hotel he always stayed at in Times Square.

"Sorry to make you wait, Harry, but we're ready to roll. I'm gonna take a nap."

"Go for it, Carter. I'll wake you up when we get there. Might as well rest up for the weekend."

What used to stir his blood in his mid-twenties didn't set him off now that he was thirty-two. Attracting guys had never been a problem for him; he'd been fucking guys since he was sixteen and walked in on Troy Latham jerking off in the shower after football practice. His dick hardened at the memory of Troy's wet lips sucking him off as hot water spilled down over them and him sinking into Troy's tight ass later on in the back seat of his car.

No, finding guys to fuck wasn't an issue. Over the years, it had been easy enough to walk away in the morning before the man had the chance to walk away from him. He'd learned long ago to hold on to that power; never let them see you cry or hurt. Never let them think you might care—it made you vulnerable, weak, and at risk. The problem was, how long could he go on taking one weekend a month to screw his brains out, leaving the rest of his life devoid of human touch?

Yet Carter smothered any thoughts of a relationship or even dating. He couldn't take the chance and disrupt Jackson's life by bringing a stranger into their little family unit. It had taken almost a year for Jacks to learn to trust him after their mother dumped him off and ran, and Carter wasn't about to jeopardize his young brother's health for a random piece of ass.

The car bumped its way onto the entrance ramp to the Brooklyn Bridge, and Carter slouched in the soft leather seat, the prospects of a nap long forgotten. In his twenties he'd been busy building up his business; he'd meet someone in a bar, and they'd hook up once, never twice. His schedule of late night meetings and constant travel precluded any serious dating. Then it seemed he blinked and here he was in his early thirties and alone.

His phone buzzed, and his lips curved in a smile when he saw Helen had uploaded a video of her and Jacks already making the promised cookies. How wrong he was—he wasn't alone. No matter how crappy a day he had, coming home to the innocence of his little brother always chased away the darkness inside, if only for a little while.

Harry pulled up in front of the hotel in Times Square, and Carter, still watching the video, opened the car door and absentmindedly said, "Good night, Harry. See you here on Sunday."

"Have a good one, Carter."

"You too."

Hefting his bags, Carter kept walking and watching the video. God knows, he didn't ever want kids of his own and barely tolerated other people's children, but when Jacks faced the camera and gave him a shy wave, Carter's heart seized up in his chest. He touched the screen as if it would bring him closer to the little boy he'd left behind.

Restless and edgy after checking in, Carter knew it was too early to go out, so he stripped and got into the shower. The hot water beating down on his tight shoulders achieved its desired effect; his muscles loosened and conversely his dick hardened. He might as well take the edge off now, Carter mused as he took himself in hand and with practiced strokes that had him quivering within minutes, brought himself to a climax onto the shower floor. His breath hitched in his throat, and he blinked several times to bring his surroundings back into focus. His strength sapped, Carter watched the running water mixed with his semen swirl down the drain.

A familiar lassitude stole through him, and Carter now craved that nap he didn't catch on the car ride over. After a quick soap and rinse off, he wrapped himself in the terrycloth robe kindly provided by the hotel, then lay down on the king-size bed and let sleep overtake him, wondering who'd be sharing the bed with him tonight.

Six hours later, Carter sat hunched over his drink at the last bar he planned on hitting up that evening. Although he'd danced and drank at several other places, no one had caught his eye long enough to make him look twice. This place wasn't a gay bar, but it happened to have an extremely good-looking male population, and Carter spotted some potential bed partners, including the sexy bartender he believed had been sending him signals, although he seemed delightfully shy about it. He liked the man's strong neck and full, plush lips and imagined them wrapped around his cock.

Noticing his glass was empty, Carter lifted it to catch the bartender's attention and winked when their eyes met. At the sight of the blush staining the bartender's face under the obligatory scruff, Carter surmised he might have found his playmate for the evening.

Carter's eyes narrowed in appreciation as he watched

the man approach him in skinny black jeans and a tight white T-shirt that clung to his muscular forearms and chest. Imagining this man on top of him in bed, sliding inside him, Carter nearly shivered in anticipation. His body pulsed with the familiar slow rise of hunger.

"Wow. Either you really want another drink, or…" The bartender quirked a brow. Carter wondered if he waxed or kept his natural happy trail down to his groin. Carter loved investigating that line of hair down a man's sculpted abs with his lips and tongue.

"Both." Carter flung a fifty on the bar. "I want another Grey Goose on the rocks now," said Carter, crooking his finger at the bartender, who sidled closer to hear what Carter had to say over the boom of the music. "And when I finish with the drink I want to take you back with me and drink you down."

Startled, the man ran his hand through the golden-brown waves tumbling over his forehead and gave a shaky laugh. "That's crazy. You're not serious." At the sight of Carter's unsmiling face, he swallowed hard. "You are serious. Shit, I can't—"

"You can do anything you want." Carter gripped the man's wrist, then slowly rubbed the pad of his thumb up and down the underside of his arm. Almost immediately the man responded, his amber eyes shooting off fiery sparks of gold. Carter pulled him closer, and the man yielded until he leaned over the bar and his lips came dangerously close to brushing Carter's. "What's your name?"

"Reed."

"Well, Reed," said Carter, pausing to lick his lips and in the process touching Reed's pouty bottom lip with his tongue. "What do you say?"

Almost laughing at the dazed expression of lust in Reed's eyes, Carter took a chance and kissed him, sucking that plush lower lip inside his mouth. Reed rewarded him with a moan of pleasure so deep and guttural, Carter almost climaxed in his pants.

When they finally broke apart, Carter made sure to keep a tight hold of Reed's wrist. "So? Are you coming with me?" Out of every man he'd seen tonight, Carter wanted Reed with an urgency he hadn't anticipated. There was nothing extraordinary to set him apart from the other good-looking men standing about the bar. Yet Carter couldn't let go of his wrist, and even now, with his heart still stuttering and Reed regaining his composure, Carter wanted to kiss him until the rest of the world spun away, rendering them both senseless again.

"Um." Reed consulted his watch. "My shift doesn't end for another hour."

"I'll wait," said Carter without hesitation. "And I'll take that Grey Goose now." He stroked Reed's fine, thin skin. "But with a twist this time."

Reed's eyes widened, and his nostrils flared. Unconsciously he leaned forward and triumph surged through Carter.

Yeah, that's right, baby. Smell me; you know you want it. Carter quirked a brow, and Reed jerked back to awareness and pulled his arm away. Shooting Carter frequent dubious looks, Reed made him his drink and proceeded to set it on the bar quick enough that Carter couldn't make a grab at him again. He backed away and began to twist at the cords of his leather bracelet.

Chuckling to himself, Carter sat there for the next hour and sipped his drink, getting just the right buzz on to the point where he could forget everything else in his life except the man who'd be coming back to his room tonight with him.

He looked up from his now-empty glass to find Reed standing beside him, wearing a beat-up leather jacket. "I-I'm finished with my shift now, but I'm not sure—"

"Not sure about what?" Carter stood and slipped his arm around Reed's waist, inside his jacket. His warmth enveloped Carter, and strangely enough, he wanted desperately to sink into Reed's arms. Reed tensed, and Carter felt the flex and play of his muscles underneath his clothing.

"I want you, you know that. And you want me too; it's obvious. It's only sex."

"Yeah, I know that, but still." Reed chewed his lip, suddenly looking very young and vulnerable, and an uneasy thought crept into Carter's mind.

"How old are you?" Carter asked and held his breath.

"Twenty-seven. I know I look younger, but…"

Relief poured through Carter. A nervous lover he

could handle. Still holding Reed around his waist, Carter moved even closer, fitting their hips together, letting Reed feel the weight of his arousal through his jeans.

"I want you to fuck me," he whispered into the startled man's ear. "Make me scream." He bit Reed's earlobe, and that gasping groan was the only sound playing in his universe. "And then I'm going to do the same to you." Reed sagged in his arms, and Carter laughed his victory into Reed's curls. "Let's go."

The two of them threaded their way through the crowd, Carter keeping a strong hold on Reed. It seemed his chosen companion for the evening proved very popular, and Carter noticed more than one man shooting him envious looks.

That's right; he's mine. Look but no touch.

Yellow cabs idled outside, waiting for the outpouring of customers exiting the bar. Carter opened the door to one, pushed Reed inside, and followed him, squashing him up against the far door.

"The West Hotel, Times Square."

The cab lurched forward, and Carter used the opportunity to cage Reed between his arms and kiss him until his head swam. This part of the game, learning the other man's mouth and tongue, was Carter's favorite part of foreplay, and he took advantage of the short traffic jam to cup Reed's face in the palms of his hands and deepen his kiss.

What he didn't expect was the intensity of Reed's

response—hesitant at first, then a shift toward acceptance where their tongues slid together. Their mouths slanted across each other, feeding off a mutual need to taste and possess. The softness of Reed's lips intoxicated, his warm, heady scent aroused him to an almost feverish excitement, and Carter found himself drowning in a desire so thick and overpowering he nearly stopped breathing.

Only the jerk of the cab stopping brought Carter back to reality.

"Yo. We're here, buddy."

The fog of lust that addled his brain lifted, and Carter fumbled in his wallet for his credit card, then ran it through the machine. It didn't matter that he was in the back of a smelly New York cab. If he could've, he'd have remained there tasting Reed's lips all night.

He pulled Reed out of the cab, and with that same surprisingly protective arm clamped around Reed's waist as before, Carter strode to the elevator, his nerves buzzing with anticipation. His lips still tingled from their earlier kisses. Reed remained silent, his eyes wide with curiosity, taking everything in. He hadn't said a word since they left the bar.

The elevator whooshed up to his floor, and within moments they reached the door to his room. Carter swiped his card key, and they tumbled inside, ripping off shirts, pulling down zippers, and tugging off jeans and shoes until the clothes all lay in a pile at their feet. Neither of them had moved from the entrance, and

Carter, fully naked, plastered himself against an equally naked and fully aroused Reed. Carter's fingers curled against the doorframe, and he buried his face in the curve of Reed's neck.

"Fuck, I want you." It wasn't that he hadn't been with another man in a month. It was Reed. Carter wanted *him*. Now. The smoothness of Reed's skin, his thick cock pressing against Carter's, the feel of his stubble scratching and burning as their cheeks slid together amped up his arousal to the point where he was about to splinter apart. Helpless, he thrust his rigid cock against Reed's, shamelessly pinning him to the door until with a shuddering cry he came, spurting all over Reed's stomach.

To his surprise, Reed took him around the waist and led him farther inside the hushed room. The maid had been in and turned down the sheets, and in a corner a dim light glowed golden, casting shadows. Carter lay face down on the bed, his head turned to the side, watching Reed watch him.

"What do you want from me?"

Spreading his legs in a silent invitation, Carter kept his gaze on Reed's face and registered his surprise.

"Oh. I thought you were kidding before."

"I never kid. I don't have the time." With a tip of his head Carter indicated his duffel bag sitting on the floor next to the bed. "In the outside pocket are condoms and lube."

Somewhere in the distance, a radio played soft music, and Carter let the familiar, post-sex languor steal through his body. Reed gave him a hard look but said nothing; he reached over to unzip the pocket and pull out a box of condoms and a tube.

"I see you came prepared for the weekend."

"Yeah," said Carter, a mirthless smile thinning his lips. "I'm a real boy scout."

Reed put his knee on the bed and leaned over to kiss the back of Carter's neck. Within moments, Carter found himself unashamedly moaning and writhing beneath the efforts of Reed's eager and agile tongue as it left a warm, wet trail down his spine.

"Oh, fuck, that's good. Don't stop." His hands scrabbled at the sheets, twisting them into sweaty knots. Everything in Carter's mind—his home, his business, even Jacks—faded away as Reed's mouth licked, sucked, and nibbled at his quivering body.

"Please," he moaned. Carter hardly recognized that desperate and needy voice as his own, and was so far gone he didn't care. "Please." A ceiling of gold shimmered above him, growing brighter with each sweep of Reed's tongue. Reed's cool, slick fingers parted his ass, and a finger brushed his hole, then sank inside, working its way in and out. It was soon joined by another, and they both kept up a steady, pumping motion while his body hummed, on fire.

"Fucking hell," he cried out, his cock once again painfully hard. His ass was up in the air, his legs spread wide, and Carter opened himself with complete abandon as he worked himself on Reed's hand, uncaring how he might look. Sparks flew from that golden ceiling, and Carter trembled in anticipation of it shattering.

"No hell," whispered Reed in Carter's ear. "I'm about to take you to heaven."

Then he was empty and bereft, Reed having removed his fingers. Carter wanted to protest, wanted to be filled again, when the head of Reed's cock pushed into his hole.

"Uhh." He grunted with the effort to relax. "Fucking shove it in me. I want it all." It was as if knowing he only had tonight, Carter wanted it as hard and fast as he could, to wring as much pleasure out of his body as possible before he had to shutter it all down for another four weeks of darkness.

If he thought Reed was about to listen to his demands though, Carter was mistaken. Reed pulled him on his knees to the edge of the bed while he stood and fit his body to the curve of Carter's back. Their torsos pressed close, and with his arm firmly wrapped around Carter's chest, Reed began a slow, sensual rocking motion, his thick cock sliding inside Carter's body, deep and strong. A wave of hunger, incredible in its neediness, rose within him to be taken, and Carter leaned back against Reed, blindly searching for his mouth. With a strong hand on Carter's face, Reed took his lips in a bruising kiss while his other hand slid down to grab hold of Carter's now-straining cock.

They kept up that rocking, sliding, stroking motion, Carter trembling with the effort of holding himself together until that golden ceiling eclipsed, showering bright shards of light behind Carter's eyes. He came again, though it was a much sweeter, less fiery release. Reed lasted only moments longer, pumping hard, coming hot and heavy inside the condom, sobbing out his climax as he collapsed on top of Carter, pushing him face down on the bed.

They lay together, the sweat on their drenched bodies drying off in the air-conditioned cool of the room, and Carter found himself dozing once again, drained from the emotions of the day and the incredible sex he'd experienced. Reed pulled out of him, and with one eye cracked open, Carter tracked him as he tossed the used condom in the trash, then went to the bathroom. He heard the sound of the toilet flush and water run, and he used the last of his strength to wiggle under the covers. For a moment he considered asking Reed to stay, but that would get awkward in the morning. Besides, Jacks always got up early, and they had breakfast together over Skype.

"Make sure when you leave that the door shuts behind you. Thanks for everything."

He closed his eyes and drifted off to sleep.

Chapter Two

"THANKS FOR EVERYTHING," mumbled Reed as he wiped down the bar. "Like I was the maid delivering towels." He flung the damp washcloth to the side, then immediately picked it up again and walked to the other side of the bar where he attacked that surface, rubbing it over and over again until the dark wood gleamed. He couldn't help it even though he knew it was a problem. Two weeks had gone by since that night, yet his dismissal, like he was the paid help, still rankled like a fresh bee sting.

And for the two weeks Reed had been jumpier than ever; his sleep was off, and he snapped at everyone at work. It had been years since he'd been this anxious and off-center, and he couldn't take it anymore.

"Can I take a five-minute break?" he asked Vernon, the owner. "I gotta make a call real quick."

"Yeah, don't worry about it. It's Wednesday afternoon; no one's drinking yet 'cept Jimmy, and he don't need nothin'." Vernon joined their regular customer, Jimmy, and sat down to listen to his old friend's latest complaint against his ex-wife.

Left alone, Reed pulled out his phone, thought a moment, then finally worked up the courage to call his doctor and confess what he'd done. Luckily she wasn't with a patient and came to the phone immediately. Hesitant at first, he explained what happened and what he'd been feeling.

"Don't be so hard on yourself. It wasn't the wisest move on your part, but I'm assuming you used protection?"

"Yeah, we did," he said, the hot flush of embarrassment heating his cheeks. Sex wasn't something he talked about with anyone; it was something he just did. And not that often. When he was a teenager his hyper behavior put off a lot of kids in school, and being gay didn't help much either. The girls all thought that meant he automatically liked shopping and wanted to be their best friend, and the few guys he knew who were gay had no interest in his friendship. Almost everything he learned was through the internet until he went away to college and started meeting guys who were more than happy to teach him in person.

"Are you upset about it? He didn't hurt you, did he?" Dr. Childs' voice changed from warmly sympathetic to sharply concerned.

"No, not at all. I mean, not unless you consider my pride. I'm upset with myself for letting him talk me into going back to his hotel room with him. Anything could have happened. I'm not usually that stupid." He tucked the phone under his ear and played with his bracelet. The soothing, repetitive movement helped calm his nerves somewhat.

"Well, sometimes we get caught up in the emotions of the moment, and we forget to think with our head and go with our heart instead. You can come in if you want, but try to learn from the experience. Sex isn't wrong, and if I'm not mistaken, it sounds like you liked this man, otherwise you would have forgotten about him already. Am I wrong?"

"Maybe. I'm so confused. I don't know if it's because I haven't been in a relationship in so long or because I was lonely and let him take advantage of me. I didn't feel this way at the time, but now I'm all panicky about it."

"If he comes in again—"

"I doubt it. This had one-night stand written all over it. And it's been two weeks and he hasn't come back."

"But if he does," she said—and Reed had heard that tone before from her; it was the sit-up-and-listen-I'm-giving-you-advice-you-need-to-take voice—"and you find yourself still attracted to him, there's nothing wrong with acting on those feelings, with the caveat to take it a bit slower."

"Thanks, Dr. Childs."

It had been smart to call. He had nothing to feel guilty about that night; it wasn't anything different than what he'd heard so many people talk about in school.

Hooking up and finding comfort shouldn't make a person feel bad about themselves. The problem, as he saw it, was if the man returned, Reed wasn't so certain he'd be able to resist him.

Drumming his fingers on top of the bar, Reed first focused on calming his runaway thoughts. Once he'd been diagnosed, the doctors had told him to find a way to center his thoughts and gain control of the anxiety that threatened to cripple him. Coupled with his ADHD that made it hard for him to focus for long periods of time, Reed often felt his life stretched out before him as a road full of obstacles, winding on forever but leading him nowhere. Learning to manage what he could and couldn't do was a way for him to control all the thoughts flying by in his head. Oftentimes he'd want to give up and simply cry.

He'd learned over the years and with hundreds of hours of therapy to channel his energy into being productive. He took painting and drawing lessons when he was younger and filled his house with his creations. After college he took a bartending course and found even with the pressure, the high-energy, fast-paced work fed into his need to keep busy. Despite everything, Reed never overcame his loneliness or the feeling he'd never measure up and never be in control over what happened in his life. Life happened to him.

Being in that hotel room two weeks ago proved his point. He may have topped that man, but Reed was not in control that night.

"You're an asshole," he said to himself.

"Now I *know* you're not talking to me."

At the sound of his father's voice, Reed couldn't help but smile. "Hi, Dad, what're you doing here?"

"I was in the neighborhood and thought I'd stop by, have a drink, and see my favorite son."

Sunlight shone off his father's salt-and-pepper curls. He and his father shared the same straight, strong nose, rangy build, and amber eyes, so Reed had a pretty good idea of what he was going to look like when he got older. Except his father's nature was calm to Reed's inner storm.

"The neighborhood, huh? I didn't know they'd transplanted Brooklyn to Times Square." Reed placed a glass of 7&7 and a ceramic bowl of salty peanuts and pretzels in front of his father. "And thanks for the title of favorite son, especially when I'm the only son you have."

His father waved his hand in the air. "A mere technicality, I assure you."

They shared a laugh, and Reed began to polish the glasses with a clean cloth. The other bartenders hated doing that job, but for Reed it fed his internal demand for repetitive activity and the drive to constantly keep busy.

"How's school coming?"

"Great. I knew spending summers working in the big hotels in Atlantic City would be beneficial. And here at this bar too; it's all part of my long-term plan to get a feel for the different skills I'd need."

Admiration shone from his father's eyes. "I'm so proud of you, Reed. You know exactly what you want to do, and nothing's going to stand in your way, is it?"

It wasn't like the two of them to get all emotional together. A lump rose in Reed's throat. "I learned from the best, you know? You gave everything to me and never let people tell you no."

His mother had bailed on their family after Reed was diagnosed early on with attention deficit hyperactivity disorder and anxiety, claiming she couldn't deal with the stress of caring for a "disabled" child. That bit of information had been gleaned from a letter he'd found one day, stuck in the back of a drawer he'd had trouble closing. Reed figured his father had tucked it away, hoping it would never see the light of day, yet keeping it as the final and only hand-written evidence that his mother actually existed. It had been hidden from sight, but from the well-worn creases, Reed imagined his father taking it out and reading it over the years, then sticking it back in its hiding place more determined than ever to make sure his son had the best life possible, despite his problems. To this day, Reed hugged his discovery to himself and never mentioned finding that letter to his father.

Determined to see him succeed and not be labeled and pushed aside, his father had rolled up his sleeves, and he and Reed did everything together, including school plays, bake sales, and helping Reed get the doctors and therapy he needed.

"Are you dating anyone? Last you mentioned you were in a study group and there might be some guys there you might be interested in."

That may have been true a month ago, but they all paled in comparison to the stranger he'd had sex with that night. He was the only one on his mind now. There'd been several nights since then when Reed dreamed of making love to him, pushing inside the hot, velvety grasp of his smooth, round ass, and woken up, the dream so vividly real his body trembled on the brink of climax. In all his life he'd never allowed himself to do something so spontaneous, and talking to the doctor he'd now seen that while somewhat foolish, it was nothing to beat himself up over. Still, he couldn't get the man's darkly handsome face out of his mind and didn't know what he'd do if he ever saw him again.

"No, I'm not dating anyone. I decided to make the choice between dating and work, and work won. Plenty of time for a social life once I graduate."

Most of the time, he and his father agreed on things. From his father's frown though, Reed knew this wasn't one of them.

"I don't understand why you think you can't have both. You're young and should be out, living your life, not spending your days studying and nights working. You need some enjoyment. Go out and meet people."

"Because…" He clenched his hand into a fist and shook his head, unwilling to go into further depths.

"Can we not talk about this, please?"

His last boyfriend was back in college—he'd broken up with him over his ADHD, claiming he couldn't deal with someone who had a "mental problem." A part of Reed still hurt from the cruelty of those two words Mason had so casually flung at him while heading out the door. Stupidly, in an effort to prove he was normal and therefore good enough, he'd stopped taking his medication cold turkey and crashed about four days later. His sleep pattern became even more erratic, and he could barely concentrate on his schoolwork. Restless didn't begin to describe his emotional state. He'd pick things up and forget why and put them down, only to pick them up again a minute later.

Only when he came dangerously close to failing a midterm exam did Reed know he had to regain control over his increasingly fragile emotional state. He made the decision to confess all to his psychiatrist and restarted his medication, resigned to the fact it was a lifelong struggle he'd have to learn to deal with. For three years he'd managed, finishing college, finding a job and enrolling in the post-graduate hotel management program.

Now, when guys he met commented on his unflagging energy and late nights of studying, he'd brush it off with a laugh. Whatever restlessness he might still have, he worked off at the gym, and Reed could see the positive results. He'd never had muscles before, and it felt good to be strong, at least physically. He might draw a bit when he returned to his apartment after work or class, losing himself in his sketches. But never again would he entrust and reveal his emotional health to another person. That part of him was not for public consumption; he had no wish to be devastated like that again. Solitude was the safest course for him.

Left by his own mother and then by a man he thought he loved, Reed knew three strikes and he'd be out. However strong he might appear, he couldn't take another blow.

Giving him a long, hard look, his father took out his wallet, and Vernon yelled from down the bar, "Don't even think about it, Walter. I told you before, family discount is one hundred percent."

This was as close to a family as he had right now: his dad and these guys at the bar. Vernon was the only one at work he'd told about his ADHD because he randomly drug-tested all the employees. Reed didn't want his antianxiety meds to show up on the test and have Vernon think he was abusing drugs for school or worse. He made light of it and never let on how it controlled his life; Reed neither wanted nor needed pity, no matter how well intended. One day he planned to control his illness, not have it control him.

"I'm fine, Dad," he said quietly. "Really. Let me do what I have to do, the way I want."

"I always have, but it's hard to see you alone; you're such a people person. And I know what it's like to be alone for too long."

After he and Mason had broken up he told the whole miserable story to his father and received a stern lecture not only on wasting himself on someone so obviously self-centered, but also on the dangers of not taking his medicine. Reed had vowed to himself if it happened again he'd maintain his privacy and not tell his father, but then became anxious that he'd upset and disappoint him. It was a no-win situation for him, as usual.

"I wish you'd take your own advice then and date." For years after his mother left, his father concentrated so much on Reed and his issues, there was little time for anything or anyone else. Once he became a teenager and needed less supervision, Reed knew his father had dated several women, but nothing serious enough that Reed had ever met any of them.

"As a matter of fact, I have been seeing someone lately."

If his father was hoping for a reaction from him, he got one. Reed knew his mouth fell open in surprise.

"Really? Who is she? Why haven't you told me?"

And from his father's soft expression Reed instantly knew this woman meant something to him.

"I met Ariel at a cooking class I registered for about a month ago. We were stationed next to each other, and the next thing I knew we were having so much fun, the instructor got mad and told us to leave." He chuckled. "We ended up having dinner, and we've been dating ever since." He stood and slid his wallet back into his pocket.

"I'm thrilled for you, Dad. You deserve the best."

"So do you." The concerned expression returned to his father's face. "Don't think I'm going to stop worrying about you because I'm involved with someone. You're still taking your medicine, right?"

Jesus. He made one stupid mistake; when was his father going to stop being his keeper?

"I'm twenty-seven, Dad, not seven. I don't need you checking up on me."

"I don't want you thinking—"

"I know, I know. I'm taking it, okay? I'll always need to take it." Reed could hear the frustration and anger in his voice, and while he didn't want to direct it at his father, whom he loved more than anything, the well overflowed. "You don't need to remind me I'll never grow out of it. I remember what happened when I stopped. I crashed and almost had a breakdown. But I'm stronger now, mentally and physically. I'm never going to let anything or anyone hurt me like that again, so stop worrying about me and treating me like a child, okay?"

Breathing heavily, Reed's heart squeezed from the distress on his father's face, yet he owed him the truth. He'd never given him anything less.

"How long have you waited for a chance to tell me that?"

No condemnation, only concern. And that made Reed feel even guiltier.

"A while," he admitted.

"Good. You shouldn't hold your feelings in. It's not a good thing for you." His father shot him a look. "Or anyone."

It seemed it was a time for confessions, so Reed decided to be candid. "You as well. I'm glad you've met someone. But you held back all these years because of me. It's your time now."

A warm hand covered his own, and Reed remembered his childhood and always having that strength to lean on.

"I'll never stop worrying about you, Reed. It's what a parent does. Once you love someone with all your heart, you never stop caring."

Swallowing past the lump in his throat, Reed gave his father a tremulous smile. "I'll talk to you later."

Watching his father walk away, his words played over in Reed's head, and he wondered if his father had ever stopped caring about his mother.

TWO MORE WEEKS passed, and Reed had all but forgotten the stranger from the hotel room. He'd joined his father and Ariel several times for dinner and was thrilled to see she was as into his father as his father was into her. After so many years alone, thinking only about Reed, his father deserved for once to put himself first.

Midterms had come and gone, and Reed was waiting for exam results in his final two classes; every buzz of his phone set his heart racing in case it was a grade. His scholarship money rested on remaining in the top third of his class, and while he'd done well in his other three classes, pride in himself and his work had him teetering on a tightrope of stress. At Dr. Childs' urging he tried yoga and meditation to calm his nerves, but while he enjoyed the stretching and quiet music playing in the background, his mind raced and he couldn't concentrate the way everyone else did in the class, so he dropped it.

When Vernon had asked him to take on a few extra shifts he'd jumped at it, eager to fill his evenings. School was on break, and he had no plans; he'd heard his classmates discussing trips, and though he wasn't exactly envious, it would have been nice to have someplace to go.

Or someone to be with, a little voice whispered in his ear.

Every night the bar was packed with college and grad students looking for easy hook-ups, and Reed turned down more offers than he could keep track of for quickies and blowjobs from men and women alike. Every advance was met with an easygoing smile and a shake of his head. No matter how lonely he was, going home to his silent apartment was always the wiser, safer choice.

The start of the weekend brought out the partiers in droves, but tonight Reed was at the far end of the bar with his back to everyone, figures dancing in his head, helping Vernon with the management end of the business rather than bartending.

"Hey, Reed."

He put a finger up; he was in the middle of counting the remaining bottles of beer to see if Vernon should order more and didn't want to lose his place.

"Wait a minute. I'll be finished in a sec."

The music pounded, and Reed bounced on his toes in time with the beat as he finished writing the numbers in the bound composition book Vernon insisted on, instead of the computer Reed tried unsuccessfully to get him to use. With that boring chore finished, he turned around to see who called his name.

"Yeah, wha..." His voice trailed off at the sight of the man he had sex with a month ago. His hair had been cut a bit shorter, but Reed would know those piercing, light-gray eyes anywhere. They beckoned. And Reed ignored everything he had worked out in his head this past month and walked over to join him at the bar, pulling and twisting at his bracelet. Realizing what he was doing, he immediately stopped and clasped his shaking hands together.

"What's your name?" Reed refused to keep thinking of him as "the man he had sex with."

"You don't remember?" He seemed a bit put out by the question.

"You never told me."

A light dawned in the man's eyes. "Oh, yeah. I guess we were too busy." His sensuous lips curved in a slightly evil yet incredibly sexy smile, and Reed once again felt that inexplicable tug of lust in the pit of his stomach. "Want to get busy again?"

Reed's mouth dried at the blatant invitation, but this time he'd had a month to prepare himself. "No, I don't think so."

The man visibly startled, and his jaw flexed; he gripped the glass in front of him tighter. "Why not? You can't tell me we didn't have fun."

The safety of the bar provided Reed with a bulwark to resist, and yet he took a step back in retreat. "I'm not interested in fun. I'm too busy right now."

"Everyone's busy; we all have responsibilities." For a moment he gazed unseeing into his glass of vodka, then gave a sly glance up. "Carter."

Huh? "I don't understand," said Reed warily, half expecting the man to grab him again like last time.

Half hoping he might.

"My name. It's Carter. Carter Haywood. Now will you come back with me tonight?" That inviting, enticing smile presented itself again.

"You're crazy." Laughing to himself and shaking his head at Carter's pushy, insistent behavior, Reed turned his back and walked away.

"You can run from me, but you can't hide." Carter raised his voice above the music. "I'll be here all night, waiting."

With a casual wave of his hand he hoped hid his rattled nerves, Reed feigned nonchalance and went to tally up the night's receipts. It was close to nine p.m., and the bar didn't close until two a.m., so it was a premature task at best, but Reed needed to collect his thoughts, and that meant removing himself from Carter's disturbing presence. It was so easy to brush off the other sexual advances from customers without a second thought—why couldn't he do the same with Carter?

Because you want him, that little voice inside him whispered. *You don't always get to pick who crawls beneath your skin and turns you on. It happens.*

And Carter happened to push all his buttons despite Reed's self-awareness that sex with a stranger wasn't his norm. He believed in getting to know a person first and spending time together before getting physical. Frustrated with his rational head warring with his suddenly enlivened libido and emotions he normally managed to keep under control welling up in his chest, he knew he was on the verge of a full-blown panic attack. He needed to get out, away from the bar for a moment.

"Damn it." He banged his fist on the register. "Clay, I'm going out back for a minute."

"Sure." The second bartender shot him a worried glance. "You okay?"

The noise in his head hit him from all sides, buffeting him back and forth until he didn't know where he was going, only that it needed to be away from where he was. Without answering, he ran through the back office and out into the alley behind the bar.

Damp with sweat and shaking, Reed bent at the waist, drawing in huge gulps of the cool night air. Shit. He hadn't had a panic attack like this in years, and it fucking scared him to death. And even as he wondered why it happened, he knew the answer. Carter. It was him, with that confident, sexy swagger, showing the world he didn't have a care or problem. Coming back to the bar after a month, right after Reed had kicked him out of his mind, Carter blindsided him, unraveling the frayed seams of his tightly wrapped psyche.

"Fucking asshole, get a grip." Reed fisted his hands and squeezed his eyes shut against the sting of tears. The curse of his overly emotional state struck with full force, another by-product of this illness he hated, controlling his life.

A touch on his shoulder caused him to stiffen.

"Are you all right?"

Shit. Fuck. Damn. Why the hell did he come out here?

"I'm fine." Reed drew in a shaky breath, trying to get a handle on his swirling thoughts. "What are you doing out here, anyway? How did you get behind the bar to come back here? You're not allowed."

Carter's strong arms pulled him around until they faced each other, and though Reed could see the concern in Carter's face, he also noticed other things. Like the laugh lines crinkling out from the corner of his silvery eyes, or the way his lips curved up more on one side than the other, giving him a crooked, endearing smile.

"Says who?" That lazy grin deepened. "I don't like people telling me I can't do something. Makes me cranky." He nuzzled against Reed's neck, the scent of his warm skin flooding Reed's senses, and to his despair his body responded.

Fighting the heated desire rising through him, Reed attempted a laugh that came out harsh and choked to his ears. "You always seem cranky." Carter thwarted his attempt to pull away by holding him even tighter.

Humming deep in his chest as he drew his nose across Reed's jaw, Carter's hand skimmed lightly down his back, and despite his promise to remain strong, Reed's vibrating body arched into Carter's touch.

"That's 'cause you keep saying no to me when you know you want me. As much as I want you."

Reed slid his hands up Carter's chest, ostensibly to push him away, yet he found himself unable to do so.

"This is crazy. You can't show up here after a month and assume I'm going to have sex with you." Yet even as he spoke, Reed sensed himself yielding to Carter, his body betraying the words even as they came out of his mouth. "I don't do this sort of thing."

"Why not?" Carter continued to hold him. "We're not young kids screwing in the bathroom, high on whatever or drunk. We use protection, and we know what we're doing from the start. If we're physically attracted to each other, it's the best thing. Sex without the hassle of a relationship. And you have to admit you're as hot for me as I am for you."

With that declaration, Carter kissed him, and Reed clung to his shoulders as if drowning, unable to contradict what he said. They did seem to have this crazy physical connection, and maybe what Carter said was true; a purely physical relationship was better than the emotional minefield of falling in love. All those thoughts spun in his mind as Carter took his face between the palms of his hands and proceeded to kiss him with such intensity Reed couldn't think of anything else at all after that, except how much he wanted another night with Carter.

Chapter Three

D AMN, HE'D ALMOST fucked up. Carter knew Reed wanted him; that wasn't the issue. Taking care of Jackson had attuned Carter to people's emotional states in a way they weren't aware, and he not only used it in business to close a deal, but to gauge the interest of the men he picked to hook up with.

In Reed's case, the man seemed skittish as a fawn taking his first steps, and Carter knew now to play the gentle, soft seducer, rather than ravage Reed's mouth, rendering him senseless like he wanted to, and dragging him back to the hotel. If after this conversation he could get Reed to come with him, he'd have him stay the night. It would necessitate him finding the proper place to have his morning breakfast call with Jacks, but the prospect of an entire night with Reed proved too enticing to ignore.

The one night they'd had together last month hadn't faded into oblivion like the other hook-ups he'd had over the years. Instead of becoming restless with his usual urges, the only man he wanted to see tonight was

Reed. Vividly erotic dreams had plagued him during the past few weeks, all of them involving him and Reed. He'd awaken, shaking and aroused, cursing himself for this strange obsession he'd acquired. He needed to see Reed again and hopefully get it out of his system.

Now, having Reed backed up against the brick wall of the building, his eyes hazy with desire, full mouth soft and temptingly open, Carter couldn't imagine forgetting anything about him. Carter groaned and covered Reed's lips again with his, kissing him, feeding off his hunger until the need to touch him crawled through his body and he was only moments away from ripping down the man's zipper and having him up against the wall, naked and hot in his hands.

Carter broke the kiss and stood over Reed, breathing hard. Reed opened his eyes and gave Carter a hesitant, shaky smile. "Um. Maybe you're right." He drew a hand through the waves of his hair, and Carter wondered about the texture—silky smooth or rough and curling? He couldn't recall and wanted the chance to rediscover.

"I am? I mean, yeah, I am." *Shit, get a grip.*

"So how do we, uh, do this?"

The wind grew stronger, finding its way through the thin shell of his jacket, and Carter shivered in the chill. He didn't relish the long, dark days of fall and winter to come. "First we go inside so I'm not freezing my ass off."

With a firm hold on Reed's elbow, Carter led him back to the bar, and he savored the overheated air wrapping around him. Once he sat down with a fresh iced vodka in front of him, Carter felt more in command, more like himself. Reed, stationed in his position behind the bar, gave him a wary glance but stood like a prisoner of war awaiting sentence.

A combination of vulnerability and passion simmered behind Reed's golden gaze, and recalling their incredible night together, Carter refused to think another man would touch Reed, kiss his mouth, and have their name on his lips. The only name Reed would call out in passion would be Carter's. One night together hadn't been enough to satisfy Carter, and he wanted, no, he *needed* more. He needed to be inside Reed. Their eyes locked, and Carter quivered as unfamiliar possessiveness seared through him. The deep earthy taste of Reed bloomed on his tongue, and the fire in his blood burned bright and sharp.

After taking a deep swallow of his drink, Carter gazed at Reed in contemplation, then ignoring all the rules, *his* rules, made a decision and leaned forward, resting his crossed arms on top of the bar. "We'll have an arrangement. It shouldn't be too difficult. I have obligations that keep me home except for one weekend per month. That's when we'll meet and spend our time together. Other than that…" He shrugged. "There's no real need for us to talk. We aren't dating or romantically involved. It's not even friends with benefits since we're not really friends." Carter narrowed his gaze. "What do you think? Can you handle it?"

As he spoke, Reed's eyes grew wider and wider, and Carter's heart sank. Even considering their night of amazing sex, Reed's inexperience showed, and what Carter proposed might be too much for him to handle. Reed might want love and that hearts-and-flowers shit. A relationship. Snorting inwardly, Carter took another drink. Relationships were nothing but another avenue for someone to disappoint him, and he'd had enough disappointments in his life.

"Yeah. I think it might be exactly what I need."

Coughing up his drink, Carter wiped his mouth on his sleeve. It took a moment to suck in enough air before he could answer. "It is?"

"Yeah."

"Yeah? You're sure?" The wheels were working in overdrive behind Reed's eyes; doubt, fear, lust, and excitement flashed in their golden depths.

"I go to school full-time and work here; I don't have time to think about relationships or lovers. They're not worth my time or effort."

Reed hesitated over the last part, and Carter sensed a story there, but it wasn't his business. There wasn't going to be any sharing of lives and cozy dinners for two.

"I think," Reed continued, "what you suggested will work for me. But I want certain things as well."

"Oh?" said Carter, his interest piqued. "Tell me."

"Last time after we…" He reddened and gnawed on his lip, and Carter thought he looked adorable in his effort to be discreet. And sexy. Actually Carter wanted him right then and wondered how soon Reed could leave so they could go back to his hotel room.

"Had sex?" Carter offered helpfully. "Fucked?"

"Shh." Reed hushed him, his eyes darting side to side. "People don't need to hear about my personal life." He leaned closer, and Carter enjoyed having his undivided attention. The smattering of freckles across his nose gave him a youthful appearance, and Carter noticed a ring of green around the rim of his golden eyes. Before he could stop himself Carter reached up and skimmed his fingertips over those freckles, watching the flush of desire rise in Reed's face.

"Carter, stop." Reed blinked and pulled away. "Last time you dismissed me like the maid when we were finished. If we're doing this, I deserve a full night."

"You can have the whole fucking weekend; how's that?" Carter stood and laid a twenty on the bar. "Are you ready to go? 'Cause I'm horny as hell and I'm all for starting the weekend right now."

Once again, Reed gave him that anxious stare, and Carter cocked his head. "Are you worried about something? You have the strangest look on your face."

Instantly Reed's eyes shuttered flat and a faint yet troubled smile tilted his lips for a moment. "No, I'm fine. I'm thinking about how soon I can get out of here without leaving them in a lurch."

"And that would be…" Carter quirked a brow. "As I see it, we have from now until around three p.m. on

Sunday when I go home. I intend to put that time to good use."

"Um, sure. I'm fine with that. But I need to get a change of clothes and stuff and get my schoolwork from my apartment. Maybe I can meet you back at your room?"

"Have you changed your mind and decided to bail?" It wouldn't surprise him, Carter realized. Reed's brain might have finally overtaken his libido and put the brakes on his unorthodox proposal. "Do you want to forget about it?"

"No, not at all."

The swift response brought a smile to Carter's face. "Good. Because I have plans for you. I'm not going to reveal what they are right now,"—he leaned forward again—"but I promise they're very dirty and involve getting naked and wet."

That glazed expression from their first meeting a month ago crossed Reed's face again, and Carter knew right then he had Reed hooked. He took out a pen and wrote his room number and full name on a napkin. "Here's my info. Whenever you're ready, come over." Without waiting for permission, he leaned over the bar and kissed Reed, once again falling into the sweetness of his lips and tongue. Hazily, he thought he could get used to this arrangement of theirs very easily with a man like Reed warming his cold hotel bed.

When he walked out of the bar he wondered if Reed's heart pounded as hard as his. Off-kilter, Carter decided to check on Jacks and make sure he was okay.

"Taxi." He stuck his hand out and jumped into the cab that immediately pulled up in front of him and gave the cabbie the name of the hotel. He pulled out his phone and called home.

"Carter, what's wrong?" The anxiety in Helen's voice rang clear.

"I was about to ask you the same thing. I had a funny feeling all of a sudden and needed to hear Jacks's voice. Is he around?"

"Of course." Her voice softened. "I think he misses you too. When we were doing his therapy today he pointed to the picture of the animals in the zoo and said, "I want to see that with Carter."

His stomach churned. Time and again, Carter kept wondering if he was being selfish in going away for even the once-a-month weekend and voiced his concerns to Helen.

"Does he seem upset that I'm not there? I don't want him to think I'm abandoning him. The doctor wasn't sure about his short-term memory, and if you think I should stay home—"

"Carter, stop."

He halted, a bit surprised at her cutting him off like that. "Yes?"

"I've seen how you are by the end of each month. You're so bottled up inside, you're ready to explode. No one can ever be there one hundred percent for another person, and it doesn't mean you don't love or care about him because you find the time for some self-care. You give everything to Jackson, so there's nothing left of yourself. I can only hope one day you'll meet someone—"

"No." Having heard this argument many times before, Carter smoothly interrupted her. "We've discussed this, and I'm grateful you're telling me Jacks is okay. I'll make sure next weekend we go to the zoo."

"I think he'd like that. Now here he is to say hello."

The cab sat stuck in a traffic jam only several blocks from his hotel, but Carter was grateful as it gave him quiet time with Jacks. It was only a little past nine p.m., Carter realized with a start. No wonder Reed couldn't leave the bar yet.

"Hey, Jacks, how's it going, buddy?"

He imagined Helen standing by Jacks's side with her warm, encouraging smile. The thought of losing her terrified him.

Carter could hear Jacks's breathing. "Hi. It's good."

He expelled the breath he was holding in a soft burst of air.

"I hear you liked the pictures of the animals in the zoo?"

When he first became responsible for Jacks's care and noticed some obvious developmental problems, he took him to a specialist who said Jacks's small stature, under-developed muscle tone and learning issues could be caused by any number of things: smoking during pregnancy, drinking or drugs, or a combination of all three. However, without their mother present, it would be impossible to tell. But Carter knew the diagnosis was more than likely correct, remembering his mother's chain-smoking and penchant for beer. He'd done some research of his own on the internet after meeting with the doctor, and the stories were heartbreaking. The blinding rage toward that woman for putting her defenseless child second to her own selfish needs almost caused him to punch a hole through his computer monitor.

But he shouldn't have been surprised. This was his mother; the same woman who'd left him at age seventeen when she deemed him capable of taking care of himself, and disappeared. If you couldn't trust your own mother to take care of you and give you love, who could you trust? No one, he decided, and Carter lavished whatever love he had inside on Jackson. Whatever Jacks needed in terms of therapy and help, Carter made sure to get him. He alone would be the one person Jacks could always rely on and never lose trust in. The two of them didn't need anyone but each other and would be just fine.

"Yeah. They're pretty."

Tears blinded him. This boy had done nothing but be born and ask for love. Carter would make damn sure he'd get it all—at least what he was capable of giving.

"How about you and me go next weekend to the zoo, and we can see them in person?"

The cab pulled up in front of the hotel, but Carter

stayed seated.

"Really?"

"Yes. Really. We'll see elephants and lions. All kinds of cool stuff."

"Yeah. I'd like that."

"I'll talk to you more tomorrow when we have breakfast, okay? And be good and go to bed for Helen." He blinked away the moisture in his eyes. "I love you, Jacks."

"Bye."

There was only a slight chance he'd get an "I love you" back, and Carter wished this was one of those times, but Jacks had hung up. With a pang, he ended the call and paid for the cab, then made his way swiftly through the crowded lobby to the elevator bank, holding back the tears he wasn't sure were for himself or for Jacks. There was little he could do for either of them to make life better.

Satisfied that Jacks was healthy and as happy as he could be, Carter focused on his upcoming weekend with Reed. He barely noticed the other people sharing the elevator with him; instead he ran over all the things he'd like to do to and with Reed that weekend.

However, he thought as he swiped his card key at the hotel door lock, nothing could be accomplished until Reed got there and got naked, neither of which could come soon enough for Carter. Like the last time, the maid had done turn-down service, and there were several pieces of chocolate on the pillow. Unlike last month, Carter had requested an upgrade to a small suite, all in the hope that he'd be bringing Reed back here and would need an early morning quiet space to have his breakfast with Jacks. He took a quick glance at the clock on the nightstand by the king-sized bed, and seeing it was only 9:20, he knew most likely Reed wouldn't be there for several hours.

Feeling grungy after all his running around, Carter peeled off his clothes, and leaving them in a pile on the floor next to the bed, walked into the bathroom. Some fifteen minutes later, refreshed and naked under the fluffy hotel robe, Carter lay down on the bed and closed his eyes for a nap, but sleep failed to come as it so often did when thoughts of his mother had taken up residence.

He tossed and turned and even pulled a pillow over his head, but it didn't help. Nothing ever did. All he could see was himself at fourteen and her face twisted in disgust when she walked into the curtained off part of the living room that was supposed to be his bedroom and found him jerking off to a picture of a boy-band singer. Or how she constantly complained giving birth to him had ruined her life: she could've been a model or an actress if only she didn't get pregnant at fifteen.

When you grew up believing you were the cause of your mother's problems, you tried to make yourself invisible and not cause any more trouble for her. All you wanted was for her to love you, and if that meant learning to steal cigarettes for her when she ran out, or remaining home alone at night by yourself even though you were afraid, you did it and never complained. You stayed out late when her boyfriends came over so she could have privacy, sometimes sleeping on the back porch because the men slept over and she didn't want him in the house at all.

But it built a fire in your belly that grew into a conflagration, consuming you and burning away any hope as the years went by. Because the other kids knew something you didn't and snickered behind your back as you walked by. Or stuck notes in your locker saying, *Your mother's a whore.*

And you knew as sure as the fact that you'd never lose your heart, that when you became an adult, you'd never let anyone talk or think about you unless it was in admiration of your accomplishments. He wanted people to fear him when he walked by. To feel his power. He closed his eyes, and sleep finally overtook him.

Awakening from a dream where Reed had him naked and spread out on the bed, Carter heard knocking at the door, and his heart thumped strongly while adrenaline buzzed through his body. With his robe hanging partially open, he peeked through the peephole, and a grin tugged his lips upward at the sight of a very nervous-looking Reed bouncing on the balls of his feet as was his habit. He'd changed from earlier and now wore a dark-green sweatshirt under his leather jacket and his golden-brown hair curled damp over his brow, as if he too had taken a shower before he came.

Not wanting to waste another moment of their limited time together, Carter pulled open the door and gave his widest grin.

"Come on in, Reed. I've been waiting for you."

Chapter Four

THE KNOWING SMILE on Carter's face made him look like the big bad wolf, ready to gobble Reed up and eat him for dinner. No man had ever had this effect on him, not even Mason, whom he'd thought he was in love with. It was why he initially hesitated in accepting Carter's invitation; but Carter refused to be ignored and Reed shivered, unfamiliar emotions rippling through him.

"Uh, yeah. Sure." Reed gulped down a breath and walked past Carter, who smelled fresh and clean, like sage and lemon. Reed too, had taken a quick shower before packing up his schoolwork and some clothes. He'd almost reached the subway before he realized he'd forgotten his pills and had to run back home, cursing under his breath all the way. The last thing he needed was to not have his medication with him when he planned on spending a weekend with a man who kept him off balance even when he took it as prescribed.

The door closed behind him, and at the sound of Carter turning the lock, Reed's heart stuttered again.

This was most likely a mistake; he'd already proven he wasn't the best judge of character. Maybe he misjudged Carter and put himself in a bad situation. Self-doubt whirled through his head, and Reed had half made up his mind to leave when Carter moved close and rested a hand on his back. Reed instinctively leaned into his firm touch and warmth, letting Carter's arm naturally slide around his waist.

Warm breath tickled his ear as Carter spoke softly. "Why not put your bags down and take off your jacket? I can't tell you how happy I am you came a little earlier than I expected." With a bit of pressure, Carter turned him toward the sofa in the outer portion of the room.

It wasn't the same standard room this time, Reed noticed. Carter had reserved a suite, and Reed hadn't ever been in a hotel room quite as large or luxurious. The outer room boasted a dining table with four chairs, a credenza with a flat-screen television, a large, comfortable-looking sofa, and two club chairs. A low light glowed from an interior room, which Reed assumed to be the bedroom. His stomach clenched tightly in response.

"Uh, sure. I wasn't working the bar, just doing some of the office work for Vernon, so he didn't care if I left." Still holding on to his waist, Carter walked him over to the sofa where Reed dropped his knapsack and duffel bag, then managed to break Carter's hold on him so he could remove his jacket. On the pretense of looking around the room, Reed walked around a bit before halting by the wall of windows overlooking the congested streets of Times Square.

"It's bizarre, you know?" He touched the cool pane of glass. "There's so many separate worlds going on all over the city. We're in this secluded bubble up here where we don't even hear the sound of the traffic. Anything could happen, and no one would realize it; love, death, every day it all goes on around us and we remain oblivious."

He sensed Carter behind him. "That's very philosophical. Is that what you're studying—philosophy?"

The disbelief in Carter's voice caused Reed to smile, but he kept his gaze fixed on the glittering light show outside the window instead of turning around to meet Carter's eyes. "No, I'm studying hospitality management. I'd like to eventually manage my own restaurant or a hotel."

"Good. For a moment I thought you were wasting your tuition money on nonsense. You'll never make any money studying that crap. It's not like you can open up a philosophy store and spend your day spouting all that bullshit to people."

Strangely enough, Carter's obvious disdain quieted Reed's nerves. "I don't know; I could see myself sitting in a nice quiet space, talking to people about their lives, thinking deep thoughts."

"Oh yeah?" Carter pressed him against the window, covering Reed with his body. He'd forgotten Carter had been naked when he entered, and Reed could feel the thrust of his cock against his ass. "Maybe you have something there 'cause I like it when you get deep." Carter kissed behind his ear, sending shivers down Reed's spine. "Deep inside me."

A surge of lust stiffened his dick, and heat flooded through him. Carter's tongue traced a slow deliberate pattern across his neck and Reed's pulse raced. "I like that too," he whispered, and Carter's lips curved in a brief smile against his ear, his breath hot and humid.

All thoughts of school and studying fled when Carter reached around and popped the tab of his jeans, then pulled down the zipper. His erection pushed out, and the simple touch of Carter's hand brushing against his boxers had him groaning out loud. There was something surreal about being so high in the sky yet half-undressed in front of a window. It was powerful and a huge turn-on, wondering if anyone else could see them. Not caring if they did.

Reed gasped as Carter began to touch him, lightly, teasingly, until he barely recognized the moaning, pleading sounds coming out of his mouth.

"Oh fuck, please." His hips pushed outward, wanting Carter to grasp him hard instead of with those barely there, feather-light strokes of his fingertips that left his nerves on edge, his body screaming for release.

Carter yanked down his jeans and boxers, and Reed hurriedly toed off his sneakers, then stepped out of his clothes until he finally stood naked from the waist down. Carter began to jack him off in earnest now, his thumb swiping over the thick head of Reed's cock, picking up fluid, while he sucked the tender skin of Reed's neck. Carter's other hand snaked down his belly to cup his balls, rolling them first, then gently squeezing them in the palm of his hand.

Waves of pleasure rolled through him as Carter continued to play havoc with his body. Trapped between Carter's arms, exposed in front of the window, not knowing who might be watching them, Reed trembled violently, certain he was about to splinter apart. Carter continued his hand-play across the tip of his cock, teasing the sensitive head, applying pressure when he perceived Reed needed more. Never in his life had Reed been so turned on, and with a hoarse cry he came, spilling hot and hard into Carter's hand, spraying onto the windowpane.

The powerful climax annihilated him, and Reed sagged against the window, uncaring of the mess he'd made. Behind him Carter fumbled, and Reed had barely caught his breath before Carter's wet and sticky fingers slid into the crease of his ass.

"Oh, God, no. I can't."

But even as he said it, Reed spread his legs a bit wider, encouraging Carter and enabling his fingers to slide inside his passage. He knew Carter wanted to fuck him and, God knows, he wanted it as well. It had been so long Reed had almost given up, thinking he'd never again crave being touched, but now this stranger had given him back his lost desire, and he wanted more.

"Fuck me, Carter; do it." Reed placed his hands on the glass, tilting his ass up, feeling like he was in one of those cheesy porno movies, but he didn't give a shit. Carter's fingers pushed in his ass, tormenting him with their wicked, unrelenting flutters. Then as suddenly as they had entered him, they withdrew, and he cried out in protest, wanting them back. In a daze, Reed heard the foil wrapper rip, and he tried not to tense as Carter pushed his slicked-up cock inside him. Slowly and with deliberation, Carter filled him; Reed had never been so stretched, so consumed. Carter didn't only possess his ass—Reed's whole body belonged to him.

It was too good, Reed thought hazily as his body began to respond and he met Carter's thrusts, pushing back hard, clenching his inner muscles tight to keep Carter's dick inside him. Too good and too long since his body felt this pulse of life within. Carter's grip on his hips intensified as he drove himself into Reed's body, and heedless of the fingers digging into his skin, Reed keened high and loud at the wondrous sensations buffeting his body as Carter hit his prostate over and over again.

"Ahh, Carter." He guessed the exact moment before Carter orgasmed; his fingers tightened further on Reed's hips while his cock stiffened. Carter continued to slam hard and fast into his body and Reed welcomed it, urging him on. A harsh cry rent the silence as Carter came, impaling himself deep inside Reed, his hot breath gusting past Reed's shoulder as Reed shuddered and twitched.

The warmth of Carter's sweat-slicked body comforted him, and Reed could've stayed plastered together a bit longer, but Carter withdrew to go inside the suite. Reed presumed it was to use the bathroom. Awkward, suddenly, as if just realizing he stood naked in front of a window in Times Square, Reed bent to gather his discarded clothing and hurried away from the windows.

After rummaging in his duffel bag for a pair of sweatpants, Reed slipped them on and lay down on the sofa to catch his breath. His ass ached, and he shifted to get comfortable. It had been a while since he'd had someone inside him and never with this powerful a reaction. He could hear the water running in the bathroom and itched to go into the bedroom but found himself strangely shy. Yeah, they'd just had mind-blowing sex, but Reed realized that Carter never said a word to him the whole time. His stomach dropped, and in that moment Reed felt a bit dirty and used. He checked his watch and saw it was time to take his antianxiety medication, and for the first time he was grateful to have it. He needed to keep on top of his meds with all the upheaval in his life right now.

Carter reappeared in the living room of the suite but remained standing by the entrance.

"Why don't you come inside? You aren't sleeping on the sofa, you know." His eyes flickered to the windows where they'd just been, then back to Reed. "I was waiting for you. I thought maybe I came on too strong and you decided to leave."

Might Carter not be as confident as he appeared on the outside? The possibility that he was plagued with the same doubts and uncertainty Reed suffered from never occurred to Reed. Of course Reed knew ADHD and anxiety amplified his own fears, but Carter need never know that side of him. He wasn't about to open himself up again to humiliation and ignorance. A brash and self-assured Carter, juxtaposed with the concerned and, dare he say it, sweet-natured man, oddly enough gave Reed a certain strength. Like he had inside knowledge to a man that most others didn't get the chance to see. A softer, more human side that caused Reed's heart to beat a bit faster.

"I was waiting for you to finish."

Carter's silvery eyes turned dark and hungry as they roamed over Reed; a shiver rippled through him involuntarily. It was ridiculous how responsive he'd become to a simple look from this man.

"We have an entire weekend; I've barely started." He held out his hand. "Come on. You could use a shower, then we can order some room service and go to bed."

Surprising himself, Reed walked up to Carter and cupping him around the nape of his neck, drew him down for a kiss that he intended to be claiming but instead turned sweetly passionate. Their tongues tangled and slid slickly, and Reed ended up with his arms around Carter's shoulders, clinging to him as their mouths slanted over each other, their breaths mingling and becoming one.

Carter broke free, gasping for air, and wiped his lips on his sleeve. "Or we could just go to bed now and forget the room service and the shower."

Reed smiled. "I think that's the best idea you've had all night."

Carter swatted his ass as he walked by. "I'm full of good ideas."

REED LIFTED HIS head from the pillow and squinted at the bedside clock. Nine a.m. He groaned and flopped back down on the pillow while simultaneously stretching the early morning kinks from his sore body. Not that he was complaining—he couldn't hold back the smile that tugged at his lips. He and Carter had stayed up into the early morning hours, mapping out the contours of each other's bodies with lips, hands, and tongues. Reed didn't think he'd ever felt so wanted in his life.

He rolled over to curl up to Carter's warmth. "Hey, how're you—"

No one was there, and the bedding was cold to the touch, as if it had been empty for a while. Still a bit fuzzy from the all-night marathon, Reed scrubbed the sleep from his eyes, disappointed Carter wasn't there with him to wake up and say good morning.

After using the bathroom and brushing his teeth,

Reed cocked his head, certain he heard voices from the outer room. Did Carter plan on inviting someone else to share their weekend? Reed had no intention of joining in a threesome and was about to walk into the living room when he heard Carter laugh. It sounded carefree—not designed to seduce, but real and from the heart. And even though he knew it was wrong, Reed couldn't help but listen in on the conversation.

"I miss you so much. I'll be home tomorrow night, and we can have dinner together, okay?"

Reed inched closer, straining to hear through the closed door. He knew he shouldn't eavesdrop, yet he wanted to know more about Carter. They might have agreed to keep their private lives separate, but Reed couldn't help his curiosity.

"I love you. Bye."

Fearful of getting caught, Reed scrambled back into bed and had settled in at the exact moment Carter opened the door and stuck his head inside. A wide smile beamed across his handsome face.

"Oh, you're finally up. You were dead to the world an hour ago when I tried to wake you."

Feigning a yawn, Reed pushed his fingers through the tangled waves of his hair. "Yeah, you kept me up late last night." He stretched and through sleepy eyes watched Carter's dark gaze roam over his half-naked body. Reed wondered who Carter spoke to. Was it another man? Reed didn't think so. A thought occurred to him: was Carter living a double life and married to a woman, pretending to be straight?

When Carter pounced on him, taking his mouth in a bruising kiss, however, Reed's head spun, and as was becoming more frequent, he lost the ability to focus on anything except the furious need that built inside him at Carter's touch. Reed forgot about the call and his doubts and thought about nothing except how much he wanted Carter again.

Chapter Five

A MONTH HAD passed, and he shouldn't be as excited as he was to see Carter this weekend, yet as Reed rushed to get dressed for work and packed his bag, he couldn't help the stupid grin he knew rested on his face. Something about the illicit nature of their arrangement made it fun and different, almost like a movie script or something in a book. Making love in front of the window last time proved to be a huge turn on and Reed spent many nights re-living that experience, until the mere thought of it gave him a hard-on. It certainly wasn't anything Reed ever expected to happen to him. He thought he was too ordinary a guy, but for some crazy reason Carter wanted him.

And God, did he want Carter. The weeks away from him were turning torturous; too many times he wanted to text him, but remembering what Carter had said from the beginning—that this was purely a sexual relationship—Reed held back and contented himself with his hand and increasingly vibrant sexual fantasies. Only once these past weeks did Reed allow his curiosity free rein, and he did a reverse look-up of Carter's telephone number, which proved to be a bust. As suspected, the phone was registered to his office and therefore provided Reed no personal information. All it did was make him more anxious, thinking up reasons why Carter could only meet him for one weekend a month.

It all came back, Reed decided, to that conversation he'd overheard the last time they were together. In their time apart, Reed had built up an entire make-believe world for Carter, one that most likely included a wife and child. Reed imagined Carter living a closeted life and using this one weekend away to live out his true need to be who he really was.

As quickly as he built up that fantasy, Reed shot it down and dismissed his crazy thoughts. All it proved was he spent too much time watching made-for-television movies. Carter was simply a busy man who didn't want or have time for a relationship. Maybe the person he spoke to was his mother. Reed imagined Carter had a nice family with loving parents.

It didn't stop him from wishing, however, that they could have a little bit of time together like a couple instead of spending their entire weekend holed up in bed. God knows he wasn't complaining about the sex. When they were together it was all he could do to keep his hands off Carter, but it would be nice to go out to dinner and walk the streets of the city. Pretend what they had was real when it was anything but.

By the time their allotted weekend arrived, Reed had worked up a plan that in his head seemed plausible, but now that he was close to bringing it to fruition, had him worrying about Carter's reaction. Would he be okay with it or dismiss it outright? What if he got angry and told him to go home for the weekend? Even worse, Carter could end their arrangement altogether. The thoughts tumbled through his mind, making Reed dizzy and ill with anxiety.

But first he had to do his shift at the bar, where hopefully he could forgo thinking about Carter, if only for a few hours. Unlikely to happen, but Reed forced himself to sit down, relax, and do some deep breathing, ultimately centering himself and gaining some control.

The weather refused to cooperate and outside sleet pelted down from a stark night sky while the blustery raw wind howled. At his last glance through the front windows Reed watched as people's umbrellas buffeted about, blown inside out, and he was grateful to be inside, warm and dry. The few desultory customers who had showed up nursed their drinks as if deciding whether to stick it out or give up and head home, hoping for a better tomorrow.

"Go on, get out of here already." Vernon gave him a nudge. "I know you got plans; I saw your bag. You've been pretty useless here all night, anyway."

"I haven't done anything." Reed poured a few glasses of beer and gave them to the guy waiting at the bar. "Here you go. That'll be eleven dollars."

Vernon snorted. "That's the point. You ain't done nothing. All you do is bounce up and down, talk under your breath, and keep checking the clock. It's like standing next to someone who's gotta go to the bathroom but can't."

With a guilty smile, Reed handed the customer his change, then turned to talk to Vernon directly. "Am I really that antsy?" At Vernon's pointed look, Reed felt his face burn and dropped his gaze to the floor, mumbling, "I guess you're right."

"It's that guy again, am I right? The one you left with last month? He's your boyfriend, ain't he?"

From the first, Vernon's acceptance of his sexuality surprised Reed; he'd expected to have to hide being gay, figuring Vernon, being older, would automatically be conservative and disapproving. But Vernon's daughter had come out several years ago as a lesbian, and she was his whole life; Clara could do no wrong. If Clara was a lesbian, Vernon told him, he had no problem with Reed being gay.

"Not really." How the hell could he explain it to Vernon without sounding like a slut or an idiot that he couldn't stop thinking about a man he met once a month to have ridiculously hot sex with?

"Oh, you're hooking up?"

Reed gaped at Vernon, who looked extremely proud of himself.

"Ha. Bet you didn't think I know what that means."

"Well, yeah." Plus, it sounded really funny coming

out of Vernon's mouth to begin with.

"I get MTV. I watch *Teen Mom*." At Reed's disbelieving stare, Vernon shrugged. "Sometimes I can't sleep and there ain't nothing else on late at night."

"This is too weird." Reed began to stack glasses underneath the bar.

"So what's going on with you two? You don't hardly see him; is that why you're so jittery?"

"Damn." Reed swore under his breath. Even Vernon noticed. He couldn't get mad at him for the things he unwittingly said. Reed had more confidence in revealing his sexuality than his psychological issues and hadn't told Vernon he suffered from anxiety, only ADHD. His mental state carried a stigma for him, not who he liked to sleep with.

His palms broke out in a sweat, and the familiar tightness crept through him, signaling his anxiety was on the rise. It was always hard to say when it might hit, but today Reed knew why. He'd woken up late and rushed out of the house without taking his medicine, and already he could see the difference in his lack of concentration and inability to start and finish one task. More than once tonight Vernon had to ask him to finish running the monthly numbers, but something inevitably distracted him, causing him to lose focus on the task at hand. Reed knew he was a mess: he couldn't keep from running his hands through his hair or twisting his fingers together. Something, *anything* to cure himself of the rampant restlessness he'd been cursed with. He'd gone home during a lull and only taken his meds about an hour ago—they were just beginning to take effect.

At times like this Reed hated his weakness and wished he could rip the anxiety from his body. Wistfully, he'd watch the other students in class sitting so calm and focused, listening to the professor speak, taking notes he knew would be neatly precise, while under his skin an electrical current buzzed and he had to force himself to pay attention.

If he wasn't twisting the bracelet he'd worn more than half his life—solely for the purpose of giving himself an outlet for his nervous energy—he doodled; anything to expend the constant energy revving through him. Mason would get annoyed at his actions and dubbed the bracelet his security blanket. He'd make a point to tell Reed he wished his oral fixation could channel all the excess energy into giving him more blowjobs. That more sex would cure him of all that anxiety. As usual, Mason turned the focus of everything, including Reed's illness, on himself. When Reed pointed it out to him, Mason laughed, but Reed failed to find the humor in any of it.

The more he thought about it, Reed realized it was better for him and Carter to spend so little time together. Anything more and his secret might be discovered. A man like Carter would have no use for someone as mixed up in the head as Reed.

"No, I'm fine with the way things are; we're both

busy and not interested in a relationship, so this works."

"Huh. Well, the way he looked at you that night, I'd say he's got it bad." Reed jumped as Vernon elbowed him in the side. "And you're pretty hot for him too. So go on, get outta here. And at least make him take you out for a nice dinner before he jumps your bones." Vernon turned away, cackling to himself.

Without another word Reed went to the office, put on his coat, picked up his duffel bag, and headed out into the rain-swept night. If ever there was a time to splurge on a cab, tonight was it, and after he hailed one and sank into the back seat, he texted Carter to let him know he was on his way.

Good. I'm waiting for you.

Maybe tonight he could talk Carter into going out and having a drink somewhere. All the meds he took precluded him from drinking too much, but if he could get Carter to relax his guard and open up, maybe he could find out a bit more about this mysterious man who'd gripped his heartstrings.

Once he entered the suite, Carter would want and have him on the bed within minutes; Reed had no doubt Carter wasn't with any other men during their separation. He was insatiable at first; it was part of what drew Reed to him. No one had ever made him feel as desired, as *desirable* as Carter did, but tonight he hoped for something different. Something more intimate.

The cab rolled up in front of the hotel, and after

paying his fare and slamming the door shut behind him, he hoisted his bag over his shoulder and hurried through the front doors. The route through the hotel lobby to the elevators had become rote by now, and the closer he got to seeing Carter, the higher anticipation sizzled through his bloodstream. He breathed deeply to calm his rapidly beating heart. His dick might be half-hard already, but Reed was determined to talk before fucking.

Before he finished his first knock, Carter had opened the door and holy fuck, Reed couldn't help but stare. Carter had let his beard grow in a bit from the stubble he usually wore by the end of the day. He looked seriously hotter than the surface of the sun, and without thinking, Reed reached out and skimmed his fingers against Carter's cheek and jaw, wondering how all that roughness would feel against his bare thighs, his balls, and brushing along his hard dick.

"You like it? I've been working nonstop on a campaign and barely had a chance to shower and eat." Carter opened the door all the way, and Reed walked inside the suite. "I'll shave."

"No." Reed dropped his bag and took Carter's face between the palms of his hands. "Not yet."

They embraced, and the now familiar wave of pleasure rolled through him as Carter's lips softened, his mouth opening to deepen their kiss. Hazily, Reed heard the door slam shut behind him, and he reluctantly pulled away from Carter, taking a step back to prevent himself from falling back into his touch.

"Why'd you stop?"

Breathless, Carter touched his swollen lips, his silvery eyes gleaming bright with a passion Reed was fast becoming addicted to.

"I was thinking—"

"First mistake." Carter pulled him close and tried to kiss him again, his beard providing delicious friction against Reed's neck. It would've been easy enough to sink down to the floor and give Carter, give them *both* what they wanted, but Reed gathered what little wits he still possessed and pushed away.

"Why do we have to rush all the time? We have the whole weekend."

"I'm not rushing. I plan on fucking you nice and slow." Carter bent to pick his bag up and started walking to the bedroom.

"Come on, Carter, stop it. I'd like to go out and have a drink or walk around the city for a while." About to take another step, Carter froze in place before turning around to face Reed. At his steely glare Reed almost faltered and gave in. But deep down there was so much he wanted to learn about Carter, things he'd never find out if all they did was screw themselves silly every time they saw each other.

"I don't want to spend another weekend locked in the room." Reed held his breath at the darkness rising in Carter's face.

"I thought we had an agreement."

"We do. I'm here to spend the next two days with

you. Only you." Reed advanced on Carter, who hadn't moved since he started speaking, and put a hand on his arm. Carter's eyes, glittering with desire only minutes before, now looked like flat chips of dark slate in his stony expression. "But what's preventing us from taking a break? You have responsibilities, I get it. I'm not asking you to bring me home with you."

At those words Carter shook off his hand and took a step back.

"You're making this more complicated than it needs to be or we agreed upon. What's wrong with the way things are?"

Words failed him for a moment, but for once Reed didn't allow the panic to take over. He focused and took the time he needed to arrange his thoughts into a coherent answer.

"Nothing's wrong. I never said there was. But I think it could be better. We're not in a relationship; I get it, and I'm not trying to force you into some little box and parade you around to people I know as some prize I've won. On the other hand, I'm trying for a little normalcy. What's the harm in going to a bar or a club? You did it before we met."

They studied each other in silence, and after a moment or two the harsh lines on Carter's face softened. Reed could almost guess the moment when Carter changed his mind.

"I guess you're right. It might be fun." He glanced down at his bare chest and thin sweats. "I suppose this means I have to get dressed."

Thrilled with his victory, Reed cupped the nape of Carter's neck and drew him in for a swift kiss that became long, sensual, and left them breathless. From the hard thrust of Carter's cock, Reed supposed they could indulge a bit before going out.

"Not yet. I think you deserve a reward for being so willing to make me happy." He tugged at the strings of Carter's sweats, and they fell, puddling on the floor around his ankles. His erect cock sprang free, and Reed could smell the heady concoction of Carter's desire that only fueled his already simmering lust. "Time to make you happy as well."

He sank to his knees, engulfed Carter's cock in his mouth, and proceeded to make them both very, very happy.

"THIS PLACE LOOKS good; don't you think?"

It was an hour and a half later, and after they'd both showered and changed, Reed had his walk through the city with Carter. To his delight, Carter even took his hand as they window-shopped past the closed stores along the street. The rain had stopped, and the street gleamed wet; while the taxis churned up brackish water at every corner, even that couldn't foul Reed's mood. They meandered up toward Eighth Avenue and stopped in front of Bounce, a club where both karaoke and dancing were featured attractions.

To his shock, Carter pulled him to the entrance. "Let's go inside."

Confused, Reed dropped his hand and held back. "You want to go in here? I don't know how to dance."

Carter had already taken out his ID for the bouncer at the door. "Don't worry. I'll show you whatever moves you need to know." His infectious grin drove away any doubts from Reed's mind, and he followed Carter into the club.

On one side behind a tinted glass door was a dance floor, and Reed's body shook from the pounding beat. Peering through the glass, he could see the swaying bodies pressed together, and Reed imagined a hot and sweaty Carter hard up against him, their hips gyrating to the slow pulse of the music. Maybe the time had come for him to learn some moves.

On the other side, raucous laughter and loud, off-key singing could be heard, and Reed guessed that was the karaoke club.

Carter tugged at his hand. "Let's listen to some karaoke before we dance."

Giving Carter a surprised look, Reed huffed out a laugh. "You? Karaoke?"

Without answering, Carter led him inside the room, still holding tight to his hand. They followed the hostess to a small round table for two, set with a flickering candle on top of a glittering cloth. The room was half-empty; there were around fifty people seated at the same small round tables scattered about the room. A waitress appeared in a scanty black tank top and leggings, accentuating her lean, muscled body. If Reed were to hazard a thought as to her day job, he'd pick dancer or maybe personal trainer.

"Good evening, gentlemen. What can I get you?" The lights picked up the slash of her bold red lipstick and the colorful feather earrings sweeping her shoulders.

"I'll have a Grey Goose on the rocks. Reed, what do you want?"

Because of all the medications he took, Reed didn't often drink, but tonight, being here in public with Carter for the first time, he felt a little reckless and decided to indulge.

"I'll have a Sam Adams."

The waitress left, and he and Carter soon became so engrossed in the hilarious karaoke, neither noticed the waitress setting their drinks down on the table. An unexpected, flirty side of Carter emerged, and Reed enjoyed the neck nuzzling and Carter holding his hand and toying with his fingers. His heart lurched with a happiness he hadn't felt in years, and he struggled to remember it was all a fantasy.

Without even realizing it, he'd finished his first beer only to find it replaced with another. It slid down his throat cool and easy, and to his surprise he watched Carter take a big gulp of his own drink.

Maybe he was nervous too.

And somehow that small chink in the armor, letting in the tiniest light of vulnerability to shine through, endeared Carter all the more to Reed.

When the group on stage had finally finished, a lull fell over the now-crowded room. Carter nudged his thigh and whispered in his ear. "Want to try?"

Reed almost choked on his beer. "Me? I sound like a dying chicken when I sing." He wiped his chin. "Do you sing?"

Carter downed his drink and stood. "Guess you're about to find out."

Chapter Six

WHEN REED HAD asked for a night out, Carter's first inclination was to refuse. He had no desire to go out in public together; after all, their arrangement had been to spend their time having as much sex as they could possibly cram into their weekend. But the disappointment in Reed's pretty golden eyes bothered Carter more than he imagined it could, and he found himself agreeing simply to keep Reed happy because he liked to see Reed smile. Another alien concept Carter mulled over as they walked together in the cold.

Once they were out and strolling through the city, Carter admitted to himself he enjoyed it. It was a rarity for him to take the time and wander about, look at restaurant menus or simply people-watch—he and Reed had even played a fun game of *Guess Where the Tourist is From*. Once Jackson had come to live with him, Carter had thrown himself headfirst into work, pushing all thoughts of personal pleasure out of the way. Jackson had to and always did come first. Carter had promised himself his brother would never end up feeling unloved and unwanted like he did.

But for this night Carter gave in, not only to Reed's wishes but his own desire to be part of a crowd; a desire he didn't know existed until he walked with Reed amid the throngs of people in Times Square. The usual hawkers were about, shoving pamphlets in their faces encouraging them to take a tour bus ride around the city or listen to a comedy act. Carter ignored them and chose to focus strictly on Reed: his animated voice, the excited sweep of his hand as he pointed out something of interest, and the sweet curve of his smile.

With some difficulty Carter forced himself to look away from Reed; not an easy task with the man so close he could see the smattering of freckles along the bridge of his nose and the vivacious sparkle in his eyes. Happier than he could recall in recent memory, an idea popped into his head as they walked up Broadway toward 50th St. A client had recently opened a nightclub that featured both karaoke and dance, and watching Reed walk slightly in front of him, Carter pictured them with their arms around each other, dancing to a slow, rhythmic beat. Inside of twenty minutes, they were seated at a cozy table, having a drink and listening to terrible singing, with Carter enjoying himself more than he thought possible. He ordered a second round, figuring it would loosen Reed up for the dancing he had planned. And, God knows, he needed the buzz.

So this is what regular people do on dates.

Casting a sly look at Reed, he whispered in his ear,

feeling him shiver and loving how affected Reed was by his simplest touch.

"Want to try?"

Reed almost choked on his beer. "Me? I sound like a dying chicken when I sing." He wiped his chin. "Do you sing?"

Carter downed his second drink and stood. "Guess you're about to find out."

What did it matter the problems he had waiting for him when he came home after this weekend? Tonight, with Reed unable to keep his eyes off him and alcohol and anticipation buzzing through his veins, Carter felt almost invincible when he took the stage. He hit the button on the machine, almost laughing at the song that popped up, "Trapped Again" by Southside Johnny and the Asbury Jukes.

How appropriate.

In the early days when Jacks had first come to live with him, Carter had spent many nights singing him lullabies to ease whatever fears he might have. He soon had the crowd clapping and singing, forgetting about their drinks when they realized he could not only sing but sing well. But Carter wasn't interested in the crowd. He kept his gaze firmly trained on Reed who, when Carter began singing, set his bottle of beer on the table and stared at him, open-mouthed, his eyes round with wonder. Shocked surprise—exactly the reaction he'd hoped for.

Carter grinned inwardly and finished the song with

a loud flourish and fist pumps, then jumped off the stage to thunderous applause, striding over to a still-stunned Reed who stood along with the rest of the people in the room. To the delight of the whistling, clapping crowd, he grabbed Reed around the neck and kissed him full on the mouth, leisurely at first and then with increasing fervor. Curbing his desire to drag Reed off to a dark corner and do lewd things to him, Carter vowed to save it for the privacy of their hotel room.

"I didn't know you could sing," said Reed, breathing hard into the curve of Carter's neck. "That was amazing."

"I'm a man of many talents—some hidden, some not."

That brought a smile to Reed's lips, which remained pressed against Carter's throat. The mere touch of Reed's wet lips against his burning skin fired Carter's lust all over again.

"Let's go next door and dance. We can be amazing together."

Reed sat in his seat, and Carter took his own chair, hitching it close enough to keep nibbling kisses along Reed's jawline. Carter could tell Reed wanted him by his rapidly heaving chest and how the bottle of beer shook in his trembling hands. He loved setting this man on edge. It made their short time together explosive and an unforgettable memory he could hold onto in the long weeks until they came together again.

"I already told you I don't dance."

Adrenaline continued to hum through Carter's veins, and he laughed. "I'm offering to be your tutor. You can pay me later for the lessons."

Reed swallowed and breathed deeply several times. Carter, sensing this was more than mere nerves, massaged the back of his neck, attempting to soothe him. After a few moments, Reed let out a shaky laugh that sounded anything but happy.

"I've never felt comfortable dancing; I'm clumsy, and don't have rhythm, and step on people's toes, and—"

"Shh." Carter placed his fingers across Reed's mouth. "This is supposed to be fun, not a chore. Let's try it, and if you don't like it, we'll leave, okay?"

When a moment passed and Reed still didn't answer, Carter sighed and cupped Reed's chin, forcing him to meet his eyes.

"Come on, just one song, and then I promise we'll go if you say the word."

At Reed's hesitant nod, Carter kissed him again and put a few twenties on the table to cover the drinks and the tip. He then took Reed's hand, and together they walked across the hall where the flashing lights and pounding music consumed him until his bones rattled under his skin. Carter stood close behind Reed and rested his hands on Reed's slim hips, both of them swaying slightly to the beat. The couple right in front of them on the dance floor drew his attention, and he nudged Reed.

Oblivious to the crowd, the two men had their eyes closed and their arms wrapped around each other, swaying back and forth. The sight of them, so free and beautiful with their love, gave Carter hope for a future where this would be the norm and not something for people to stare at like a science experiment.

"That's going to be us." Carter slipped his arms around Reed's waist and snuggled his pelvis in the tempting curve of Reed's ass. They fit together perfectly, and Carter closed his eyes for a moment, losing himself in a world he never gave himself permission to enter.

"I—I can't do that."

Feeling Reed quivering in his arms, Carter took his hand and led him to the far corner of the dance floor where tall columns as well as the thicker darkness hid them from sight.

"Is this better?" He smoothed the hair from Reed's damp face and kissed his cheek. He didn't understand Reed's fear over a simple dance, but he wouldn't push him to a breaking point or give him an ultimatum. If he'd learned anything from living with Jackson, it was to introduce new experiences one small step at a time. Anything too overwhelming and Jacks shut down, and it seemed Reed might have that same issue as well.

The song ended, and new music came on. A slow, rhythmic beat pulsed through the air. All the lights in the club dimmed, and Carter took advantage of the darkness to pull Reed close. At first he stiffened, and Carter whispered encouraging words in his ear. "Come on, baby. It's only you, me, and the music. That's all you need to remember."

Reed glanced up, almost shyly it seemed, then pressed himself tight against Carter's chest, burying his face in his neck. Confused as to Reed's response, Carter held him close, and they simply stood and rocked together, the music enveloping them. He hummed the tune in Reed's ear and settled his arms around his shoulders, their hips matching the beat.

"See? You're doing it. That's all there is to dancing. Letting the music come alive inside you. The rest is all instinct."

Reed nodded, his cheek lying flat against Carter's shoulder now. A small shudder ran through his body, and Carter pulled him closer, molding their bodies together, and smiled to himself as the unmistakable hard ridge of Reed's erection brushed up against him. Reed's brain might not think he knew what to do, but his body certainly did. And Reed's body wanted him as much as he wanted Reed.

They stayed hidden behind the columns, Carter holding on to Reed until the flow of the music took over and the motion of Reed's hips began to match his, roll for roll. Their bodies picked up the beat, arms twining around each other, and Reed leaned his head back, opened his eyes, and gave a smile of such pure, unfettered joy, Carter's heart surged. It seemed like years since happiness had touched him, sweeping against him like a paintbrush colored with all the pleasures of life.

He grabbed Reed by the waistband of his pants and popped the button tab while at the same time brushing his lips to Reed's smiling mouth. "I want you," he said, the pace of his breathing quickening as his hand swept across the warm smooth skin of Reed's firm stomach. "Right here. Right now." Carter unzipped Reed's jeans halfway, slid his hand inside Reed's boxers, and grasped his thick cock.

And apparently Reed wanted him as well—the wide head of his cock slick and sticky with precome was all the proof needed. It coated Carter's fingers, making it wonderfully easy to slide his hand up and down the hot soft skin of Reed's cock. It was dirty, illicit, and Carter's dick ached, tightly encased in his jeans.

"Fuck," moaned Reed, throwing his head back while grasping hold of Carter's biceps for support. "What the hell..." He bucked against Carter, thrusting into his hand, while his breaths came in short, hard pants. "Faster, damn you."

Reed's fingers dug into his muscles, but the pain only added to Carter's pleasure. "Come on," he muttered, working Reed's cock with swift strokes, adding just enough pressure by pressing his thumb over the sensitive, flared tip. Carter gripped Reed's dick, feeling the heavy veins and soft skin sliding over the rigid length as he continued to pump him. The zipper gave a bit more, and he dug his hand farther down Reed's pants to fondle his balls, giving them a squeeze; Reed moaned loud enough for Carter to hear. A single strobe light hit Reed's face, and he looked debauched, his eyes wild and mouth open and panting.

Carter reached up with his free hand to cup the nape of Reed's neck and drag him down so their lips could meet, and Carter took his mouth in a brutal kiss of possession. His other hand kept busy in Reed's pants, and he slid his thumb over the leaking head of his engorged cock, giving it a wicked twist. "Give it to me, Reed. Hold me and let go."

"Oh God, oh fuck." Reed collapsed against Carter's shoulder, his teeth nipping at Carter's neck. He jerked against him twice, and Carter's hand filled with fluid while Reed's gasping breath gusted past his ear. As promised, Carter held on to Reed as his climax ripped through him, his body shuddering and twitching in the aftermath as his dick continued to unload in Carter's hand. Carter kissed the top of Reed's head, the damp curls tickling his nose, but Carter held tight. The promise he'd made was to hold on to Reed, but when had it happened that he no longer wanted to let go?

The music stopped, and Carter realized they were somewhat more exposed than before, now that the lights weren't as dim. He withdrew his sticky hand and gave Reed, who looked ravaged yet more gorgeous than Carter had seen him before, a rueful smile.

"Guess I'd better go find the bathroom." He gave Reed's crotch a pat. "You need to zip up as well." He licked his fingers, the salty-strong taste of Reed coating his tongue. "Umm, delicious. Thanks for dessert."

Blinking and with a tired smile, Reed obeyed and followed him into the men's room where Carter washed up. Reed took him by the arm and spun him around so they faced each other and kissed him full on the mouth.

"Thanks. You made that one of the best experiences of my life."

There was a light in Reed's eyes Carter hadn't seen before, and once again he wondered at Reed's inexperience. His own childhood had been far from normal, but even as a teenager Carter hadn't had much of a problem finding guys who wanted to have sex.

Something about Reed spoke of innocence and vulnerability, even though Carter knew he was no virgin. But those thoughts began to tread dangerously into personal territory and by his own rules remained off limits. He refused to cross the line into learning a hookup's past love life and history. Even now, he knew more about Reed than any other man he'd ever slept with. More than with anyone ever before, he'd let down his guard with Reed, but it was now time to head back to reality.

"I'm happy to help." He captured Reed's face between his hands and enjoyed the sweet taste of his mouth. Carter could've spent the rest of his evening drowning in the pleasurable taste of Reed's soft lips, but someone walked past them, causing him to stop and recall they were in a public bathroom. With a not-too-guilty shrug, he took Reed's hand and led him back out to the dance floor.

"Do you want to go back to the hotel now?" They stood together, and Carter toyed with Reed's fingers, surprisingly content. Reed bounced on his toes to the music. "I'm game for whatever you want."

Reed took their entwined hands behind Carter's back, sliding both their arms around Carter's waist and hugging him close. His need for touch was an endearing quality.

"I guess it wasn't so bad, then, going out for the evening?" He grinned and nudged Carter. "Although staying in the suite has its definite advantages; I'm not going to lie."

"Now that you mention it," said Carter, "I—"

"Carter? Is that you?"

A man, roughly thirty years old, long dirty-blond hair lying in damp strands along his forehead, stood in front of them. His powerful legs spread in a wide stance, his muscular arms, bare in his thin black tank top, gleamed with a fine patina of sweat.

Carter cocked his head, trying to place the man. "Yes? I'm sorry. Do we know each other?"

A lazy grin carved deep dimples in the man's handsome face. "Wow. And here I always imagined that night was so memorable. It's Trent? We, ah, hooked up about six or seven months ago." He reached over and traced the V-line of Carter's open-neck shirt. "I was watching you both before on the dance floor, and you two were so fucking hot together." Trent tipped his head at Reed and turned on a smile intended to seduce the pants right off him. "I'm up for a threesome if you are."

Carter stepped back, closer to Reed, and out of reach of Trent's touch. The only hands he wanted on him were Reed's, and somehow hearing this Trent guy talk about watching him and Reed together tainted a pleasurable experience. Besides, he had no desire to upset Reed with an obscure, random hook-up from before they'd met.

"I don't remember you, and right now Reed and I are together, and I have no need for anyone else. So thanks, but no thanks." Without waiting for a response, Carter took Reed's hand and pulled him out of the club and toward the coat check.

"Sorry about that. I don't remember him at all."

Reed said nothing as they put on their coats. When they walked out into the freezing cold, Reed, his face miserable, shoved his hands inside his jacket and tipped his head back toward the club.

"If you want to be with him, it's okay; I understand. I'm fine with stepping aside, but I'm not into threesomes."

"We had a hook-up. One I have no intention or desire to repeat, got it?" Carter grasped Reed by his shoulder. "I'm with you, and that's where I want to be."

"I guess, but I don't want you to feel obligated. I can pick up my stuff at the hotel and be out of your way. He seems more your type."

"My type?" He breathed white puffs of cold air

between them. "Right now my type is sexy, shy bartenders."

Reed smiled slightly and shrugged.

"C'mere. Obviously I didn't prove it to you well enough in the club." It wasn't until he held on to Reed that he noticed he was shaking.

"Are you all right?" He slid his arm around Reed's shoulders and gazed into his face. Reed's teeth chattered, his eyes staring round and dark. If Carter didn't know better, he'd swear Reed was scared to death.

"Hey, what's the matter?" He rubbed Reed's cheek with his, hoping to soothe him.

"I don't feel so well."

And, Carter decided after staring hard at Reed, he didn't look well either. They were only a few short blocks from the hotel, yet Carter didn't hesitate a moment before hailing a cab, pushing Reed inside, then climbing in after him. It didn't take more than seven minutes to traverse the five blocks, which for a Friday night was miraculous, but the traffic-light gods were on their side.

Carter paid the fare, and after wrapping a protective arm around Reed, took him upstairs and into the suite, murmuring comforting words in his ear.

"Don't worry. It was hot in there, and you probably didn't have enough to eat before you came to meet me."

He led him into the bedroom, and after stripping him, tucked him into bed and turned down the lights. The whites of Reed's eyes glinted in the half darkness, and Carter remained standing by the side of the bed, looking down at him. By rights he should be annoyed; they were together to have sex and nothing more. If he were smart, he'd tell Reed goodbye in the morning—forget about him and find someone else. Someone like Trent. But his mind rebelled and Carter dismissed that idea. He didn't want Trent. He didn't want anyone else but Reed.

"I'm sorry." Reed lifted himself up on his elbows, the sheets falling to his waist. "I, uh, don't know what came over me. I know you're disappointed."

Swallowing heavily at the sight of Reed's naked chest, Carter shrugged. "Don't be. One night won't make a difference."

"Thanks. I'm sure I'll make it up to you in the morning."

"It's fine," said Carter, as nonchalantly as possible. "I'm going to check some emails and be right back." Before Reed had a chance to respond, Carter turned his back and walked away.

This arrangement that had started out as purely sex was rapidly veering off course, and he had to find a way to bring it back to center. The emotional dancing in the club, his surprising jealousy at the thought of anyone else but him touching Reed, and how even now he wanted to protect and take care of Reed, all evidence pointing to them getting too close, too fast. The signs were there for him to pull away.

He stretched out on the sofa in the living room and

opened his computer to check his email. Sure enough, there was a video that Helen had uploaded of Jacks and her, making pizza for dinner, and Carter smiled and settled down to watch his little brother, happy to be able to put aside, at least for a while, his burgeoning feelings for the man waiting for him in his bed.

Chapter Seven

NOVEMBER FADED TO December, and Reed anticipated winter break and the holidays although he had nothing planned except for his weekend visit with Carter. At the beginning of the month Ariel had invited his father and him to Massachusetts for the holidays, but Reed had already promised Vernon he'd work, plus he didn't want to miss his time with Carter. He and his father had always kept the holidays low-key since his mother had picked that time to bail out on them.

Where other kids had family dinners and decorating to look forward to, the first few years after his mother left, Reed held out hope she might return and say it was all a mistake. Or at least send a card. Every day he'd come home from school and look through the mail for a card or a letter from her, at least acknowledging his existence or that she remembered she had a child.

It took several years until he finally stopped looking and convinced himself he no longer cared. His father had tried to make Thanksgiving a happy holiday—

they'd watch the balloons get blown up and go to the parade unless it was raining, but with only the two of them across the table from one another at the meal, there was always a reminder of what was missing. And Reed always held out hope at Christmas that maybe his mother would come home, or at least send a card, but inevitably he'd be disappointed and feel guilty, knowing he should be excited with the tree and presents.

At thirteen, when he realized he was gay, he wondered if she already knew and used that, in addition to his other problems, as another excuse to leave. He went so far as to try and date girls and even kissed a few, but hated it. They did nothing for him, not like seeing the boys swimming in the pool in their swimsuits or the football players in their tight uniforms.

And though he'd dreamed of settling down with a special man and falling in love, Reed suspected he wasn't the type of person someone would fall in love with. Not when everyone he'd ever been with had found it so easy to walk away from him and not look back. College guys had been after easy and uncomplicated sex, and though Reed had often hoped it might turn into more, deep in his heart he knew love wasn't going to be found in the bathroom stall of his college dorm or in the darkness of an anonymous fraternity guy's bedroom. Mason's cruelty had been the last straw, and then Carter had caught him in a vulnerable moment when all Reed yearned for was to be wanted by someone.

There was something forbidden and exciting about

meeting Carter in a hotel, like a rendezvous in one of those old-fashioned spy movies, and he strode through the hotel lobby with long, eager steps, anxious to see Carter after another long and lonely month. As usual, Reed only had to knock once before Carter opened the door and pulled him inside. He barely had time to drop his weekend bag before he found himself pinned up against the wall, Carter's tongue ravishing his mouth. One thing he never doubted was how much Carter wanted him.

"You're late." Carter sucked on his lower lip and hunger surged through Reed, making him weak at the knees. Carter continued to kiss him until his bones melted and his head spun, dizzy with desire.

"I'm half an hour early." He toed off his sneakers while Carter popped open his jeans and unzipped his fly.

"Stop disagreeing with me and get naked. I've been dreaming of your ass for a month now." Carter yanked his jeans halfway down his thighs and sank to his knees. "Take off your pants, turn around, and spread your legs."

A thrill shot through Reed at Carter's demanding voice; his hands shook slightly as he pulled off his jeans and boxers and stood naked from the waist down. "Have you joined the police force? Is this a strip search?"

"Turn around, Reed."

Carter's darkly passionate tone sent a shiver of anticipation through him and he complied, standing silent, facing the wall. He jumped at the first brush of Carter's fingers against the crease of his ass, and instinctively he widened his stance and dropped his head, breathing faster.

"Perfect," muttered Carter under his breath, and then Reed felt hot breath and the scratch of a rough, stubbled jaw against the smoothness of thighs. Every nerve ending screamed as Carter's hands cupped his ass and spread him wide, exposing him fully.

"Oh God." Reed moaned, then cried out at the press of Carter's slick tongue at his opening. His fingers curled spasmodically against the wall as lightening shot down his spine. Carter fluttered his tongue, then pulled away, causing Reed to whimper in frustration.

"Fuck." He reached down to grab his cock and gave himself a few hard tugs to take the edge off, but it wasn't working. He needed Carter's mouth back on him. "Do it."

"You like this? Tell me how much you want it." Carter thumbed his hole, and Reed thought he might pass out from the desire rocketing through his body. "Tell me." He twirled his tongue around the rim, but it wasn't nearly enough to satisfy Reed.

"Carter, please." He struggled to stand and had to place a hand flat up against the wall or else he might crumple to his knees. Carter's finger slid down his crease, then delved inside his passage, sliding in and out, unerringly knowing where to place pressure to give Reed the maximum amount of pleasure. Sparks went off behind his tightly closed eyes, and he moved his hips in rhythm to the magic of Carter's wicked, knowing fingers.

"Please, what?" Carter slid his hands up Reed's hips and nuzzled against his ass. "I want you to beg me for it." Hot air blew against his sweat-slicked skin, and Reed shivered from both anticipation and desire. When Carter slid his tongue into his passage, curling it up inside him, wave upon wave of pleasure slammed into him, and Reed came hard, shooting into his hand and splattering the wall.

Carter quickly stood and covered Reed with his body, sliding their hands together, blanketing him as he shivered and shook in the aftermath of his climax. He gasped for air, listening to the soothing sound of Carter murmuring words he was still too wrecked to make sense of, but the mere sound of Carter's voice and his weight comforted.

"All good?" Carter stepped back and turned him around so they faced each other. Reed couldn't help it; he wanted Carter's arms around him again. He reached out and cupped the nape of Carter's neck, drawing their faces close.

"Let's take a shower. I need to get cleaned up, and you need to get taken care of."

Carter's silvery eyes darkened, and he licked his lips. "I like the way you think. Come on." Carter's hands rested on Reed's hips, tickling at his waist.

"Don't be in such a hurry," said Reed as they

stepped into the brightly lit bathroom. He turned on the taps and watched Carter strip out of his clothes. "We have all night." He pulled off his shirt and dropped it to the floor.

"Oh, I know, and I intend to use every minute to its fullest."

Carter pushed him into the shower, and he yelped at the splash of water down his back.

"Hey."

Carter joined him and pushed him up against the wall. "Is there a problem?"

Reed felt the thrust of Carter's very hard cock and laughed. "Not any longer." His laughter ceased as Carter covered his mouth in a possessive kiss.

WINTER SUNLIGHT PAINTED watery, lemon-yellow stripes across the carpet of the bedroom. Reed squinted at the clock, and when he saw the time was eleven a.m., he sat up so quickly his head spun. He was alone in the bed, of course, Carter being an early morning riser as Reed had come to learn. But today Reed had plans, and though he'd slept later than he would've liked, he was now wide awake and ready to go. Strange how he'd slept better these stolen weekends with Carter than any other time in his life.

After taking a piss and brushing his teeth, he found Carter on the sofa, sipping coffee and reading the newspaper. His hair lay sleek and wet against his shirt collar, and his freshly shaven jaw gleamed where the sunlight hit. Remembering the delicious friction of Carter's stubble against his balls and ass, a small sound of dismay escaped him, which caught Carter's attention. He glanced up and smiled.

"There's coffee. I didn't know what you wanted, so I got a bunch of stuff." He gestured to the table, and Reed's eyes widened at the sight. There were coffee cakes, miniature danish, muffins, and bagels, along with an impressive bowl of fruit. A large thermal carafe of coffee and a pitcher of milk rounded out the contents of the breakfast tray.

"Are you expecting guests? 'Cause there's enough here for five more people." Plus, Reed decided as he picked up a bagel and spread on the cream cheese, the sugar alone would send him spiraling into the next stratosphere. Too much was always a trigger for him, and he tried to keep away from eating crap.

"Hmm," said Carter, handing him his coffee. "Maybe I did go overboard. But I like having choices. Choices make life interesting." He picked up a muffin and took a huge bite out of it.

"Well, today you are my prisoner, so you have no choice. I have a surprise planned."

Instantly wary, Carter swallowed what he was chewing and set his coffee cup down. "I've never been thrilled with surprises. What is it?"

"We're going to do something really touristy and fun."

"What are you talking about? I thought we were—"

"What, going to stay in and screw all weekend?"

A lazy grin curled Carter's lips. "Well, now that you mention it…"

"Last month you made me go dancing, something way outside my comfort zone." So far outside as to be revolutionary. The entire night played out as a surreal fantasy for him.

Carter picked up his coffee and took a sip. "You seemed pretty comfortable to me. At least while we were out on the floor."

Reed's cheeks heated. He'd lost count of how many times he'd replayed their dirty dance in his head this past month and jerked off to the memory of Carter's hands down his pants while the other people in the club remained oblivious to what went on beneath their noses. It never failed to give him a hard-on.

"That's not the point. I did it because you wanted to. This is something I want, and it shouldn't be a big deal."

"Fine," said Carter, tossing back the rest of his coffee. "Let's do it." He took another bite of his muffin and chewed noisily. "I'll be right here when you're ready."

"Didn't your parents ever teach you not to talk with your mouth full?" Reed meant it as a joke, but Carter's wide smile faded and his eyes darkened with pain.

Obviously he'd hit a nerve. "I'll be ready in a few minutes," Reed muttered. "Just going to jump in the shower." No use in asking Carter what was wrong as he'd never reveal his precious hidden life.

Before Carter had a chance to change his mind, Reed raced from the room. He didn't bother to shave and within fifteen minutes had showered, dressed, and was back in the living room, relieved to see Carter sitting with his phone, a sweet smile playing on his lips. Unnoticed, Reed stood for a moment, watching who he knew to be the real Carter—his eyes lit up bright with life, laugh lines fanning out from the corners. It struck Reed with a pang how young and surprisingly vulnerable Carter seemed when he dropped that confident, brash exterior. Pain and happiness danced together in his chest, and Reed knew if he answered the call of his heart, it would tell him how deeply he'd come to care for Carter.

"What's so funny?" He walked behind Carter and bent over his shoulder to take a peek.

"Uh, nothing." Carter clicked the screen to dark and flipped the phone in his hand so it faced downward. "Ready?" He pasted on a huge, fake smile. Having witnessed Carter's spontaneous happiness, Reed wondered at his need to pretend.

Reed wondered if there would ever come a time when he'd breach that impenetrable wall Carter trapped himself behind. Perhaps a day like he'd planned, free of anything except living in the moment, would be the balm to soothe Carter's troubled soul and give him some much needed calm.

He held out his hand. "Yeah, come on, let's go."

They walked out of the suite, zipping up their coats, and Carter asked, "By the way, where are you taking me?"

"Trust me?" Reed pushed the elevator button, then leaned against the wall, holding Carter's dark gaze.

Carter quirked a brow, then shrugged. "Sure. How bad could it be?"

They descended in the elevator to the lobby, and Reed decided to splurge on a cab when they reached outside. The air flowed past them, bright and chilly, and he didn't relish being half frozen before they reached their destination. Besides, Carter normally paid for practically everything on their weekends together, and it chafed him to continually accept his generosity. Even though it was something as minor as a cab ride, Reed looked at it as something small he could do for them both.

"Rockefeller Center, please." He spoke into the little plastic divider to the cabbie, who wordlessly nodded and took off.

"You're kidding me, right?" The disbelief in Carter's voice rang out in the back seat of the cab.

It was the response he'd expected, which was why he'd kept it a secret until Carter sat trapped with him in the midst of crowded Saturday traffic.

"No. We're going to look at the tree and then go ice-skating at the rink. Be total tourists in our hometown."

"I've never seen the tree or even bothered to go near

Rockefeller Center during the holiday season. Way too crowded from what I see on TV."

How sad. In addition to going to parades and zoos, every winter he and his father would make the pilgrimage into the city to see not only the tree in all its glory at Rockefeller Center, but the holiday windows along 5th Avenue, ending up ice-skating at the rink and then sipping hot chocolate in the café.

"Well, today that's about to change."

Carter scowled but said nothing, falling back against the seat in a huff while Reed studied his uncompromisingly hard face. He didn't believe Carter was truly angry; more likely, he didn't like having the decision-making power wrested from him. It didn't take Reed long to figure out even in their brief times together that Carter lived a very orderly, rigid life. His willingness to submit in the bedroom evidenced to Reed his inner desire to be taken care of, to give in and let others be in control.

The cab dropped them off, and after he paid the fare Reed stood for a moment, amazed by the sheer enormity of the tree and the crowds surging around him, jostling him to get in a better position to take their pictures. What if the tree fell on them? It would instantly crush them all, and he'd never have fallen in love or had anyone tell him they loved him. It all closed in on him, and he began to shake.

"Are you all right?" Carter squeezed his arm, peering at him, eyes wide with anxiety. "You're very pale and look like you're going to be sick."

Forcing himself to relax, Reed swallowed hard against the panic struggling to break free. His heart sank when he did a fast playback of his morning and realized he'd not only forgotten to take his medicine, but in his haste to get to Carter yesterday, he'd left it at home. He didn't know if he'd need to make an excuse to go back sometime during the day to retrieve them or deal with the situation as best he could. Two days without his meds shouldn't hurt him too much, but being with Carter meant he had to watch what he said every moment and that increased his anxiety. It occurred to him that this was becoming an issue whenever he saw Carter; perhaps his subconscious fought against him and sabotaged his best efforts to remain on track. Reed resolved to remember and fight against himself.

From one moment to the next, Reed could never be certain how Carter would respond in a situation, his mercurial nature making it almost impossible for Reed to figure out what went on behind those silvery gray eyes. Sometimes Reed wondered if Carter allowed anyone to see beneath the sleek and polished exterior he showed to the world.

"I'm good."

His breathless words tumbled out, and Carter shot him a concerned look, but he didn't say anything further, just took him by the arm and walked as close as they could get to the tree.

"It's pretty magnificent, isn't it? I never knew." He

took out his phone and took several shots, smiling slightly at the screen.

Reed wasn't sure if Carter expected him to answer, but there didn't seem to be a need to. Carter remained tapping on his phone, and Reed wondered who Carter sent the pictures to.

Hoping to lighten the mood, Reed nudged Carter's shoulder. "Hey, how about we take one together?" He waggled his phone at Carter. "Let's do a tourist selfie like everyone else."

Without waiting for a response, he slipped an arm around Carter's shoulders and took several pictures in rapid succession, as if anticipating a refusal. Shockingly, Carter not only acquiesced but mugged for the camera, making silly faces and flashing a peace sign over Reed's head. Reviewing the pictures, seeing Carter so relaxed and happy, Reed's heart squeezed tight, as if knowing these times were infrequent and ones to hold on to.

"Let's go ice-skating before it gets overly crowded." The rink, though not empty, had yet to fill up with skaters, and Reed wanted nothing to break this magical time they'd woven together.

"Okay." To his surprise, Carter took his hand, entwining their fingers. "I haven't been on skates in years."

"Oh yeah?" Reed kept his tone light and teasing. "I guess I'll be skating rings around you, then. Hope you can keep up. Will I have to pick your sorry ass up off the ice?"

Carter's gray eyes glowed, and he yanked Reed to

him, leaving Reed breathless. "I have other plans for my ass tonight. Ones that involve you getting much more up close and personal with it." His eyes bored holes into Reed's, daring him to disagree. As if Reed would. Or could. The darkness usually lurking within Carter had transformed into something more tangible and alive.

Here he'd thought he'd be the one in charge this afternoon, having made all the plans, yet with a deft twist, once again Carter had come out on top. It didn't matter to him, not with Carter smiling at him, his teeth glinting white in the frosty sun, so heartbreakingly handsome it almost hurt Reed to look at him. Like a grinning fool, he stood in the circle of Carter's arms, oblivious to the surge of the crowd around him.

"Let's go get the skates." Carter broke the spell and tugged Reed forward.

Childish shrieks split the air along with the recorded music playing for the ice skaters, and Reed hummed a tune under his breath as he and Carter walked to the ice skate rental concession and waited in line. After they collected their skates, they sat side by side, sliding their feet into the skates, tying them tightly. Arms linked, they laughed together as they wobbled to the entrance of the ice-skating rink and waited in line to enter the ice, and for the first time in forever Reed forgot about being anxious and inadequate and concentrated on the moment.

Hand in hand they swept onto the ice recently smoothed over by the Zamboni, and Reed's mouth dropped open in wonder.

"You skate beautifully."

Carter let go of his hand and skated in a circle around him, arms tucked behind him in the small of his back, his eyes never leaving Reed's.

"I taught myself years ago." He held out his hand; Reed took it automatically, and they flew together, weaving in and around the others on the rink, past little children slipping and sliding, and others practicing spins, loops, and toe flips.

From his first time on the rink Reed had loved skating; the crunch of ice beneath his skates and the wind rushing against his cheeks breathed magic inside him. He felt happy, normal, and in control over his body. Having Carter with him made it even more pleasurable; each moment clicking by like the shutter from a photographer's camera and Reed only hoped it managed to capture the brilliance of the day.

He sneaked a glance at Carter's face and at the pure, exhilaration of his smile, and a swell of something indefinable rose up inside him. Elated over his ridiculous, unexpected happiness, Reed forgot the piercing cold and Carter's earlier moody, secretive behavior.

"Come on." Once again he grabbed hold of Carter's hand, and together they sailed across the rink. For far too long, he'd succumbed to pain and uncertainty; they made for sad companions. Now Reed learned joy was what you made of it, and holding Carter's hand tight in his, Reed realized he was happy; for the first time he lived life as part of a crowd instead of always standing alone.

After executing some impressive spins, Carter pointed to the café at the edge of the ice rink. "Let's get something hot to drink. My toes and face are freezing."

"You look cute with a red nose. I should call you Rudolph," Reed teased Carter as they headed toward the exit.

"Don't even think of it," he warned. "Whenever we watch…" Looking stricken, Carter furtively glanced over at him, possibly to gauge his reaction, then started to babble about childhood holiday shows as if to fill up the silence blooming in the air between them.

With a frozen smile, Reed dropped Carter's hand once they reached the walkway out of the rink. Without speaking, they returned their skates, put their sneakers back on, then walked to the café they'd spotted earlier from the rink. A few paces in front of him, Carter reached the café first, pulled open the door, and held it for Reed to pass through. When they were inside, Reed planted himself in front of Carter, challenging him to listen to what he had to say.

"You know, I'm not stupid. I'm aware you have a life outside the two days a month we spend together. You don't have to hide it from me; I'm not a crazy person who'll begin stalking you, if that's what you're worried about."

Reed didn't expect an answer and was shocked when Carter bit his lip and spoke, more openly and honestly than he had before. "I'm trying; I really am. But there are things I can't and won't share; not with you, not with anyone. I never pretended with you; from the very beginning I was upfront about what I was willing to talk about."

Gone was the carefree, happy man who'd held his hand on the ice, skating circles around him. Those ever-present shadows that had faded over the course of the afternoon reappeared, shuttering his eyes, making Reed want nothing more than to wrap his arms around Carter and burrow close into his warm flesh. He wanted to see that light in his silvery eyes and his joyful, relaxed smile.

Even with Carter's variable moods and prickly behavior, Reed thrilled to his touch whenever they were close. It drove him crazy not understanding why Carter refused to open up to him, considering how hot and bright their attraction burned between them. There were times he caught Carter watching him with a mixture of confusion and tenderness, and Reed knew Carter felt the pull between them as well.

Before he could answer, the hostess approached, holding menus in her hand.

"Table for two?"

Carter cocked a brow and posed the question to him. "Sure; right, Reed? We're staying, aren't we?"

He forced a smile. "Yeah." He had no right to complain if Carter refused to tell him about his life; Reed had secrets of his own. Secrets he'd make certain to never reveal, aware of how Carter valued strength.

Following the young woman into the warm and fragrant restaurant, the voices in Reed's head clamored, taunting him, shouting out his inadequacies as if he could ever forget. They let him know when Carter eventually would choose someone, it would be a man he'd be proud to introduce people to, not a trembling mess of a man, such as him, who needed medication to make it through the day without feeling as if he were being pulled in eight different directions.

But Reed wanted to defeat those voices. Dr. Childs told him he was so much more than his illness and not to give in to the temptation of striking off on his own without his meds. Doing so would only feed the beast of his anxiety, enabling it to break free and consume him. For years he'd chosen to disregard her warnings and play by his own rules, contributing to his problems by failing to take his medication properly. He resented the drugs—hated that they were a necessity, like breathing, air and water.

They sat at the small café table and Carter tapped his hand. "Hey are you with me? You look a hundred miles away."

"Yeah." Reed blinked and smiled faintly.

"So, are we good?"

Reed studied Carter's face, his features fast becoming indelibly inscribed in his mind. The slight crooked smile, that sardonic tilt of a dark brow and those eyes the color of moonlight. One night last week Reed attempted to draw Carter from memory and failed miserably. He didn't want a flat, one-dimensional picture of Carter, he wanted the real man, alive and warm next to him.

But if Carter knew the real Reed, would he still want him with the same intensity?

Chapter Eight

"I THINK IT would be wonderful for you to take Jackson to school today. It would give me a chance to work up something more challenging for his therapy." Papers in hand, Helen peered at him over her glasses. "He's made incredible strides in the past few months; surely you've seen it."

Carter allowed himself a grin. "I have. And I know I haven't thanked you enough—"

"Oh no." Helen interrupted him. "This has nothing to do with me and everything to do with Jackson stretching his fledgling wings. I'm so happy he's met these new friends. He's become a whole new person."

The bond between Jackson and two boys he'd tentatively made friends with several months ago had strengthened into a fierce friendship as only school-aged children could accomplish, complete with Saturday movie play dates, video game playing, and pizza parties. Despite Jackson's overall progress, Carter hadn't yet agreed to the sleepover requests, wondering if it was too fast, too soon.

"I agree. Do you think I held him back these last few years? I didn't mean to hurt him in any way. You know that."

They weren't often demonstrative with each other; perhaps Helen sensed his need to keep his distance from people. But today she put her hand on his and squeezed it tight.

"You were doing what you thought best for Jackson's benefit. You've sacrificed almost your whole life these past three years. Because of you he feels safe and secure and ready to test the waters of friendships." She tightened her grip even more. "Did you ever imagine he'd be at this place when he came to you those years ago? I have to confess I hadn't ever seen such a sad little boy." She took off her glasses and wiped her eyes with a napkin.

For Carter, it was hard to believe Jacks hadn't always been with him, where each smile became a small victory to be won at the end of the day. Without him the kitchen table would be empty, no schoolwork, books, or pictures stacked haphazardly across the surface. There'd be no toys spilling out into the hallway or piled in the corner of the living room. From the moment their mother showed up and left Jacks, Carter had been consumed with making sure he got it right even if he had no idea what right was. But for certain he already knew about wrong. That would be his own life. No structure, no love, no family dinners or bedtime stories. With every breath, Carter made sure Jackson would have what he, Carter, lacked as a child and so much more—friends, security, and love. And if it meant that for Jackson to live a stable, healthy life Carter would have to give up thoughts of a relationship, he was fine with that. From childhood, being alone was all Carter knew.

Jackson's art therapy had evolved as well—from the dark and sad pictures he drew when he first came to live with Carter, forever depicting a lonely child standing in a corner, to the more frequent bright and colorful scenes of birds and animals and groups of happy, smiling children. Jacks's doctors informed Carter these were all signs the therapy was successful.

"I have you to thank for his breakthroughs; I never could've done any of this by myself. I know I don't say it often enough, but you've been a godsend, Helen."

"All Jackson needed was someone to love him and be a steady presence in his life. We might never know what he went through as a young child, but my guess is your mother didn't provide much stability for him, and the trust issues he has are going to take several more years to work through. But you *are* making headway. Slow as it may seem, this is the right way."

The thought of his mother being a stable presence in anyone's life almost choked him with laughter. The government required a license to drive a car and own a dog, but to bring a child into this world and be a parent—there you were on your own. It had been a while since he thought about his childhood; he didn't believe in dwelling on the past. Instead, he focused all his energy on shielding his little brother from all the people who might hurt him. *Trust no one* had been his motto for years and it had served him well.

"I'll always be there for him. He's part of my life, and I'll never give him up. I know he's making progress, but it's taken him so many years to get to this point, I won't let anything get in the way of him leading the most normal life possible."

The first time he took Jacks to a child psychiatrist, the doctor stressed the main objective was for Jacks to comprehend Carter wouldn't disappear on him like their mother had. Stability and security were the key words the doctor repeated, and they'd become Carter's mantra. The doctor also warned Jacks might have a hard time learning to trust Carter. For all that their mother was a neglectful person, she was still the only parent Jacks had ever known and Carter was yet a stranger.

From his own childhood, Carter remembered the never-ending procession of men his mother brought home, how he would try to make them like him by doing whatever they asked, only to have them vanish overnight, each replaced by someone new. His mother believed any one of those men would be her meal ticket out of a life of poverty and hopelessness. Even at his young age, Carter knew better. When he grew up, he promised himself, watching his mother move from man to man, no one would ever use him or take advantage of him again.

"Speaking of leading a normal life, you need to take a page from your own book, Carter. Have you ever thought about settling down?"

There was no condemnation in Helen's voice, only sadness. Over the past few years, as they'd grown closer taking care of Jacks, Carter confided to her his need to get away, sensing she'd never judge him, and he was right. Above all, she wanted him to be happy.

"I have, yes, as a matter of fact. I'm seeing someone with a similar mindset—neither one of us wants anything permanent." Thoughts of Reed, his sweet smile and open heart, stirred an odd yearning within Carter. Nothing sexual, which startled him the most. Yes, he wanted Reed as much now as the first time he saw him, maybe even more if that was possible, but it had blossomed into so much more than mere physical desire. Mundane, silly things occurred during the workday and often he found himself wanting to share them with Reed. He'd be a click away from sending a text or funny joke to Reed, or once or twice a dirty picture, then catch himself and wonder what the hell he was thinking. This wasn't part of their arrangement.

"Whomever you're seeing on those weekends you disappear has changed you. You're lighter and more at ease. I've noticed the difference immediately, and I'm wondering if Jackson does too. Part of his recovery might be the fact that you're much calmer now. You should seriously consider bringing this man around one day to meet Jackson."

He shook his head before she finished speaking.

"No, I don't think that'd be wise."

"Why not?"

He didn't know why. Over the months that he'd been seeing Reed, the excuses he'd made in the past no longer seemed relevant. Things between him and Reed had accelerated from simple (okay, not simple, pretty amazing) sex in a hotel room to dancing and then ice-skating in public where the time flew by instead of dragging. Their weekends together had progressed from all sex, all the time, to dinners out, then cuddling on the sofa in the hotel suite, watching a movie. They went to museums, browsed through the shops in SoHo and Tribeca, and on the last Saturday afternoon they'd spent together, Carter had scored almost-impossible-to-get tickets for a Broadway show and surprised Reed with them.

Time slipped away and six months had passed from the first time he'd spotted Reed in the bar that Friday night, and now they were on the cusp of spring, yet Carter didn't feel bored or restless. Instead, the opposite occurred. He anticipated his weekends with Reed and thought about him more than the work he had waiting for him at the office. Nothing about these escalating feelings had to do with their sex life. It was being with Reed, watching his animated face as he relayed a funny story about what happened during his shift at work, or listening to him sing in the shower, his voice painfully off-tune but so cheerful—these were the moments

Carter hung on to like a lifeline while they were apart. Because before he caught his breath, their weekends were over and once again he was back with Jackson but still alone.

Now that Jacks had started spending so much of his weekends with his new friends, Carter tried to catch up on whatever work he'd brought home with him from the office, but more often than not he'd spend a good portion of the day thinking about what Reed might be doing when they were apart, or planning their next weekend together. Instead of concentrating on his campaign, Carter lost himself in pictures of the two of them in bed or on one of their expeditions in the city. He'd catch himself and grow angry, dismissing his thoughts of a more permanent situation between the two of them as stupid. Their arrangement worked exactly how he'd envisioned it, and yet here he was, getting personally involved.

"My weekends have nothing to do with what I have here at home. This is my reality, not what happens on that one weekend a month."

Helen's brows arched in surprise. "Are you ashamed of him?"

Her question startled him. Ashamed of Reed? Impossible. More likely the other way around if Reed ever discovered Carter's less-than-normal childhood and what he'd been through.

"Not at all. He's a good person—too good for me in fact. You know the type—perfect childhood, loving home, good parents and schooling." He fidgeted, uncomfortable in his own skin, memories of his past struggles burning like acid in his blood. "He'd be ashamed of me and the life I led." The man he'd become never forgot the boy he left behind.

"Oh, Carter. People don't get to pick and choose their childhood. You made the best of a terrible situation. No one could fault you for that."

And no one ever would because he'd never tell. None of the men he'd ever been with cared, and he certainly wouldn't confess to Reed who was so damn perceptive sometimes it scared him. Reed would be the one who'd want to discuss and dissect; to probe and question until Carter's whole shameful life lay bare and he'd probably end up humiliating himself by crying.

"I have to get Jacks to school, or he'll be late." If there was one thing he hated talking about, it was his childhood, but he gave Helen an awkward pat on the shoulder as he passed, not wanting her to think she upset him. "Thanks for the talk, but I think we're both doing as well as we're able."

Avoiding her mournful eyes, Carter walked to the kitchen where Jackson stood at the table, placing his textbooks and notebooks in his backpack with precision. Every morning he went through the same ritual; each book had to be stacked in size order, and every notebook was color coordinated to match the covers Jackson made for each textbook.

"Ready to go, buddy?" He held out Jackson's down

jacket and scarf. "Better wear this; it's still cold out today. And you took your medicine, right?"

Jackson scowled. "I'm not a baby."

Surprised at this unexpected resistance, Carter found himself at a loss for words. From the first, Jackson had been a compliant, uncomplaining kid, who always did what he was asked without question. Now Carter noticed little things: Jackson balking at his chores or at being told to brush his teeth at night before bed. Having no desire to confront him, especially right before taking him to school, Carter decided to make light of it.

"Of course you're not. I'm being overly careful, but humor me."

Without answering Jackson took his jacket and walked away. Relieved to see he'd wound the scarf around his neck, Carter followed him and watched as Jacks said goodbye to Helen. He hugged her back and kissed her cheek, even giving her a smile. Stupid him, the little signs were what he wanted most from his brother yet rarely received.

The disappointment must've been evident on his face as Helen came over to whisper in his ear while Jacks finished zipping up his jacket and pulled on his gloves.

"He loves you. Sometimes it's harder to show the ones you love the most how you really feel about them. My theory is he's gotten more comfortable with you; less afraid you'll leave him or send him away, but he's not sure how to show you affection. He's never had a father or a strong male presence in his life before. In this society, boys are taught, even at his age, not to show emotion. Jacks may be afraid to let you know how much he really loves you."

He nodded and left without answering, Jackson at his side. What Helen said made sense, and Carter struggled with the concept of becoming more loving. You couldn't teach that, it had to be inside you. Funny how Reed popped into his mind. Reed knew how to love; Carter sensed he possessed an endless source waiting for the right person to set it free. At the corner, he automatically took Jacks's hand and waited for the light to change. The little hand in his felt so right and he held it tighter. Carter worried at his ability to show love, even to Jacks, whom he loved more than anything he thought possible.

The school was several blocks away, and they fell into step with the other adults and children streaming down the block. The old gray concrete behemoth loomed ahead of them, its iron gates surrounding the schoolyard. The first time he approached it years ago, it intimidated even him, but Helen reassured him it boasted wonderful teachers and award-winning special programs geared to Jackson's needs. The reason he left Manhattan and moved to Brooklyn was so Jackson could have this school and a yard to play in.

From the start, Carter had been determined to mainstream Jacks. Because they had so little to work on, and having no medical history, his doctors did the best they could in diagnosing and treating Jacks, and now

Carter believed he was seeing the fruits of their labor. More confident and with a growing self-image he'd only begun to explore, Jackson may have finally reached a milestone.

Two boys rushed up to them, and Carter recognized them from earlier play dates.

"Hi, Henry, David. How're you boys doing?"

"Good," said one he thought was Henry. "Can Jacks come over today after school? We can do homework, then play."

He needn't bother asking Jacks if he wanted to go. The shining eyes and hopeful smile on his face spoke volumes. For a moment a small ding of jealousy darted through Carter. There used to be a time when Jacks preferred his company to anyone else's, and he mourned the loss of having his little brother not only as a bright and lively little companion, but as a way to keep his own life busy, meaningful, and less lonely.

"I don't know…"

Don't be an idiot. This is what's right for Jacks.

Immediately contrite, he forced a smile back at the boys watching him, with Jacks's gaze the most pleading.

"All right, sure. I'll text Helen and let her know. But you have to be home for dinner, okay?"

His words were lost in the chilly air as the boys cheered, then sprinted ahead to join the growing swell of students entering the schoolyard. Jacks hadn't even said goodbye to him, and Carter stood on the sidewalk, feeling rather forlorn and forgotten.

"Don't worry," said a voice tinged with laughter in his ear. "They all leave us in the end."

Shaken out of his pity party, he found himself staring into the eyes of a familiar woman around forty, wrapped up in a big down parka, her brown curly hair caught up in a messy bun.

"Was I that obvious?" He gave a weak laugh and rubbed his chin. "I don't get the chance to take Jacks to school that often, so I thought it might be special for him, but I guess not."

Smile lines fanned out from her sympathetic eyes. "You shouldn't think that. I'm Michelle, Henry's mom, by the way. We've met, but I'm not sure you remember me with all the running around that went on when you dropped Jacks off."

"Yes, I remember now." Henry's house was an old Victorian with sprawling rooms, two large dogs racing about, and a hodgepodge of mismatched but comfortable furniture. To Carter, it immediately spelled family, security, and warmth.

"Boys are like that. And Jackson is a lovely child. I can't imagine it's been easy, but you've done amazing things raising him."

At his quizzical look, she explained. "Henry's been in class with him for two years now, so I've seen Jackson's growth. He's gone from scared and shut down to a young boy on the brink of stepping out in the world. And you've done this all alone, except for Helen?"

"Yes." His phone buzzed, and he quickly glanced at it, noting he had a meeting at ten o'clock. "I've been raising him for the past three years since our mother left him with me."

"Helen mentioned you've done everything by yourself. Not even a girlfriend to help you sometimes?" Her prodding became obvious at this point.

"Not likely. I'm gay."

"Really?" She almost squealed in her excitement. "Well, if you're interested, I'd love to set you up with my brother. He needs a nice guy."

Before he knew what he was saying, the words came tumbling out. "I'm seeing someone, but thanks."

What the fuck?

Before Michelle could bombard him with questions, he cut her off. "Uh, it was nice to talk to you, but I have to get to work. I heard Henry ask Jacks over after school, so Helen will be by to pick him up." Before she could answer, he hurried away, weaving past the stragglers outside the gates. Reflexively he stuck out his hand as soon as he saw a cab approaching and had the door open almost before it came to a halt. Sweating now, after sliding into the back seat, Carter unbuttoned his heavy wool coat and took off his gloves.

"Second and 73rd." The driver took off without a word, for which Carter was grateful. Upset with himself over his abruptness with Henry's mother, he wondered if she thought him rude, then, more importantly, remembered he had to text Helen to pick up Jacks at

Henry's house after school. He sent her a quick text, then slid the phone into his pocket and leaned back in his seat, allowing himself to think about Reed, as he so often did now when he was alone.

What would be so bad if he did start a relationship with someone…with Reed? Immediately as he thought it, he shut it down. He'd have to be fucking crazy; Carter knew he was a moody, workaholic asshole whose sole focus in life was taking care of Jacks and being the best at his job. Except for Jacks, he put himself and his needs first. Now would probably be the worst time to bring someone new into Jacks's life, at the precise time when he was beginning to find his way and take those first tentative steps toward independence.

His phone buzzed, and he glanced at it, surprised at the sight of Reed's name popping up on the screen with a text. Reed? Why would he be contacting him? They barely texted, except to make arrangements for their weekend, which was still two weeks away. Two very long weeks of cold showers and lonely nights, where he often had disturbing dreams of him and Reed together in his house, raising Jacks. Being a family.

You made a mistake

His heart fluttered in his chest, and his fingers inexplicably trembled as he texted him back.

What?

You texted me

No I didn't.

I think you meant it for someone else.

Alarmed, he scrolled up and saw Reed was right; he'd made a stupid fucking mistake. He always made it a habit to delete old texts and only kept the ones from Helen, Lucy—his PA, and now Reed. Maybe he was worked up from the whole morning and Jacks beginning to pull away from him, but whatever caused it to happen didn't matter. He'd sent Reed the text meant for Helen about picking Jacks up after school.

For a second Carter hesitated, debating if he should disclose Jacks's existence to Reed. He had no doubt Reed would be sympathetic, caring, and want to help in any way possible, and therein lay the problem. Having a steady man meant easy and uncomplicated sex; he wouldn't have to think about finding someone for the weekend because that someone would already be there. And Reed had agreed to their arrangement, claiming he had no interest in a relationship or getting involved. Now Carter wasn't so sure Reed understood how much distance Carter needed between them.

He shook his head in disgust. Nothing had substantially changed for Carter to consider including Reed in his life. With the new friendships he'd cultivated, Jacks needed him and the secure family Carter had tried to create now more than ever. Introducing Reed would upset their delicate family equilibrium. Getting Jacks settled with his friends had to be the main goal now, not

Carter's neglected cock. And if Reed couldn't or didn't get it, fuck it all.

Thanks for letting me know.

And like the coward he was he exited out of the screen without waiting for Reed to answer and re-sent the text, this time to Helen. Carter spent the rest of the cab ride into the city wondering why he felt so miserable.

Chapter Nine

"It sounds to me like you really like this man despite your rather unorthodox dating arrangement," said Dr. Childs, taking notes on her computer. She glanced up and peered at him over the monitor. "Have you thought about broaching the subject of maybe taking it to the level of a real relationship with him?"

"No." Reed fidgeted in his chair, the brown swirls of the office carpeting capturing his attention. He pulled on his bracelet, then feeling her assessing gaze on him, stopped and folded his hands tightly in his lap.

Reed hated lying to Dr. Childs and had the suspicion she saw right through him no matter what he said. He had a problem—a big one with only one way out as he saw it. Each time he left Carter, his body humming, the taste of his kisses lingering on his lips, Reed played out a scenario where he and Carter would eventually fall in love, but then he mentally slapped himself and woke up from fantasy island. From the first, Carter hadn't lied to him; their so-called relationship centered on available sex and nothing more. To be fair, Carter had never led Reed on to think any differently. The tenderness he'd shown him was, Reed guessed, natural to Carter though he doubted Carter recognized it within himself. It had nothing to do with falling in love. That walled-up man could never open his heart to him or anyone else.

"You've been seeing him for how long now?"

"Six months, I think. Six weekends if you wanted to get technical. And I know little to nothing more about him than the first time I met him."

A frown drew her lips down in a pinched line. "I don't understand why you allow yourself to be treated like this. You deserve so much more than to be hidden away and treated like a pet."

His face heated from her rebuke. "Is that how you see it? I thought we were having a pretty typical open relationship."

Dr. Childs sighed, and came around from behind the desk to sit next to him. His stomach twisted into knots, and Reed was certain he wasn't going to like what she had to say.

"I've been treating you almost fifteen years now, Reed, and I'd like to think we have the type of relationship that goes beyond mere doctor-patient."

Dr. Childs had been with him through his teenage years of doubt and angst when he questioned everything—his mother's abandonment, being gay, and sometimes why he was even born at all.

"We do. I trust you more than anyone else." He'd

opened up to her about his relationship with Mason and how hurt he'd been over the name-calling and their breakup. It was Dr. Childs he turned to, to help him understand his problems weren't his fault; that the panic attacks and his hyperactivity weren't shameful. They were a part of him, like a patchwork quilt. And if he became a bit undone every once in a while, he had her to help teach him how to piece himself back together.

"I used to wish you were my mom." He fiddled with his hair, directing his gaze once again to the ugly carpeting. "I hope I never do anything stupid to make you leave me."

"Oh, Reed." Her comforting, gentle hug reassured him like it always did, that unlike his mother, she'd always be there for him. "I'll never leave you even when you no longer need to see me on a professional basis." She took off her glasses to discreetly wipe her eyes, then replaced them.

"But you can't still think your issues led to her leaving your family. You know it had nothing to do with you, your diagnosis, or anything other than her own problems she wasn't willing to face. I see how far you've come and how strong you are now. You'll never go back to being that sad, scared young man again. Don't fall back into that way of thinking."

In his heart Reed desperately wanted to believe her words; he *knew* she was right and being older should make it easier, not harder to get through each day. And he had so many successes to look back on; he was at the top of his class, had a steady job and a handsome, fascinating lover. On the outside he lived a wonderful life. Inside, however, Reed could never quite let go of the feeling he was a complete mess, a fraud, and unworthy of happiness.

"I don't know." He picked at a rough cuticle, almost welcoming the sharp spurt of pain. "If I was normal—"

"You *are* normal." Her sharp tone jerked his attention back to her face, drawn tight now with uncharacteristic anger. "There's nothing that says everyone is supposed to be like everyone else—you are not meant to be a cookie-cutter stamp of another person. We're all a compilation of chemistry and biology and that indefinable quality that makes each one of us unique and special in our own way. That includes our physical and psychological makeup. But what we all have in common is the universal need to be loved and accepted for who we are. And you will find that one day, with the right person."

Thinking on all Dr. Childs said, Reed remained silent. She cupped his jaw, forcing him to look her directly in the eyes. "You know I trust you to make the right decisions. What do you know about Carter? Have you looked online to find out anything about him or his background? I worry about you being in a physical relationship with a person who has no public footprint or connection. These days I know my grandchildren tell me that's the first thing they do before they go on a date, almost as much for safety reasons as for social history. You have a right to know who the person is that you're sleeping with, Reed. For your own protection if nothing else."

Reed wondered, if he'd had a mother or grandmother like her in his life growing up, would he be as screwed up as he was today?

"Carter doesn't have a Facebook or any real social media presence aside from his business. I didn't dig too deep 'cause I thought it would be a little creepy. But I think he has a child." He stopped there, feeling somehow as if he'd let Carter down by revealing this, even if it was only to his doctor.

"A child? Do you think he's married and cheating on his wife?"

"He said no, but I don't know for certain. I don't think he's lying to me."

The skeptical quirk of her brow left no doubt as to her opinion. "And how are you handling this? I know you—is this affecting your sleep and ability to focus in class? You're taking your medications as prescribed, correct?"

Not exactly. Abandoning the decision he'd made at the skating rink to take his medication properly, over the past few weeks Reed once again made several attempts to slowly wean himself off the pills, this time by lowering the dosage, not going off the meds cold turkey. That mistaken text he'd received disturbed him, not so much for the fact that Carter might have a child from a previous relationship, but that he refused to speak to him about it, or share anything personal. It wore him down and Reed once again listened to the voices whispering in his ear, *Not good enough...never good enough.* He didn't tell Dr. Childs since he already knew she'd disapprove.

This time his body reacted more slowly, and Reed felt quietly optimistic, only to have his confidence shattered when the familiar side effects kicked in. The loss of focus coupled with his inability to stick to one task was the worst; he couldn't even read a book without the smallest noise or something else distracting him. Reluctantly and almost tearfully, Reed once again began his regimen of pills, but this time, he didn't recover as quickly. Perhaps the on-again, off-again dosages wreaked havoc with his system; he'd begun to suffer from terrible insomnia, worse than ever. He barely slept at all, and spent half the night questioning whether he was worth Carter's time or if he should even continue with school.

Already knowing her disapproval and what she'd say to him from the last time, Reed chose to keep it to himself rather than discuss it with Dr. Childs. He figured as an adult he should be capable at this point to handle his own problems without rushing to the doctor every time the slightest thing bothered him.

"I'm fine; everything's good."

Even worse than lying to his doctor, was the lying to himself. His fear of needing an increase in his dosage fed into his anxiety, eating away at his nerves from the inside out, causing him to question everything and second-guess all his decisions. Late at night he'd lie awake, listening to the traffic noises slowly fade as the hours ticked by until only his heartbeat steadily thumping broke the silence.

Never the fool, Dr. Childs' all too knowing gaze pierced right through him to that place he didn't let anyone touch; the one full of ugliness and self-doubt; that black and lonely place where a child still sat and waited for his mother to come back and tell him she never meant to leave and that she loved him.

"Really."

His wide smile obviously satisfied her for the moment, and she returned to her chair behind her desk. Inwardly he sighed with relief while shame at lying to one of the few people he cared about and trusted choked him. He really was a shit to lie to her.

As if she could read his mind, she peered over her glasses once again to speak directly to him. "It's not uncommon, you know, for medications to need adjustment as you grow older. I'd be more surprised if you didn't need an adjustment; don't think you need to keep things from me out of fear. It doesn't mean you're not progressing; I can't stress enough how well you're doing."

"Except for my love life." He laughed and stood, hefting his backpack onto his shoulder.

"Once again, that's your choice. You have as much power in this arrangement as Carter does; remember that. Don't let him ride roughshod over you."

"I won't. I gotta go."

He ducked his head and hurried out so she couldn't see his hot cheeks. A wave of desire hit him strongly at the thought of riding Carter like he did their last weekend together. Every sexual experience with Carter left a lasting impression on him. Two weeks later and he still recalled the fullness and the stretch of Carter being inside him, but it was all worth it. He literally tore the sheets he'd twisted in his hands. More amused than angry, Carter had caught him by the wrists, ripped the ruined sheets into pieces, and bound him to the bed where he spent hours sexually teasing him until Reed begged for Carter to fuck him. Laughing at his plight, Carter kissed him with surprising tenderness then untied him and they made such sweet and passionate love, their bodies moving together in perfect synchronicity until Reed lay boneless, too exhausted to do anything but smile.

The elevator doors opened, and he smiled automatically at the people as they moved to the back. He'd finished his classes for the rest of the day and now had to go to the bar to start on the backlog of paperwork Vernon had waiting for him. Exiting the building, Reed stood for a moment while the crowds hurried past him, jealous of all the people around him who had someone they could count on in their lives, then headed off to work.

SEVEN HOURS LATER, Reed blew out an exhausted breath. It was inexplicably busy at the bar tonight, and his feet were killing him. Guess he could blame it on the good weather. He was starving, having skipped lunch and forgotten about dinner, and so tired from lack of sleep the past week, his ass was seriously dragging. Plus, the bar was filled with happy couples who couldn't keep their hands and lips off each other. It reminded him again of how alone he was despite having Carter in his life.

Admit it, you wouldn't mind if Carter was here, sticking his tongue down your throat.

And why shouldn't he be here? Reed threw down his cleaning rag with a frustrated growl. For six months they'd been seeing each other and practically had sex on a public dance floor—why the hell should he be so worried about sending the man a damn text?

That odd text he'd received by mistake confirmed to Reed what he'd suspected from the beginning. No matter what he said, Carter either didn't want anyone to know he was gay, or he was still married. Perhaps the time had come for Reed to delve a bit deeper into Carter's life. But first, to hell with Carter making all the rules. If he wanted to text him, he would.

Shaking his head over his own stupidity, Reed pulled his phone out of his pocket, and before he could talk his way out of it, sent a simple text to Carter.

Hey, what's up?

When the phone remained silent after several minutes, Reed shoved it back inside his pants, only to pull it right back out when he felt the buzz in his pocket.

Reed? What's wrong?

Therein lay the problem. Why should Carter think something was wrong if he texted?

Nothing. I felt like saying hi to you.
Oh. Hi.

Carter's great conversational skills obviously didn't translate over to texting.

What are you up to? I'm at work, and it's crazy busy.
So how do you have time to text?

Wiseass. Reed grinned, and his fingers flew over the keypad.

Because I get a break, dumbass, and I wanted to spend it with you instead of watching couples make out.
I'm in bed.
Alone?

Shit. Reed's fingers hovered over the phone. Did he really ask that?

I'm talking to you, aren't I?
That doesn't answer the question, though.

You're right.

Bastard. Reed worried his bottom lip and stared at the phone. When it seemed nothing further was coming, he slipped the phone back into his pocket only to pull it right out again and send the message he'd wanted to for a while.

Why are you playing this fucking stupid game?

The text was read and in a minute his phone lit up with a call.

Carter.

"What is it?"

"Your text sounded angry."

He couldn't help but laugh. "How can a text sound angry?"

"Trust me. You haven't spoken with pissed-off clients. Remind me to show you one day."

"Yeah, well, I need to get back to work."

"You said you were on a break a minute ago. Come on." Carter's voice dropped, softly persuasive. "Talk to me."

"You never answered my question."

"What? If I'm home or with someone else? Is that the gist of it?"

"Well, yeah," Reed said, a bit reluctantly. Easier to feel brave over text, but with Carter's voice in his ear, all Reed wanted was to slide his hand down the soft skin of

Carter's back and feel the play of muscles under his fingers. With a sinking feeling, Reed recognized the signals. Despite their initial agreement, Reed had fallen for Carter, and from Carter's flippant tone, it was obviously one-sided.

"Never mind," Reed said, disgusted with himself. "It doesn't matter."

"I'm surprised to hear from you. I didn't realize we'd decided to start talking in between our weekends."

"Is that a problem?"

He waited for Carter's answer.

"We discussed this from the beginning. I'm not looking for a relationship, Reed."

"I hardly think texting someone once or twice a week to say hi, how're you doing, constitutes a marriage proposal."

"No. But I don't want to lead you on to think that anything more than what we have right now is possible."

"I didn't ask for anything more, dammit. But if I'm sucking your dick one week, I sure as hell don't see an issue with me asking how your fucking day at work went the next."

The lashing out felt cathartic, almost cleansing.

"Well," said Carter, irritatingly calm and amused. "You're really angry, aren't you?"

"I get it. You're some big important executive, and you don't need everyone to know your business. I'm not asking for that. But sometimes it gets lonely, and I wouldn't mind—"

"I understand. Really. And it's okay. I have to admit..." Carter paused for a moment, and Reed pictured him stretched out in bed, his dark hair spread out on the pillows. "It was nice hearing from you. And to answer your question, yes."

"Yes what? I've forgotten what my question was."

Carter chuckled in his ear, a warm and inviting sound, and Reed wished he was curled up in own his bed so they could have some dirty phone talk. Or, better yet, curled up next to Carter.

"I'm home alone. In my bed."

"Are you married? I can't keep seeing you if you're cheating on your wife." He held his breath, waiting for the fallout.

"God, no, I'm not married. Never have been. Is that what's been troubling you and why you decided to text me?"

A sigh of relief, yet still no answers. "I wish..." Reed stopped, knowing it was useless.

"Don't."

That solitary word fell flat, and all good humor fled. Reed heard a longing and sadness in Carter's voice he hadn't heard before.

"Wishes can't always make dreams come true."

His breath caught in his throat. "I'm the last person you have to tell that to, trust me." He gave up on dreams and wishes when he found out why his mother left.

The phone remained silent, and Reed wondered if Carter had disconnected. "What do you want, Reed? I thought we were having a good time, but something's obviously bothering you. Do you want to end it?"

No, he wanted to cry out, and he gripped the phone tighter in his sweaty palm. *I want you to tell me the truth about yourself. Your hopes and dreams.* A tiny part of his mind whispered, *I don't want to be alone anymore. I want you to fall in love with me.* But he held back, struggling as always not to give in to his emotions, and instead posed the question right back to Carter.

"Do *you*?"

"I think—"

A voice in the background from Carter's end interrupted his answer. Reed strained to hear but couldn't make out the words, only that the voice was high and light. Was that his child? The boy named Jacks from the text? He could tell Carter had placed a hand over the phone to shield the sound. Unashamed of the eavesdropping attempt, Reed strained to listen but could only make out garbled noise. Obviously Carter didn't want him to hear whoever it was.

"I have to go."

"But—"

The phone went dead, and Reed was left staring at the inanimate object in his shaking hands. Goddamn it. Before he could stop himself he threw the phone to the ground, watching it bounce around on the floor. Instead of picking it up, he kicked it across the bar, getting a vicious kind of satisfaction in watching the screen fracture. He bent down, and without even looking to see the extent of the damage, shoved the phone in his pocket and turned to a stunned Vernon, who stood several feet away from him.

Reed sat in the front seat on a roller coaster of unrestrained emotions, incapable of holding back or holding on. If he didn't leave the bar right now, he'd splinter apart and end up lying in pieces on a dirty barroom floor. A pathetic Humpty Dumpty.

"I can't—I gotta…" His breaths came in sharp gasps and sweat poured down his face. Indiscriminate sound rushed in his ears, all the laughter and chatter in the bar melding together to form white noise. He caught sight of Vernon's shocked face, and before he lost it altogether, he squeezed his eyes shut.

"I gotta go. I'm not feeling well."

"Sure, kid. You want me to call your dad?"

Oh, God, that's all I need. Reed hunched his shoulders, wishing he could crawl into his skin, pull the world over his head, and remain buried like a fossil. "No, I'll be all right." He finally drew in enough air to steady his breathing and halt the shaking.

He slanted a look up at Vernon and gave a feeble smile he hoped would satisfy the man and wipe the worried look from his face. At twenty-seven years old he shouldn't feel like a broken child, but that's how it was sometimes. His illness was the master puppeteer and he merely the disjointed marionette who flopped up and down while anxiety played on the strings of his life.

"See?" Reed straightened up to his full height and

forced his trembling lips to smile. "I'm fine." The fact that his disease could consume him like this still, after all the years of treatment and medication, tormented him. So many times over the years he believed he was finally getting a handle on it—and even though Dr. Childs told him he wasn't going to outgrow his anxiety and ADHD and he should stop fighting it—understand its effect on his mind and body, and work through it, a part of him still secretly hoped one day to wake up cleansed and new. Reborn as someone else. Someone normal.

"You don't look fine. You're all sweaty and pale, and a minute ago I thought you were gonna heave all over my bar."

"I'll see you tomorrow, then?" He grabbed his jacket from Clay, the other bartender, who'd gone to the office to get it for him. "Thanks, man."

"No problem. Go home and get some rest, dude. You look like shit."

Without answering or waiting for Vernon to say anything further, Reed left the bar, kept his head down, and walked briskly to the subway entrance. Lucky for him the train was entering the station as he swiped his MetroCard, and he also managed to snag a seat in a corner. All things that, had he been in the right frame of mind, as a native New Yorker would've put him in a good mood. Instead, he huddled up against the wall of the subway car and wondered if he had enough courage to do the smart thing and call it quits with Carter.

Chapter Ten

ON ONE OF those longed for spring days, when you knew you were finally out of the clutches of the long, cold winter, but crisp coolness still bit through the morning air, Carter's already thinly stretched nerves teetered on the breaking point. For over a week Jacks had been having night terrors again, and last night had been one of the worst yet. He'd cried late into the night that he was being good and to please not send him away. It broke Carter's heart to fucking pieces, thinking his little brother still didn't feel safe after everything he'd tried to do.

Carter stayed up with him, holding his shaking body, reassuring him that they'd always be together and nothing and no one would ever come between them. Ever. Only reverting to their routine of three years earlier when Jacks had first come to live with him and Carter singing him lullabies had settled him down to sleep.

Once Jacks stayed asleep, and for the rest of the week, Carter had made up a makeshift bed on the floor to stay with him and watch over him while he slept. He'd catch a quick catnap but nowhere near a full night's rest. Although he'd rarely had a peaceful night of sleep, this arrangement began to wear on his nerves, and he longed for his time with Reed in their private haven.

Somehow, the hotel suite he and Reed shared for their weekends had become more comfortable than his own home. On Saturdays the maid, blushing a hot pink and looking everywhere but at them, had to kick them out of the suite to make up the bed and clean the rooms. As if they needed to hold on to the memories of their weekend together to get them through the rest of the month, their final lovemaking on Sundays turned greedy and more physical. Often the mattress lay tipped off the bedframe to one side, the sheets strewn about, and the air had that unmistakable scent of *someone got well fucked in here.* Their mutual desperation to hold on to each minute and every piece of one another transferred into furious, desperate sex, and Carter relished each bruise and mark Reed left upon his body with his lovemaking.

With Jacks clingy, and having little time for anything other than his care, Carter found himself tempted to call Reed, to talk to the only person who didn't know Carter the businessman or Carter the caretaker, but simply Carter the man. On several occasions he even pulled up Reed's number and stared at the screen but in the end decided against it, not willing to lead him on. After that unexpected text from Reed, Carter suspected

Reed might have developed feelings for him; not love, because how could Reed love him? He didn't know Carter, only the man Carter allowed him to see. The real Carter was nothing but ugliness; a fake and a fraud.

If your own mother didn't want you, why would anyone else? And so Carter remained behind that impenetrable wall of aloofness, content in his make-believe image of strength and mystery. But in those early, silent hours, alone with nothing but the truth mocking him, Carter could confess he wanted nothing more sometimes than to be held, or told he was wanted…needed…loved.

That's when the devil, who resided permanently on his shoulder, would poke at him and laugh, calling Carter a stupid romantic fool. He wouldn't recognize love if it kicked him in the balls, and most likely it would end up being almost as painful. There was no point in wishing for love anyway; he'd gotten through his life so far without it, and except for Jacks, he'd never allowed himself to love anyone. Life was about fighting through the day and getting it done. Rinse and repeat.

But Reed upended him. Reed, with his gorgeous face and that mouth Carter could explore for hours, reveling in his plush lips and honey-sweet tongue. All the sweetness disappeared, however, once they were alone and in bed. The hesitancy and jitteriness Carter spied sometimes in Reed vanished, leaving behind a man who took control and gave Carter the most intense sexual experiences of his life. Like himself, Reed was a study in contrast, only Reed's face was an open book, somewhat like Jackson's. He couldn't hide his emotions—they were right there, shining from his eyes.

His fingers skimmed over the surface of the phone screen, tracing pictures of the two of them. First a silly selfie shot Reed took with Carter's phone as they skated around the ice rink, then one he took the last time they were together of Reed while he slept, his hands tucked under the pillow and one long, naked leg exposed. The warmth of his fiery kisses remained fresh in Carter's mind, as if he'd left him only that morning. Carter turned in his makeshift bed, the white emptiness next to him stretching out in a barren expanse of loneliness.

Rather than call Reed and break his own rules, Carter remained content to stare at his phone, awash in remembrances of their nights together, knowing all too clearly their time together was running short. This was the longest he'd ever spent with one man, and he waited for the time when they'd grow tired of each other's company. Reed texting him to talk that one time seemed to be an excuse to get closer. Soon there'd be demands on Carter's time he wouldn't be able to fulfill because of his responsibility to Jackson.

Strangely enough, Reed had never brought up the text Carter had sent him by mistake, but Carter suspected it sat somewhere in Reed's mind, ticking like a time bomb waiting to explode. Reed was too smart and sensitive to forget something like that, but Carter wasn't about to reveal Jacks's identity to anyone, not even to

Reed who'd managed to somehow infiltrate the impenetrable wall between his personal and home life. He buried his head in the pillows and willed himself to get a few hours of sleep.

In the morning, by the time Helen showed up to take Jacks to school, Carter had recovered from his nighttime maudlin reminiscing, his armor of invincibility firmly back in place. Jackson and his night terrors were what mattered, not stupid, silly dreams of Reed and himself playing house.

Helen's expertise with special-needs children proved invaluable as he navigated these unfamiliar waters of prepubescent behavior and childhood friendship dynamics. The moment she walked through the front door he asked her about Jacks's newest string of nightmares, not even waiting for her to remove her jacket or talk about the weather.

"It's not uncommon, Carter. He's growing up and on the edge of puberty; his body is undergoing hormonal changes he doesn't understand. Plus he now has friends and has to learn to socialize and be in a group where he isn't the main focus of attention all the time. He may have some learning delay issues, but he's a very smart young man and highly attuned to the world around him. Maybe something happened at school that bothered him. If you'd like me to ask the paraprofessional when I pick him up, I will."

"Would you, please? He has to know he's safe here and protected. Last night he kept telling me he didn't want to leave and please don't send him away." Carter turned away so she wouldn't see the tears burning his eyes. "I'll do anything to make sure he's safe."

"Of course." She squeezed his arm. "You've done remarkable things for him; you have to know that. I'll make sure to find out if anything is going on."

There was so much Carter couldn't tell her—how he owed her everything for the help she gave him, how lost he'd be without her guidance. But it wasn't his way to be warm and fuzzy although he tried his hardest with Jacks. Instead he gave Helen a brief, tight smile and headed out the door, forcing his mind to shift to the day ahead and his business; at least there he was always in complete control. The office ran with the tight military precision he required. He might not have control over his personal life, but he damn well would in his professional one.

Which was why, when he arrived at the office and found himself waiting for his first clients to show up, his already strung out nerves frayed to the breaking point, Carter snapped at his secretary, whom he usually treated like gold. He hated when people were late; it showed a lack of professionalism and consideration.

"Lucy!" he yelled out from his office to his secretary. "Where are you?"

"I'm right here, Carter. No need to holler."

Lucy McCrae had been with him since he started Haywood Public Relations with the idea of internet advertising marketing. No matter where people went, they had their phones; why not use their location to push ads to local business onto their social media accounts based on their shopping history? As a single mom, always looking for ways to save money, Lucy had given him the idea to offer business discounts through coupon codes on their smartphones, and the business took off from there.

Instantly contrite, Carter backed down. "I'm sorry. Rough night."

Lucy, one of the few people who knew about Jackson's existence, gave him an understanding squeeze of his shoulder and a small smile.

"I'm sorry. Is it Jackson?"

Lucy might know about his brother, but that didn't mean Carter wanted her sympathy. Care and concern, no matter how generous, grated on him.

"It's all fine. But where's my first appointment? They should've been here ten minutes ago. I have another meeting at ten and then lunch with that couple who're flying in from Florida."

"Don't worry; I'll make sure everything runs smoothly for you." Both her smile and pat on the shoulder were meant to be comforting, but Carter didn't need words, he needed action.

"Please. I promised Jackson we'd go for ice cream tonight, and I can't be late."

Absolutely nothing would keep him from leaving the office at his designated time of six o'clock in order for him to be home for Jacks. And, of course, to relieve

Helen. She could only stay in his home so much. He made it known to the people he did business with that they should not expect evening phone calls or late dinners with him. When he was home, his time was solely devoted to Jacks and would be more than ever now if his brother continued to show signs of feeling unsafe and insecure.

"You won't let him down, I promise." There was genuine warmth in her voice, and she cocked her head. "I hear the elevator. I'll bet that's them." With a quick tug at the sleeves of her blouse, Lucy hurried out of his office, heels tapping on the wooden floors.

Thus began his whirlwind day of back to back (to back) meetings and phone calls with barely a break even for the bathroom. At noon he left to meet with Dan and Carole Grabowski, the potential clients from Florida, who'd never been to New York City before and wanted to see the sights. He took them in a limo, and as they wove their way through the streets, he pointed out landmarks: the Empire State Building, Macy's Herald Square, Madison Square Garden, and of course Times Square. In the daylight the sheer crowds and facades proved overwhelming, even for a New Yorker like himself. Carole wanted to see some of the theatres on Broadway, so Carter had the limo wind its way through the streets so she could take pictures of the famous marquees. The car turned the corner on West 52nd St., and the bar where Reed worked came into view as they drove up the block.

The limo sat idling, stuck in typical noontime traffic, and Carter took the opportunity to pitch his sale one more time.

"How about we head back to my office, and we can talk about what I can do for your business?"

The young, tanned couple from Coconut Creek looked at one another and shrugged.

"We don't need that—you more than explained everything here today. I'm satisfied, and I know Carole is too," said Dan. "I like your no-nonsense style, and we're anxious to break into the New York scene. Why don't we stop and have a drink and something to eat over here and toast the deal? I don't need to be persuaded. We're ready to sign."

The zing of another success and pride in himself and his business rushed through him. The potential for this company was huge; New York City was at the beginning edge of a healthy-food revolution, and he planned for Dan and Carole's business to appear at the perfect time to take advantage of it.

"I didn't think you guys drank alcohol. Not healthy enough."

Carole quirked a brow. "We most certainly enjoy our cocktails," she said with a knowing smile. "How do you think we stay happily married?"

Carter still had an hour and a half before his next telephone call, and making nice with the clients was all part of the job. He leaned forward in his seat to tap on the divider.

"Can you pull over, please, when you get the chance?" The driver took the opportunity of a small space and maneuvered into a No Standing Zone spot. "Thanks. You don't have to wait."

"Are you sure, sir? You have the car for the next hour and a half, and then I'm scheduled to drive them back to the airport."

Damn. "That's right. Tell you what. We'll be ready in an hour; try and grab yourself something to eat."

"Very well, sir." They got out of the car and stood on the sidewalk. It was a beautiful spring afternoon and the sidewalks hummed with hordes of people. Carter assumed Reed was in class and wouldn't be working, and he was proven correct when they entered and he saw only one older man behind the bar.

During daylight hours the bar looked completely different than in the evening party atmosphere. Several other people had the same idea as they did, occupying two of the booths along the side wall, with drinks and lunch plates in front of them, while the bar hosted several older men, their attention captivated by an afternoon ball game on the overhead television.

The bartender came to take their orders. "I've seen you in here before, haven't I?" He stared hard at Carter for a moment before recognition dawned on his face. "Oh, right, you were with Reed. He'll be in shortly."

A warning alarm buzzed inside Carter; the last thing he needed was for Reed to think he was forming an attachment to him by dropping by during the week.

That wasn't part of their arrangement. "You must have me mistaken. We'd like to order please; we're in a bit of a time crunch."

They placed their drink orders, and the bartender walked away, glancing over his shoulder with a frown. Carter didn't miss the dubious look he received but ignored it and turned back to his clients, giving them a half smile and an indifferent shrug.

"I have that kind of face people think they recognize, but they're usually wrong. Now let me outline what I have planned for 'Chop to It.'" He kept talking, taking out from his soft leather briefcase the pad he'd brought with him to finalize their agreements. Using that and the charts he had previously downloaded from his computer to his phone, Carter smoothly outlined his plans to make their custom salad and fresh juice restaurant the next New York sensation.

The drink Carter ordered sat in front of him, remaining largely untouched as his enthusiasm for the project grew, and to his surprise almost an hour had passed by the time they finished ironing out the fine details and agreements. He took a sip of the now watery vodka and grimaced. A fresh drink appeared on the table in front of him. Grateful to the bartender, he glanced up from his notepad to thank him, only to be shocked by the sight of Reed standing in front of him. The memory of their last weekend together sent a surge of lust through Carter, disturbing in its intensity. He shifted in his seat, uncomfortably hard.

"Hi," said Reed, a hesitant smile curving his lips.

"I'm sorry, we're busy here."

Carter's shoulders tensed, and he sat stony-faced. He knew it was a mistake to come here; he needed to shut this down immediately before Reed got the wrong idea and assumed Carter was here to see him. "I'll let you know if we need anything else."

An embarrassed flush stained Reed's face, and his fingers clenched spasmodically at his side.

"I—You don't—" Reed stuttered, then swallowed, and as his Adam's apple bobbed up and down Carter had a crazy desire to lick Reed's throat and taste that all-warm skin. Instead he kept a tight rein on his emotions even as he watched Reed struggle with his own. Like that night in the club, Carter's protective instinct flared, and he wanted to reach out and comfort Reed, but chose the coward's way out and let Reed flounder, hating himself for not helping and for being the cause of the problem in the first place. Carter's heart hurt almost as much watching Reed struggle as it did when he watched Jacks.

"Sure, whatever." Reed spun around and hurried back behind the bar. From beneath half-lowered lids, Carter watched the older man pat Reed on the back and Reed jerk away from his touch with an irritated wave of his hand. A moment of shame swept through Carter when Reed, obviously still upset at the slight, closed his eyes and stood still, then, heaving a great sigh, began polishing a huge stack of glasses sitting on the bar.

Carter turned back to pay attention to his clients with a practiced, smooth smile, although on the inside he felt like the shit he was.

"I think that about wraps up what we wanted to accomplish. I'm thrilled you want to work with me, and I look forward to helping you take New York City by storm."

His phone buzzed, and it was a message that the driver had arrived back outside to take Dan and Carole to the airport. Since they wanted a chance to pick up some souvenirs before their flight, they planned to head directly to the airport. He walked them out to the car and shook their hands in farewell. Dan held the door for Carole, then climbed in and leaned out the window to speak to him one final time.

"Send me the contract today. I'll sign it when I get home tonight, and we'll be up and running."

"Excellent. You'll be hearing from me before five o'clock."

Carter watched them drive away, then pumped his fist in the air.

He hurried back inside, and to his surprise the large stack of glasses in front of Reed had vanished, and Reed stood furiously polishing the bar even though to Carter's eye it gleamed spotless. Unaccustomed shame washed over Carter at Reed's obvious state of distress. He looked distraught, pale, and nothing like the confident man who'd held him down in bed and made him scream his name in passion.

Before he could stop himself, Carter strode through the bar and took hold of Reed's wrist, dirty washcloth and all. No surprise, however, when Reed yanked away from Carter's grasp and turned away, his body stiff with tension.

Carter had no choice but to speak to Reed's back. "I'm sorry, but it was a business meeting, and I don't mix business with pleasure." Even as he spoke the words, Carter heard how weak an excuse it sounded.

Vibrating tight with anger, Reed threw the washcloth on the floor and faced him.

"It wasn't that. I don't... You..." Reed's chest heaved, and he looked as if he was holding on to the edge of his rapidly deteriorating self-control.

Without thinking Carter went into protective mode; his only thought now was to calm Reed down from his overwrought state.

"Shh. It's okay. Take deep breaths and relax." Like he did when Jacks had bad moments, Carter kept his voice soft and soothing, hoping to temper Reed's anxiety, and after a few moments it worked; Reed's breathing steadied, and he was able to draw a deep breath and speak again.

"I don't like this, this,"—he waved his hand in the air, his lips thin with anger—"whatever you call what we have going on between us. I understand your need for holding your professional life separate from your private life. I get that."

"Then what's the problem?" Carter genuinely didn't

understand.

"It was the way you dismissed me, like I wasn't worth the time you took to speak to me. It brought me back to our first night together when you thanked me for sleeping with you, like I was the hired help. I'm a person, Carter, with feelings. We may only be hooking up, but that doesn't mean you get to ignore me in public. Or think it's crazy for me to text or call you sometimes. There's no reason to be ashamed of me, yet you are. I'm a human being with real feelings, not someone you simply fuck once a month and forget."

Standing at the bar listening to Reed unburden himself, Carter understood the damage he caused by his selfishness, but he didn't have the ability to change course. "Will you sit down with me? I have a meeting to get back to at the office, but maybe we can talk before I leave."

For a moment Carter thought Reed might refuse. The sharp line of his jaw remained tense with anger, and a muscle ticked in the smooth skin.

"Please?"

Reed gestured to the table Carter had sat at with Dan and Carole. "I have to clean the table anyway, so you might as well sit." Without waiting for a response, Reed walked off and Carter trailed behind, admiring the fit of the snug, dark-wash jeans across his ass.

Carter liked the slightly dominant side of Reed that surfaced every once in a while. It usually had to be coaxed out of him, but now he seemed in full command. And for Carter it was a huge turn-on. Perhaps it was the result of fending for himself since he was a child and now being so tightly cordoned off from any personal contact except for Jackson that made Carter secretly long to cede that control to someone else.

When he reached the table, Carter slid back into his seat and picked up the drink Reed had placed before him earlier. It disappeared in two healthy gulps. Instead of sitting down across from him, Reed chose to remain standing, his usually vibrant eyes dark and shadowed.

"You know what? I can't. I think I'm done with this…arrangement, or whatever it is we have going on between us." Reed waved his hand in the air while Carter sat in shock, trying to absorb what he was saying. "It's causing me undue stress, and I don't need it."

"Reed," Carter began. "I didn't—"

"Stop." Reed cut him off. "Don't say you didn't mean it because you did. And it's fine. It's your life, and you have the right to live the way you want. However,"—Reed shook his head sadly, looking down at Carter, who suddenly couldn't find enough air to suck in a deep breath—"it's not the life for me." He placed a check on the table. "You can pay Vernon. I've got work to do in the back." Without another word, he turned on his heel and strode away, disappearing through the doorway behind the bar.

Stunned, Carter sat at the table littered with dirty plates and glasses. Without bothering to look at the check, he tossed a wad of twenties on the table. He had a meeting to get to and couldn't begin to wrap his head around what Reed said. Chalk it up to him once again disappointing someone. Someone he didn't want to admit he'd begun to care about.

Because it wasn't Reed that Carter was ashamed of, it was himself. Like he knew he'd do from the start, he'd hurt a truly nice person. It was why he didn't do relationships; no one deserved to get stuck with a person like him—someone who was blind to anything other than his own needs and wants. There was little Carter could find about himself to be worthy of love; the seeds of self-loathing had been planted early and dug their roots far and deep into his psyche.

His life was a riot of threads, the younger years creating a spider web spun out to include Jackson, his business, and the carefully drawn persona he allowed the public to see. He couldn't possibly add another circle to include someone like Reed, who'd rightfully demand and deserve all of him. His past and his present. His heart.

His past had been nothing to remember after he left home. Lucky enough to have his high-school diploma, he worked wherever he could, sleeping in parks and shelters until he found a steady job in the mail room of an advertising firm, where he listened and kept his eyes and ears open, taking in everything he heard and overheard. He could work there by day and go to college at night. After four years he took his savings and his information, and with his new name, left to make it big in New York City. Calvin Hastings had become, legally, Carter Haywood.

There were times he believed his own carefully crafted backstory of parents who died young, leaving him to be raised by elderly relatives. The lines of reality blurred, so he wasn't certain he could tell where the Carter Haywood he created and his true self became separated.

Fear and crushing self-doubt crawled through his veins like a sniper on a rooftop, sweeping through him, but he blocked them, like he did all his mistakes and the ugliness trapped inside him. No time to sit and reminisce or beat himself up over what might or could have been. From the first Carter knew there was a chance feelings might develop when he made this arrangement with Reed. He'd been willing to risk it and try because of their undeniable physical attraction.

But now all that was done, and surprisingly it wasn't him who wanted it to end but Reed. Pain shot through him like a cramp, and he almost gasped out loud, it hurt so badly. Maybe he was sick, or something was breaking apart inside him.

He might be several years younger, but Reed was the mature one in this twosome, for Carter could easily have imagined keeping up this arrangement for years. He left the bar, hailed a cab and settled into the back seat; then, as they drove away, craned his neck for one last look through the rear window of the cab and heaved a sigh of regret. Whatever love he had, needed to be reserved for Jackson; his heart wasn't available for a double occupancy.

That didn't stop him from thinking about Reed, no matter how busy he got after he'd returned to the office; for the rest of the day his mind wandered from discussions of market forecast projections and sales demographics to recalling the weight and press of Reed's lithe, naked body as he pushed inside him, or his own hoarse cry when they climaxed together. And as quickly as the image rose in his mind, Carter dismissed it.

Some things weren't meant to be.

Chapter Eleven

HE MIGHT HAVE meant it when he told Carter they were finished, but that didn't make Reed any less miserable for having said it. And as the days went by and Reed's life slipped back into its usual monotony of school and work, he wondered what Carter was doing and if he missed him. Every morning he checked his phone, foolish with hope that he'd see a text from Carter with an *I miss you and I want to see you*. His phone remained depressingly blank, and Reed lectured himself to stop acting like a lovesick jerk.

Once again he'd fallen for a man who didn't have a heart to give. And while Carter wasn't cruel as Mason had been, their tentative relationship, for want of a better word, proved much worse. He'd treated Reed with tenderness, making him feel wanted and special. Reed fell for him, without realizing until he stepped off the ledge that he was plummeting headfirst toward earth without a safety net.

Even his father noticed his miserable emotional state and brought it up when he came to the bar for dinner one night, about two weeks after his confrontation with Carter.

"What's wrong? You look like shit. Do you feel okay?"

Reed reached over and pinched a few fries off his father's burger plate. Because he hadn't been sleeping well, Reed decided to halve his medication the past few days, and his appetite came roaring back to life; he'd already plowed through a towering pile of nachos yet the emptiness remained inside.

"Yeah, school and stuff."

"Ask him about the stuff," said Vernon, joining them. "He's doing great in school, told me he got all A's on his tests. It's that bastard he was seeing."

His father turned a curious eye on him, and like he was four again Reed squirmed under his regard. "You didn't tell me you were seeing anybody. What happened?"

Everything. I fell in love, then told the guy I didn't want to see him again.

"Nothing." Taking time to decorate his French fry in a patina of ketchup, Reed avoided looking at his father. "I saw someone a few times, but it didn't work out." He glared hard at Vernon, daring him to contradict what he said.

"Why are you bullshitting your father?" Obviously Vernon didn't put much stock in Reed remaining angry with him. "This guy kept coming into the bar, and he and Reed began seeing each other. Then one day he shows up with his fancy clients or somethin' and pretends like he don't know Reed. Piece of shit, I say."

Reed groaned his frustration and gulped down his club soda. Angry as he was with Carter, he'd begun to wonder if he'd been too quick to break it off with him. From the beginning Carter had made him no promises. If he wanted to keep his business and personal life separate, he had that right. The times when it was the two of them had been pretty damn special. He chewed on his fingernails and stared off into space, recalling how Carter's mere voice and touch broke him down to the core.

Despite Carter insisting the two of them weren't in a relationship and never would be, he still noticed little things, things only someone who cared would pay attention to. If Reed had mentioned he enjoyed eating something, merely in passing, Carter made sure to have it in the suite, waiting for him when he showed up after work the next weekend they spent together. One time he complained of a stiff back from studying, and Carter surprised him with stress relieving bath salts they both enjoyed in the oversized jetted hotel tub.

He'd also given him small gifts—nothing expensive, but thoughtful ones, like a special reading light to cut down on the glare.

"For all your studying," Carter said with a smile when Reed opened the box. *"You don't want to strain your eyes, although you'd look sexy as hell in a pair of glasses."*

Things like that made Reed so curious about

Carter's personal life and why he tried to make it all about the sex yet showed a surprisingly sweet side as well. And even though he'd been the one to end it between them, Reed needed that final closure, that understanding of why—why Carter presented himself to the world as a cold businessman, devoid of feelings, when Reed knew him to be the exact opposite. Reed supposed it was the anxiety in him that needed those details wrapped up nicely before he could move on. He could never be satisfied until he had all the facts and the hows and whys clear in his mind.

"Reed. *Reed.*" He came back to the present to find his father and Vernon staring at him.

"What?" He brushed his hair back in his typical nervous gesture, noticing his hand trembling. The signs all pointed to his stress levels at the maximum he could endure. Perhaps he needed to visit Dr. Childs and ask her for advice, more as a mother figure than as his therapist.

"We've been calling your name. What's wrong? Is Vernon right? Did this guy mistreat you?"

"No. He's wrong. He and I…I'm fine." Irritated at having to discuss his love life in a bar with his father and his boss, Reed shut down. "Everything's fine. I need to serve those people over there." Without a backward look, he strode to the waiting customers and decided to get a grip on his life and stop allowing everyone—Dr. Childs, his father, Vernon, even Carter—to make decisions about what was best for him. Happiness didn't fall into your lap—that was for fairy tales and movies. Sometimes you had to fight for the right to be happy, which might make the ever after all the sweeter.

But putting himself out there, taking that initial step scared the hell out of Reed. The anxiety spiked, crowding out his best intentions. Sure, taking a risk meant a chance to succeed. But what if he tried and failed? What if he lost it all? Throughout the rest of his shift, Reed wrestled with himself, still uncertain what to do, hating the doubts that continued to plague him.

Later that night when he'd gotten home from work and showered, Reed sat in bed, cup of tea in hand, and began to search for anything he could find on Carter Haywood. Maybe Dr. Childs was right and he should do a little deeper research into Carter's background. It might give him better insight into the type of man who on the outside seemed to have everything yet Reed knew for a fact led a hollow and lonely life. The nights they spent together, Reed, up often at night from his medicines, studied Carter in his sleep. Restless and wakeful, Carter would sometimes cry out or reach for him, and Reed drew him close, feeling the pounding of his heart. Warm and comforted, they'd both fall asleep, if only for a little while.

Reed bypassed all the usual stock articles which seemed to repeat the same carefully constructed biography: "came out of nowhere to take the PR field by storm" or "has an uncanny knack for predicting the hottest new trends before anyone." The only personal fact about the man, if you could call it that, was the last line of his bio, which merely stated in one succinct line: "Carter Haywood lives in Brooklyn."

Surely there had to be more to Carter than his resume and sharp business skills. And though it was weird to obsess over a man who was almost a stranger, in some ways Reed knew him better than anyone else, having taken the man inside his body. For that reason alone, he couldn't walk away as easily as he should. He hadn't had that many lovers and none who'd stirred up these mixed emotions.

It all made him want to hold on even tighter, no matter that he was the one letting go.

An hour passed and he'd dug a bit deeper, a trend becoming obvious in the charitable contributions made by both Carter individually and his firm—all were to children's charities. *He's not a complete bastard,* thought Reed. Deep down he knew there was way more to Carter Haywood than a winning smile and a boatload of confidence. Carter might be only thirty-two, but the shadows hiding in his eyes told a story of a lifetime already lived. It hurt Reed to have to dig for bits and pieces of the life story of the man he'd spent entire weekends with and made love to.

Then again, Reed hid some pretty big secrets about himself from Carter as well.

A several-years-old headline in an online newsletter grabbed his attention, and with mounting excitement, Reed read the blurb, his tea growing cold. It acknowledged a gift of ten thousand dollars to an organization dedicated to helping children with disabilities, on behalf of Carter Haywood and Jackson Miller.

Reed fell back on his bed with a whoosh of accomplishment. That name, Jackson, could be the full name for Jacks, who was the child Carter asked someone to pick up from another child's house in the text. If it wasn't Carter's child, maybe he was a brother or a cousin? Reed hated having to play a guessing game, but instead of getting angrier at Carter, all he felt was deflated and unhappy. He couldn't understand why Carter continued to hold him at a distance.

In the beginning he had respected Carter's need for privacy and anonymity and made no attempt to delve into his personal life; their meet-ups sounded sexy and intriguing, and Reed was more than willing to play along. But Reed had never been into sex for the mere physical release.

In every prior relationship, he'd craved an emotional connection before becoming physical with the man; that had always been his problem. He didn't have it in him to casually give his heart away. Reed thought he'd reached a point where he could turn off the needy side of his personality and remain as coolly detached as Carter. He'd tried and held strong for several months, but Carter's tender attentiveness and the incredibly passionate sex they shared broke down all his best intentions. Reed fell harder than ever before.

But this last time at the bar had hurt. Hurt badly.

Because the one thing Reed had been denying for a while was that he'd developed feelings for Carter; how could he not? They may only have been together a handful of times, but their days and nights were spent crawling inside not only each other's bodies, but their minds, hearts, and souls. Reed knew what Carter sounded like as he slept and the sounds of pleasure he made stretching awake in the morning. How his jaw tensed and his neck arched and strained in an effort to hold himself together as he climaxed deep inside Reed. Even now, Reed could hear Carter's wickedly seductive chuckle echoing in his ear when Carter cornered him in the shower, spread-eagled him to the tiled wall, and proceeded to take him apart with his soft, flickering tongue.

He refused to delve too deep inside his own heart to see if it remained intact or if he'd already given a part of it away to Carter. But tonight Reed made a decision, one he hoped he'd have the guts to keep once the morning came. After his class he planned to visit Carter's office and let him know both of them were worth so much more than anonymous fucks in hotel rooms. More importantly, Reed disliked the thought of Carter finding other men to replace him if he'd taken Reed's brush-off seriously. As a matter of fact, he fucking hated it.

Somehow Reed had to persuade Carter that once bodies were engaged, hearts were sure to follow. And, if he was willing to take that chance with Reed, then there might be a way for them to move ahead. Together.

Don't be intimidated. The mantra played inside Reed's head the next afternoon when he entered Carter's office building. After the obligatory sign-in at the security desk, he waited by the elevator, whistling tunelessly under his breath, foot tapping with nervous energy. It was only after he realized people stared at him that he stopped, understanding his behavior might make other people uneasy.

The elevators whooshed him up to the twenty-first floor, disgorging him into a brightly lit hallway where he followed the signs to the doorway marked "Haywood & Associates." The door opened up to a waiting area where an enormous dark wood desk stood as a barrier to the offices behind it. A red-headed woman in her mid-fifties sat behind it, staring intently at her computer while she sipped from a large mug that said: *Wine—the Other Venti Drink.*

She looked up and gave him a brief yet friendly smile.

"May I help you?"

His heart pounding, Reed ran a shaking hand through his hair and swallowed. "Uh, yeah, I mean, yes. I'd like to see Carter, please."

At her slightly shocked expression, Reed realized she had no idea who he was or how he knew her boss. "I mean, Mr. Haywood."

Her eyes narrowed. "You don't have an appointment, do you?"

"N-no," he answered, growing more intimidated by the minute, "but if you tell him Reed is here, I think he'll want to speak to me."

"I'm sorry, but Mr. Haywood is on a business call, and then he has another call right after that. I can take your name and information and have him get back to you."

Brisk, efficient, and warning him off, Reed decided. That only made him more determined to see Carter.

"I'll wait, thanks." He turned his back and began to walk over to sit down in one of the chrome and leather chairs set about in the waiting alcove, when she called out to him.

"That will be impossible. Mr. Haywood has client meetings all day. He doesn't have a free moment."

"I'm sure he has to have lunch or take a break." This woman had no idea how recalcitrant he could be when someone tried to tell him no.

"He had a lunch call. Now please. Give me your number, and I'll make sure to have him call you."

Her phone buzzed, and she picked it up and tucked it under her chin. "Yes?" She listened and began scribbling notes with her right hand while manipulating the keyboard of her computer with her left.

Reed took that as a sign that she couldn't stop him if he took off looking for Carter, so without giving it a second thought, he strode right past her desk to the back of the office suite. He heard her call out to him but ignored her, and with the blood rushing to his head, hustled down the corridor, checking the doors to see if one had Carter's name on it. All he could see were conference rooms, a file room, and a door marked "restroom."

The hallway curved around, widening to a double door with Carter's name on a placard. Finally. Without stopping to think, Reed pushed it open, stepped inside, and closed the door behind him. A thrill shot through Reed at the sight of Carter in his formal business attire of navy suit, stark white shirt, and bright-green tie. To the bar he'd always come casually dressed, and Reed remembered him with his clients—he'd had on a dress shirt, no tie and unbuttoned at the neck. And of course, Reed knew what lay beneath all the clothing: long limbs, lean muscles, and warm, naked flesh.

"What the—" Carter stood, a flush rising to stain his cheeks.

"Hi. I came to talk to you."

Reed walked closer to the L-shaped desk with three computers and multicolored files stacked in neat rows across the top.

"Haywood, are you there?" A disembodied voice carried from the computer screen, and to Reed's dismay he realized Carter was on a video conference, not a simple telephone call.

"Yes, yes, of course I am, Grant," Carter said in a soothing voice.

There was nothing soft about the look Carter shot him, and chastened, Reed sank into a small chair positioned off to the side of the wide desk. This was the Carter from their last encounter at the bar: cold, hard, and strictly business. The hotly passionate man who held him in his arms and kissed him senseless during their weekends together was nowhere to be found. Before him sat a man he didn't know and didn't like very much. This Carter made him anxious, and the stupidity of his actions finally sunk in.

"I was saying that I believe the demographics being what they are now, with more people choosing to live in the city and have more than one pet, they will be driven to buy your pet food because they believe in high quality, natural ingredients, and having the best for their animals, who they consider part of their family. And we can push your ads to their smartphones and tablets when they're in their favorite grocery store as well as any pet store."

"Good. That's what I want to hear. Let me think about it, and I'll have an answer for you tomorrow."

"Of course. Take your time, and give my best to Sharlene."

Carter clicked the keyboard and then exhaled long and hard, his chin falling to his chest. Reed tensed and was about to open his mouth to speak when the phone buzzed and without even looking, Carter reached for the phone and hit the button.

"Yes."

A woman's voice filled the room, presumably the secretary up front. "Carter, a man came in and—"

"It's okay, Lucy. Do me a favor, though. Hold my calls, okay?"

"But you have—"

"I know." For the first time Carter looked directly at him, and Reed sucked in a breath at the hard glint in his eyes. "I'll let you know when I'm ready. It won't take long."

Dismissed again. That choking sensation returned, the one where so many important things to say became twisted up and caught in his throat, yet he couldn't get the words out fast enough. While Carter gave his secretary instructions, Reed talked himself down off his emotional cliff.

"Why are you here?"

Carter's harsh tone, one he'd never heard before, jolted him back to reality. He'd been so busy inside his own head he hadn't realized Carter was off the phone. Damning his shaking hands, Reed studied Carter's hard, unforgiving face, trying to find some semblance of the man who whispered his desire while setting his body aflame.

"I, uh, um…" Thoroughly rattled now, Reed couldn't answer. Furious with himself and his escalating anxiety, he blinked back the tears that threatened to humiliate him even further and attempted a deep, calming breath.

"Here." Carter sat next to him and poured a cup of

water from a pitcher on his desk and gave it to him. curving his palm around Reed's to steady its shaking. "Take your time."

Several moments passed before the tightness in Reed's throat eased, allowing him to swallow. Reed finally raised his eyes to meet Carter's, which to his surprise gazed back at him, soft with understanding.

"I'm sorry. I don't know what happened."

Liar, but now was not the time for a true confession to his screwed-up mental state.

"Don't worry about it. I used to feel like that when I took debate class in school." The tiniest hint of a smile broke through. "I'd want to throw up in the bathroom right before class."

"I can't imagine anyone winning an argument against you. You're pretty persuasive."

Carter's eyes dimmed. "I couldn't win you over. You left."

Reed set his cup on the desk, then hitched his chair around to face Carter, and the rush of words exploded before he had a chance to think. "I left because I can't be your shadow lover anymore. I'm sorry I misled you, and I really thought I'd be able to do it, but when you brushed me off like that in front of those people, it hurt me. Badly. More than I thought it would."

He stopped, and Carter took his hand. "Feel better now?"

"A little. But not enough."

The sound of his breathing filled the room. Carter

dropped his hand.

"What do you want from me? I can't make you promises."

"I'm not asking for forever. I'm looking for respect from the man I'm sleeping with. But it all comes down to you."

Reed watched Carter's jaw work but couldn't stop and pressed onward.

"We have something, something more than physical, at least. I know you've felt it."

At that, Carter smiled and slid his hands up Reed's thighs toward his crotch. "I love feeling you."

Annoyed, Reed moved away from Carter to stand in front of the immaculate desk and looked down at him as he spoke. He'd expected this response and was prepared. "Don't make a joke of my feelings. I get you have a very private side; I'm not saying you have to introduce me to the family and invite me over for barbecues. But like I said before, I'm not your dirty secret to hide away in hotel rooms and never think about except for those two weekend nights. I deserve more than that and so do you."

"I can't give you more than one weekend a month; I'm sorry."

The tightness in his chest released a bit. "You've made that clear enough from the beginning. But I won't be with someone who's cheating on a wife or another lover."

"I'm not; I've told you before I don't have a wife."

Carter closed in on him, pinning him to the desk. "I barely have time for myself; there is no wife, husband, or other lover. There's only you. And I have no fucking idea what to do about it." Carter held him close, and his misgivings melted away.

How could it be wrong when Carter's arms around him made everything right in his world?

"It's become more than sex for me, Carter. I can't lie to you."

Reed found it hard to breathe, never mind talk, with Carter's lips so close to his. This wasn't panic or anxiety, though. This was something new and wondrous, leaving him shaking in the aftermath of realization.

Love.

"I don't want you to lie, and I'm not lying either when I tell you I was fucking miserable thinking of someone else touching you." Carter leaned him back over the desk, his chest pressing against Reed's, and there it was again; that furious pounding of Carter's heart that told Reed everything he needed to know, even if Carter didn't understand it himself.

Reed kept his thoughts to himself, knowing now was not the time. "That didn't happen; it couldn't. I don't want anyone else. Do you?"

The harsh lines around Carter's mouth deepened with his frown. "No. I want you. I want you right now as a matter of fact. So fucking bad. Do you feel it?"

"Yeah." Reed reached down and traced the bulge of Carter's erection through the fine wool of his trousers, feeling it twitch and thicken beneath his fingers, and thought how easy it would be to take Carter in his mouth and give him pleasure. Instead, he caught Carter's face between his hands and took his mouth hard, pouring everything he couldn't put into words into his kiss. Carter moaned his approval, his hands roaming, pulling up Reed's sweater to splay against the naked skin of his back.

So fucking good. Reed wanted to give in right then and bend over that desk, but he refrained, knowing if he did it this time, Carter would come to expect these types of "visits." Reed wanted more, and not without regret, pulled away.

"Next time we see each other it will happen, but it won't be over a desk in your office. Can you try to find the time to be together more than only one weekend a month?"

Carter leaned against the desk and wiped his mouth, slanting a haunted look of regret at Reed. His tie lay pulled off center, and his now wrinkled shirt had come untucked from his suit pants. Those full lips Reed couldn't get enough of pouted, red and kiss-swollen, and his silvery eyes drooped, heavy-lidded with lust. He looked beautiful but broken, and Reed ached to hold him.

"I—don't know…" Carter turned and braced his hands on the desk, his back toward Reed. "You don't understand."

"Help me to, then." Reed laid a hand on Carter's

back, feeling not only the power in his shoulders but the dampness of sweat and distress. "I won't run away. Talk to me and let me try, if I can."

In a television show or movie, Carter would turn around with a smile and they'd kiss and everything would fall into place. Life didn't imitate art, however, and Carter remained facing the desk, unyielding and silent, incapable of opening up to give Reed what he needed.

So in the end this visit had proved useless, and Reed would be damned if he'd humiliate himself any further.

"I see." He heaved a sigh, then walked over to his chair and picked up his knapsack, which lay discarded on the floor. "You know, I thought you were the smart one. You have it all; money, your own business, and that enviable confidence I always wished I had." He hefted the knapsack to his shoulder and put his hand on the doorknob. "But now I see how wrong I was. You're no better than me and probably worse."

He opened the door. "At least I know what I want and I'm not afraid to admit it." Without waiting for a response he left Carter's office, closing the door behind him with a thump.

Chapter Twelve

A WEEK HAD passed, and he'd heard nothing from Reed, but realistically Carter didn't expect to. From the way Reed left it between the two of them, he'd made it clear that unless Carter acknowledged the existence of their as-yet-to-be-discussed relationship and made more time for the two of them, Reed wanted no part of Carter.

He soldiered through the days like always, signing a few big contracts that normally would have him feeling good about life but instead brought him little joy. All Carter thought about were Reed's parting words and that final, devastating kiss, so filled with desire and passion he swore he still tasted it on his tongue. For all his seeming naiveté, Reed had nailed who Carter was—a fraud. Better off without someone whose wise eyes so easily pierced his shield.

That didn't stop his dreams from betraying him. Carter dreamed of Reed, in a world that didn't exist for him. A world awash with color instead of grayness. One of joyful noise, not the great dark void he lived in.

Fuck it. Carter swept a file off his desk, sending reams of paper fluttering to the floor, and rested his head in his hands. He didn't need anyone. He had Jacks, and his brother's welfare came before anything and anybody. Sex he could find anywhere. He only had one family, and Carter was determined not to let his little brother down.

In fact, he wanted to see if Helen had found out why Jackson had such trouble sleeping lately. The pediatrician told him to keep a chart of Jacks's sleep habits and to let them know if there were any other changes in his daily routine.

He picked up the phone and called Helen.

"Carter? Is everything okay?"

"Yes, of course. I wanted to know if you'd gotten any information from the school that might shed some light on Jacks's sleep problems. The nightmares haven't gone away."

"I have a call in to the head administrator. As soon as she gets back to me, I'll let you know."

He knew he could count on her. Helen had never let him or Jacks down.

"Thanks. I don't mean to push, but…"

"You want to find out if anything's upsetting him, I understand. I do too. But to put your mind at ease a bit, I stayed for a while after drop off and the new boys Jacks has made friends with have introduced him to other children, which I personally think is good for him."

Alarm surged through him. "Who are they? Are they

nice kids?"

"Very nice. Henry and David you know, and there is another boy and two girls; they all live within half a mile of us here. It's a good sign."

Helen's words didn't reassure him. "Maybe they're teasing him or treating him badly. What do we really know about what's going on?"

"Carter, stop. You're being ridiculous."

Was he? Maybe. He had no basis for comparison. Raising a child had never been in his plan; he had no idea what he was doing. And a child with disabilities? He had no fucking clue if he was doing it right or wrong. All he knew was to give Jacks his love, and security, and do everything he could to protect him from the world.

"But how do we know? I don't want him hurt."

"Oh, Carter, life isn't always going to be kind, you know that. And Jacks is a pretty resilient kid, for all his problems. I think he's ready to take this step, and you have to let him, even if it means stumbling a little. I see how much he wants these friends."

"I'm smothering him, is what you're saying."

"I don't think—Wait. I have another call. Maybe it's the school. I'll call you back."

The phone went dead in his hands, and Carter stood scowling. It was how Lucy found him when she opened the door.

"Carter, your next client is here."

He gazed at her as if he'd never seen her before. Was

this what it all came down to? Meeting after meeting, call after call, and for what? It seemed even Jacks was trying to find his place in the world, a place that no longer included Carter as the focus. Reed only wanted him if he was willing to tell him everything, but he couldn't. The whole world he'd painstakingly built was slipping away bit by bit.

He had no answers.

"I'll let you know when to bring them in after I finish this call from Helen."

For now, he'd focus on his business, the one thing in his life he had total control over and had never let him down.

WALKING INTO HIS house to see Jackson's face light up with a smile made every miserable part of this day irrelevant. Never one to be demonstrative, tonight Jackson got up from the kitchen table where he and Helen had been going over his homework and gave him a hug.

"Hey, buddy." Carter smoothed Jacks's hair off his face. It was like staring into a mirror of innocence. He and Jacks shared the same dark hair and silver eyes, but there was no taint of disappointment or hardship on Jacks's smooth cheeks. "How's it going?"

He didn't expect a response, so when Jacks took his hand and led him over to the center island, Carter prepared to listen to Helen give a recap of the day. He settled down on his stool, and Jacks handed him a sheet of paper with math problems.

"I did them all."

Frozen with shock for a second, Carter recovered and quickly glanced at Helen who unsuccessfully tried to blink back the tears which streamed down her face. Afraid to break the magic, he swallowed hard and kept his voice steady.

"You did? That's awesome."

The brilliant smile on Jacks's normally somber face was as if Christmas, New Year's, and winning the lottery all happened simultaneously.

"The teacher said they were all right." His legs swung under the counter top. "Can I have mac and cheese for dinner?"

Helen answered him, but Carter barely heard her response; he couldn't take his eyes off the paper. Jacks had done some fraction work and several complicated-looking logic problems. At every parent-teacher conference they'd praised Jackson's intellectual capabilities but confided he had trouble translating what went on in his mind, putting it down on paper, and verbalizing his needs. To come home and find a set of math problems written and have a conversation about them blew Carter away.

A hand touched his. "In the phone call today the paraprofessional told me she thinks these new friends of his are not only bringing out Jacks's need for social interaction but are helping him in other ways as well.

His sleeplessness could be his body and mind adjusting to overstimulation from all the new experiences. I knew once he found his niche and other children he felt comfortable with, he'd blossom. Isn't it wonderful?"

With a stab in his heart, Carter watched Jacks happily eat the dinner Helen had prepared. The occupational therapy he'd had several years earlier had helped him with his dexterity and muscle tone, and he had little trouble handling his utensils or pens and pencils anymore. Now he was learning to branch out emotionally and take tentative steps toward creating a social life. This breakthrough should have thrilled Carter, but instead it filled him with dread.

As much as he wanted Jacks to soar, Carter feared a crash.

"What if they decide they don't like him anymore or don't want to play with him? You know how sensitive he is. I've tried to shield him from how miserable life can be, but I can't do it all for him." He ran his fingers through his hair. "No matter how much I want to protect him."

"What if they love him and it all works out? How can you keep him from it?"

A soft rain pattered against the windows, and Helen went to shut the blinds.

"How long has Jacks been with you now, three years?"

Carter slid off his stool and went to the refrigerator to get a bottle of water. "Yeah. I found you right afterward."

"Oh, I remember." She chuckled and shook her head when he offered her one. "I don't think I've ever seen anyone so scared yet so determined to do things right."

He glanced over at Jacks who, having finished eating, was now scrutinizing the workbook that lay open before him on the large center island in the kitchen. Everything in his life from that day forward had been planned with Jacks's needs in mind. Carter had always wanted a home with a large kitchen and a big center island. He'd never planned on having children of his own, but having devoured family television shows as a child, a big kitchen where everyone sat around at the end of the day spelled home. As soon as Jacks came to live with him, he'd had one installed.

He felt a tug on his arm.

"Can I have dessert?" Jacks gave him one of those increasingly more common smiles. "Helen bought ice-cream pops."

If this kept up, Carter would buy him an ice-cream truck just to have Jacks happy and feeling safe. "She did, huh? What flavors?"

"I don't know; I'll check." He tore off, running over to the refrigerator and flinging open the freezer door. "Vanilla and chocolate. I want chocolate. Can I, please?"

At Carter's nod, Jacks brought the box over to him and laid it on the center island. "I don't want to rip the box. Can you open it?"

Recalling Jacks's need for precision and order, Carter understood, and he showed him where the little pull tab was. "Here. Pull that, and it will open the side of the box."

Jacks did, but a little of it stuck and tore the side off.

"I'm sorry; I didn't mean to ruin it." Looking devastated, Jacks blinked back tears. "Now it won't close right."

"It will; it's fine, see?" With the patience he'd taught himself in dealing with Jacks, Carter took out an ice-cream pop and then pointed out the little tab. "That fits in the little slot, and that's all there is to it. So don't worry."

"Are you sure?"

"Totally. Now go eat, and then after we go over your homework, you get to pick what we do tonight since you did so well in school today."

That was their everyday routine—dinner, dessert, homework, and then family time. He was helping Helen with her coat when Jacks, whose face was covered in smudges of chocolate, piped up, "I told my friends I'd go on the computer tonight."

Carter heard Helen's swift intake of breath, and he too needed a moment to respond. Before now, surprisingly, Jacks had never shown any interest in computer games.

"The computer? For what?"

"When I was over at Henry's house he taught me to play this game called Minecraft, and it's so fun. I want to play. Can I?"

"Minecraft?" Bewildered, he turned to Helen. "Do you know what that is?"

Chuckling, she finished buttoning up her jacket. "Oh, you're in for it now. It's all the rage with the kids; I hear them talking on the playground, and it's like the black hole once they get started."

Carter couldn't have cared less; this newly talkative Jacks, one who asserted himself with a circle of friends, was all he'd hoped for the past three years and never thought he'd see. Despite the doctors advising him that it would take time, Carter had never believed they'd reach a milestone like he considered this day to be.

"Sure, buddy. After cleanup and homework I'll get you set up."

Helen left, and after he made himself a sandwich, he and Jacks cleaned up the kitchen. Armed with a big cup of coffee, he poured Jacks a glass of orange juice, and they sat down to tackle vocabulary. Jackson's mind was anywhere but on the paper in front of him. After several attempts to settle him down, Carter issued an ultimatum.

"If you don't finish the list of words, you're not playing the game."

Jackson pouted but set his jaw in determination and powered through the rest of his words while Carter ate. After testing him, Carter was satisfied he understood and closed the workbook. Helen had proven correct again when she told him once Jackson felt safe and secure enough, he'd be like a little sponge, sucking up as much information as he could take in.

"All finished. Let's get you going on your game."

The biggest smile he'd seen yet broke across Jackson's face, and he danced around Carter as they walked to the living room where he had a desktop set up.

"I got really good at the game; wait until I show you."

Carter created a profile for Jacks on the computer and then watched him sign in to the game with deliberate keystrokes, tongue caught between his teeth. An animated screen appeared, and Carter had zero desire to figure out the game that so entranced his little brother. But after settling down on the sofa and listening to Jacks's satisfied "Yes!" and cheers, it was clear at least he was having a good time.

Carter opened his laptop and attempted to work on the new Chop to It account, but his mind refused to concentrate on salads and juices. How could it, when he wondered what Reed was doing tonight and if he had started seeing someone else yet. The thought of someone else touching him, never mind fucking him, nearly blinded him with a wave of pain so strong he physically felt it in his chest. The screen blurred before his eyes, and he wanted to throw up. What the fuck was wrong with him? It had never been difficult to walk away from any other man without a second thought. But Reed was nothing like any other man.

Different from his usual pick-ups, Reed had neither

the swagger of the sexually confident serial clubber nor the polished appearance of the urbane, Upper East Side sophisticate Carter typically bedded. But none set his blood on fire like Reed did, his sleepy golden eyes heavy with lust as he took Carter deep inside his body, or gazing up at him from his knees while he sucked Carter off, his glistening lips wrapped around Carter's cock.

What Reed had said to him in his office was the truth: Reed was by far a better man than Carter and much less of a coward. But fuck it, he had reasons. Reed couldn't know the fruits of Carter's three-year-long journey sat in front of a computer tonight having the time of his life. None of that would have been accomplished if Carter hadn't been there every step of the way, being there for Jacks, protecting him, and always loving him.

Jacks's brilliant smile alone made every sacrifice worthwhile.

An hour later, Carter shut his laptop and stretched. "Okay, buddy boy, time for bed."

Usually amiable, Jacks scowled. "Not yet. I'm still playing."

Remembering what Jacks's doctor and Helen had said, that defiance was normal and even good for Jacks, Carter remained firm yet calm. "It's a school night, and we both need to get some sleep. Say good night, and you'll see everyone tomorrow."

Jacks stuck out his lower lip in a pout. "We were in the middle of something."

The full conversations he and Jacks now had disconcerted Carter a bit; Jacks had gone from mostly silent and agreeable to talkative and recalcitrant. Carter understood testing limits came naturally to a child and wondered if this was a precursor to the rebellious teenage years. He gazed longingly at his liquor cabinet.

"I said now. Let's go. It's already past nine, and you should've been in bed already. Shut it down yourself, or I'll do it for you."

They glared at each other for a second; then Jacks relented and slowly typed out a message to one of his friends and powered the computer off. Without a word, he stood and walked away.

"I hope you aren't mad at me, but if you're going to start using the computer, we'll need to set some house rules for its use." Carter followed Jacks up the stairs and to the bathroom, where Jacks wordlessly took his toothbrush and began to brush his teeth.

"I'm glad you're making friends, Jacks, but I'm not going to let them change our schedule and way of doing things around here." Carter sat on the edge of the bathtub while Jacks spit and rinsed his mouth, then washed his face and hands. "We can adjust things, but that doesn't mean you get to decide how and when you do your homework and therapy and go to bed."

"Everyone else goes to bed later; why can't I? I'm going to be eleven soon."

The doctor had told him Jacks's independence day would come, but living it far exceeded the anticipation.

"We haven't really talked much about these new friends of yours. You're having fun, right?"

The smile lighting up Jacks's face told Carter everything he needed to know, yet he wanted to hear the words from his brother's lips.

"So much fun. Henry's my best friend." Jacks turned to meet his eyes. "And he said I was his yesterday at school." He bit his lip. "I never thought I'd have any friends, 'cause I'm so short and didn't talk a lot."

Everything Carter had worked for these past three years couldn't have prepared him for this moment. It was like a punch in his stomach to hear his brother's voice, still somewhat babyish yet struggling to find its strength.

"What made you start talking?"

"I wanted to make friends. I wanted the kids to like me."

All along, Carter had been living a lie because he claimed to never be swayed in matters of the heart. But listening to Jacks talk proved him wrong. The pain in his chest could only be caused by his heart breaking.

"So you always could talk, you chose not to, huh?"

After a split-second hesitation, Jacks nodded.

"Why, buddy? Do you feel like you can tell me?" Carter didn't want to push, but he wanted to know.

Jacks didn't answer for a moment. "Cause Mommy said I shouldn't. I was really sick when I was little and missed lots of school. She'd get so mad at me when she had to take me to the doctor all the time and get my medicine. Lots of time she forgot and then would get mad when I'd get really sick and have to go to the hospital."

Spots danced before his eyes; only then did Carter remembered to breathe.

Jacks continued in a monotone voice. "She told me I was too much trouble and to shut up, that no one wanted to hear me complaining if I didn't feel good, especially her boyfriends." His voice got small and tight, as if he fought not to cry and it took all of Carter's fortitude not to hug him close and make the pain go away. Instead he continued to listen to Jacks's poignant story.

"We moved so much and I used to get scared going to new schools, but she and her boyfriends would make fun of me. When I stopped talking, she stopped yelling at me, so I figured it was better that way. After a while, I didn't want to talk to anyone. None of the kids I ever went to school liked me anyway so it didn't matter."

"But," Carter prodded gently, "how come you didn't start talking when you came to live with me?"

When several seconds ticked by and he didn't answer, Carter squeezed his shoulder.

"It's okay, buddy. You don't have to tell me if you don't want to."

"Mommy said I shouldn't. That if I was loud or got in your way…" Jacks's voice trailed off and he traced the drops of water in the sink with his fingertip.

"What?" said Carter. "I won't get mad, promise."

"She said you'd get mad and send me away to live with a strange family."

Goddamn her.

"Even after all this time you think that?" Shocked, Carter turned Jacks around to face him. "You know I love you, don't you? I love you more than anything. More than myself."

"Yeah, but I didn't know that at first. You were always tired and upset, so I stayed quiet. I wanted to stay so bad but I didn't know you. So I didn't talk. I was used to it, so it was easy."

Taking a deep breath, Carter took a moment to gather his thoughts. *Easy now. This could mean everything.*

"Oh buddy, you can be as loud as you want, if you keep talking. Don't hide how you feel from me. You can tell me anything."

He hugged Jacks close, loving the little boy smell of him.

Jacks gave him a hug back, then unzipped his jeans. "I have to pee."

"I'll be in your bedroom with your pajamas." Carter hurried out of the bathroom to Jacks's room and smiled when he saw Helen had already set out a pair of pajamas for Jacks. He heard the toilet flush and the water in the sink run and thanked God he ingrained proper hygiene practices in Jacks. Watching Jacks dragging his feet as he entered the bedroom, Carter bit back a smile. God, he loved this kid so much.

"Here you go, buddy."

"Thanks." Jacks took off his clothes and put them in the hamper at the foot of his bed, then slipped on his pajamas. Carter noted he still had the skinny, wiry frame of a little boy and recalled the physician making a point at his last checkup that a bone-age test should be done to see if Jacks was delayed in that respect. Before he forgot, he pulled out his phone to make a note, then slipped it back in his pocket.

Jacks had already climbed into bed and lay snuggled in the pillows, his eyelids drooping, half-lidded with impending sleep. "Henry asked me again if I could sleep over this weekend. He's having a party, and I really wanna go. Please, can I, Carter? I promise to go to bed on time from now on."

Despite knowing it would be good for him, Carter still hesitated but couldn't pinpoint why. Was he afraid of letting go because it meant possible hurt for Jacks, or was he being selfish to try and keep Jacks close to stave off his own inevitable loneliness when Jacks was gone?

"Please?"

Resistance proved futile under that sweet pleading.

"Okay. Tell Henry tomorrow you can go. I'll bring you over on Saturday."

Jacks flung back the bedcovers and hurtled himself in Carter's arms. "Thank you. I love you."

Dazed and holding back tears, Carter hugged Jacks tight. "I love you too, buddy. So, so much."

IT FELT STRANGE to be without Jacks on a Saturday evening. He'd dropped him off around lunchtime and made sure to speak with Michelle, Henry's mother, about his medication and gave her his cell phone number.

"Don't hesitate; if you need to call me, it doesn't matter what time."

"Don't worry, Carter. Go have fun with your boyfriend." She gave him a wink. "Maybe you can have a sleepover too."

"We broke up." Damn. What was it about this woman that he kept revealing pieces of himself to her?

"Oh, I'm sorry. Well, that offer to fix you up with my brother still stands."

"Thanks, but—"

"You miss your boyfriend. I saw how much you cared about him when you mentioned him weeks ago. It showed in your eyes. Well," she said with an impish smile, "now you have the whole weekend to try and get him back. If that's what you want."

He had no fucking clue what he wanted anymore.

Carter spent the rest of the afternoon listening to Michelle's words run through his mind. Giving up all pretense of finishing the work he brought home on Friday specifically to keep him busy on Saturday night, Carter vacillated between going to Reed's bar, plunking himself down and refusing to move until they talked it all out, or downing the bottle of vodka staring at him from atop his liquor cabinet and passing out on the sofa.

"Fuck it," he said and grabbed his leather jacket. Before he could change his mind he shoved his keys and phone in his pocket and ran out the door, hearing the lock click behind him. He walked the two blocks to where the stores were and only had to wait a few minutes before a cab came by with its light on.

"52nd and Seventh," he told the driver, and the cab sped off. Traffic was a bitch as usual, especially getting through the mess in downtown Brooklyn, but soon they were over the Brooklyn Bridge and heading north on the West Side Highway. For about the tenth time Carter checked his watch and saw the time hadn't moved much past the last time he looked at it. Still not yet eleven p.m., and Saturday night in the city barely got its feet wet to party at this time. He wondered how Jacks was doing and checked his messages. The last picture he'd gotten was all the boys in the basement, having pizza and ice cream.

Jacks looked so happy Carter's heart squeezed. Never having had this as a child himself, it was what he worked so hard for these three years to accomplish. Still, he couldn't help but worry, and the fact Michelle sent updates every hour made him her number one fan for life, even with her well-intentioned nosiness.

Forty-five minutes later the cab pulled up in front of Reed's bar. "Here you go."

"Thank you." Carter swiped his credit card and slammed the car door behind him. For a moment he stood on the sidewalk gathering his wits, heedless of the annoyed glares from the passing crowd, getting bumped by various elbows. What was he thinking? He had no right to come here when he wasn't any more certain things had changed from the last time he saw Reed. Yet that didn't stop him from walking in and pushing his way through the crowd until he reached the bar and spied Reed chatting up a good-looking man drinking a beer from an iced glass.

Fucking poser. He ground his teeth and sidled up next to the preppy douche who, from the smirk on his face, thought he had Reed in the bag.

Think again, asshole.

"Hi." He leaned on the bar. "Can I have my usual?"

"He's talking to me. Wait your turn."

Carter flicked his gaze over the man as if he were nothing more than an annoying fly. "I wasn't speaking to you; I was talking to Reed." He turned his attention back to Reed who hadn't moved and stood staring at him, white-faced and trembling. "I really want to talk to you. Can we…later?"

"Wha-what are you doing here?" Reed gulped out his words. His hands nervously played through the thick strands of his hair, and Carter wanted to bury his fingers in those curls.

Fuck, he had it bad.

"Things have…changed, and I needed to see you." By this time the other guy had lost interest and walked away with his drink. "I have tonight free and tomorrow too."

"So you came here thinking I'll go to bed with you because you made time for me one night?" Reed's mouth was set in a stubborn line, and a muscle ticked beneath the fine stubble covering his jawline. Carter recalled its roughness against his stomach, the hot, wet suction of Reed's mouth sliding up and down his cock, and his hunger for Reed had Carter throbbing painfully in his jeans. He discreetly pressed the heel of his hand against the zipper, welcoming the painful yet arousing burst of pleasure.

"No, I've been thinking about what you said in my office, and you were right."

Never one to make it easy for him, Reed crossed his arms and widened his stance. "Go on. I don't have all night. I have work to do."

The other bartender glanced their way, frazzled by the crowd. Carter didn't wish for either Reed or the other man to get in trouble. "I'd rather talk to you alone, so if you want, I'll wait for your shift to finish."

"Uh, yeah, that would be best. I get off at one."

"I have no other plans."

With a troubled glance, Reed went back to serving the people while Carter stayed at the bar, sipping the drink Reed eventually placed in front of him. Carter spoke to no one and nibbled at the dish of peanuts and pretzels to stave off his hunger. With all the excitement over Jacks's first sleepover, he'd forgotten to eat dinner himself. He wondered if he could order something at the bar.

"What is it? You look pained."

Reed stood in front of him. Funny how certain qualities of Jacks's reminded him of Reed; how whenever Reed was in his arms Carter had an overwhelming need to protect him. Maybe it was a sign of how much he'd come to care about Reed without even realizing it.

"I, uh, didn't eat dinner, and I'm a little hungry."

"I can have the kitchen get you something; how about some sliders or chicken wings?"

"Sounds good; whatever. I appreciate it."

Reed placed the order on the computerized screen, then hurried to the other side of the bar to serve more customers. After several minutes nursing his drink, he felt a tap on his shoulder.

"Are you waiting to get served?"

The man looked close to sixty, with gray streaking the dark curls of his neatly trimmed hair. His weathered face bore a friendly smile, and laugh lines fanned out from his amber eyes. Something about his face and build reminded Carter of Reed, and he wondered if they were related.

"Yes, I ordered some food."

"They have great bar food here. I hope you tried the chicken wings." He sidled in next to Carter and leaned his hip against the wide wooden railing.

"I think I did. The bartender is a friend and ordered me a plate."

The man slanted a look down the bar, then focused

back on him. Carter finished his drink and played with the edge of the glass, wishing Reed could get off early but understanding why with this crowd he couldn't shirk his responsibilities. That solid work ethic was one of the things he admired most about him.

"Clay or Reed?"

"Pardon me?" He squinted at the man's face.

"Are you friends with Clay or Reed?"

"Uh, Reed. Do you know him?"

The man smiled. "I do. He's my son."

Chapter Thirteen

REED EXITED THE kitchen with Carter's plate and stopped dead outside the swinging doors. Shit. What was his father doing here? Wary, he plastered a smile on his face and approached him and Carter.

"Um, hi, Dad. What brings you here so late at night?" He set the plate down in front of Carter and picked up his empty glass. "Another Grey Goose?" Not bothering to wait for a response he poured a healthy splash over ice, slid it over to Carter, then took a bottle of beer for his father and snapped off the bottle cap. Anything to keep his hands busy.

A smile curled Carter's lips. "Your father and I met unexpectedly."

"So I see." He quirked a brow. "Dad?"

"I haven't heard from you in a while and figured if the mountain won't come to Muhammad…" He chuckled and held out his hand for the beer.

"I've been busy," said Reed defensively. "Between school and work I hardly have a minute."

"Is that all you've been busy with? Or should I say

who you've been busy with?"

Carter choked on his drink, and Reed groaned inwardly. "Subtle, Dad. Carter is only a friend."

Looking unconvinced, his father drank some of his beer, then placed the bottle on top of the bar. The music continued to play in the background, its pumping rhythm feeding the heat of Reed's blood, enhancing every movement Carter made. From their first meeting they'd had a strangely special connection, but unable to decide what Carter's visit tonight meant in terms of a potential future, Reed remained silent.

"Vernon is in the back. You want me to go get him for you?" The cocktail napkin shredded between his fingers, and he quickly shook away the clinging bits of paper before his father could mention it.

"There's no rush. I was having a nice conversation with…Carter, is it?" At Carter's nod he smiled. "I was about to ask Carter how you two know each other."

Oh, Christ. Reed sent Carter pleading signals with his eyes, hoping his usually astute antennae picked up his distress.

"Oh, I've been coming to the bar now for several months, and Reed is my favorite bartender by far. It's like he anticipates my needs before I even know what I want."

Thankful the dim lights in the bar hid his somewhat pained expression, Reed tipped his head to the back. "Really, Dad. Vernon would get upset if he knew you were here and didn't say hello. Besides, Carter was just leaving, weren't you?"

Looking crestfallen, Carter's grin faded. "Oh. I thought we could maybe hang out later."

"Why don't I text you when I get off shift, and if you're around, we can make plans."

That was as close as Reed would get to saying he'd see Carter later. The last thing he needed was for his father to draw conclusions about a relationship that no longer existed.

Perhaps recognizing he'd been dismissed, Carter slid off his stool, and leaving the platter of food mostly untouched, took some bills out of his wallet and placed them on the bar. "I hope to hear from you. I think we have some things to discuss."

At Carter's words, hope flared within Reed that Carter had listened and thought over what they'd talked about in his office and decided to let Reed into his life.

"You think, or you know?" He'd never been this daring or demanding, but Reed had never wanted to give anyone his heart before. He thought when he'd fall in love it would be soft and sweet, a coming together of two people who'd discovered each other. Instead it had proven to be messy and difficult, full of tears and hurt, of longing and thwarted desires.

Looking startled for a moment, Carter's expression turned from hopeful to determined. "You're right. I know we need to talk, so call me. I'll be waiting in the usual place." He made his way through the crowded bar, quickly disappearing from sight.

"You can't tell me that man isn't in love with you. Why didn't you tell me you were in a relationship?"

Reed had almost forgotten his father's presence and could've groaned out loud.

"It's strictly casual, Dad. We don't know each other very well." He took a rag and began to wipe down the bar, studiously avoiding his father's eyes.

"You don't have to know someone long for them to fall in love with you or you to love them. It's in the way they lean toward you, watching your mouth as you speak, or how their eyes light up when you enter the room. The brush of their hand on your shoulder when they pass you, or taking hold of your hand when bad news happens. Not having to ask if you're upset—knowing it because they know you. Love has nothing to do with sex and everything to do with the heart."

Reed stopped his pretense of wiping up the bar and clutched the rag in his shaking hand. "When did you stop loving my mother?"

His father slid onto Carter's vacated seat. "I'm a funny man. It takes a lot to make me angry. But hurt my child, and I am done with you forever." Dirty rag and all, his father placed a hand over his, and the memories of holding on to him while riding the roller coaster at Coney Island, of jumping the waves at the beach flooded through Reed.

"I'm sorry. I shouldn't have asked that."

"Don't be. The minute she walked out and left you, she became dead to me. Stop loving me—that I could handle. But how do you walk away from your child?"

"I wasn't what she planned on."

"No one has the right to claim perfection, and who's to decide what's perfect and what's not, anyway?" His father's grip tightened. "I wouldn't trade one minute of you as my son for anyone else. You are my perfection, the only child I could ever want, and it hurts to think you still doubt yourself."

He would not cry; he would not cry. Reed braved a watery smile. "I don't know that I do. I never let other people see the real me because I'm afraid to show them who I really am."

"Who you are is kind and loving; a wonderful son and friend; a hard worker and a person who values someone for their heart, not their bank account. If a man doesn't want you knowing that, he's not worth it."

Maybe he lost out on a mother, but he certainly hit the jackpot with his father. "Thanks, Dad. I think maybe I needed to hear that right about now."

"You want to know what I think?"

Reed extricated his hand and picked up a neglected chicken wing from Carter's abandoned plate, then set it back down. "You need to ask? Not like you weren't going to tell me anyway." He licked the sauce off his fingers.

Slanting a look at his father, they shared a laugh, and Reed's heart lifted. Whatever happened between him and Carter, he always had his father.

"Talk to this Carter; don't be afraid to tell him everything. I saw how he watched your lips and how he focused on your eyes." He finished his beer and laid a ten-dollar bill down. "It's your time, Reed. Take the brass ring right in front of you and grab it tight."

Without waiting for him to answer, his father walked away, leaving Reed with his scrambled thoughts. Mechanically, he served drinks and smiled at the customers, but when one a.m. rolled around and his shift had finished for the night, Reed grabbed his jacket with a hurried "goodbye" and knew where he was going.

NOT QUITE SURE what he planned on saying when he got to the hotel room, Reed knew what he wouldn't be doing. When he texted Carter after he left the bar to say he'd like to talk, and Carter immediately responded that he was at the hotel, Reed knew what Carter had in mind. A night of endless sex to blur reality and make everything better on the surface. Only when the dawn broke and they had to face each other, their ugly truths would remain. For Reed to move forward, the time had come to peel back the surface to expose his core; if Carter would do the same, then he recognized they had something worth fighting for.

One knock and Carter wrenched the door open. "Come on in."

Nervous as their first time, Reed's breath caught. Carter's haunted eyes held his, and lines not there the last time they were together etched grooves next to his mouth.

"What's wrong?" Reed grasped his arm. "You look awful."

"I should be happy you wanted to talk to me, yet I'm not sure..." Carter shook off his hand and left him standing at the door to return and sit on the sofa. A half-full bottle of liquor stood on the coffee table, and Reed remembered Carter said earlier he hadn't eaten anything.

"Are you drunk? You never ate the food I gave you at the bar." He followed Carter but remained standing by the entrance to the small living area. This was a different room than Carter normally reserved, a bit smaller and on a lower floor, without a view of the skyline. Reed's concentration wasn't on hotel amenities, and he focused on Carter sitting disconsolately on the sofa.

With a wave of his hand, Carter dismissed his concern. "Nah, I had a sandwich from room service. Can you come sit down, though?" At Reed's hesitation, he gave a rueful laugh. "Don't worry. I said earlier it was to talk, and I meant it. I'm not going to jump you." He patted the seat next to him. "Please?"

Relieved he wouldn't have to waste time fending Carter off, Reed joined him on the sofa. "If you're not drunk, I have to tell you, you look like shit."

Carter expelled a breath and leaned back with his eyes closed. Reed took this time to study him, wondering at the measure of a man and why he, above any other, had the power to make Reed want to break his silence about his illness and tell him everything.

"I fucking hated these past weeks. All I imagined was you hooking up with someone else, and it drove me crazy. I know I don't own you and have no right to feel that way, but I can't help it."

With his heart hammering in his chest, Reed fidgeted with his hands, wrapping and rewrapping the cords of his bracelet around his fingers, but even this didn't soothe him like it normally did.

"You're not saying anything new, though. I wasn't happy either, thinking of you here with another person. That doesn't mean I can continue on the way we have."

Carter opened his eyes. "It wasn't supposed to be like this, was it? We were supposed to hook up and then forget about each other."

Reed smiled sadly. "You're kind of an unforgettable guy."

Carter tilted his head on the sofa pillow, and their eyes met. "So are you."

Silence shimmered between them like heat rising from the ground on a summer day. Reed's heartbeat thundered in his head.

"What do we do about it? Anything?" He wet his lips. "Or nothing and say goodbye?"

Carter inhaled deeply, his fingers curling into fists at his side. "I'm going to tell you something that might upset you. If you still want me afterward,"—his unexpectedly shy, endearing smile ripped through

Reed—"we can see about moving forward."

What could it be? Was he an escaped convict, a murderer? He'd sworn already he didn't have a wife or a child. "Go on. I'm listening."

And Carter began to speak, his voice soft at first, then rising with pain and determination. As Reed listened to his heartbreaking tale of neglect, of a childhood without any love whatsoever, he ultimately understood Carter better and why he walled himself off from people and from life. No one could let him down or use him if he remained alone and apart. But what a sad way to live. Carter had so much love brimming inside him, waiting to be unleashed.

"So now you know," said Carter when he'd finished his story. He took a deep swallow of his drink and cradled the tumbler between his hands. Hands which Reed knew from experience could be harsh and rough, or soothing and loving. He'd never met a man who was such a dichotomy.

"I never thought you were an angel. None of us walk around with untarnished halos. Stop trying to think you need to be perfect."

"You don't understand."

"Then help me to." Frustrated, Reed stood to pace the room. "We're human, we're allowed to make mistakes."

"My mother having children was a mistake."

Children? "You have siblings?"

Carter nodded but said nothing further.

In order to keep the conversation going, Reed continued to ask questions. He'd already assumed from that errant text a few months ago Carter had a child in his life. Maybe he'd finally open up, and instead of giving the story like a puzzle in bits and pieces, he'd tell Reed the whole truth.

"You said you changed your name. Why?"

Carter opened his mouth, but instead of speaking, took another sip of his drink.

The small hesitation from Carter told Reed he still had unresolved issues about that subject.

"It's okay. I'm not judging you."

"Doesn't matter if you are or aren't. I'm too busy judging myself." The empty glass dangled from his long fingers, swinging between his knees.

"Sometimes talking about things helps you feel better about them."

"Sounds like that philosophy stuff again. Are you sure you're not studying psychology?"

That comment hit too close to home for Reed. "Not at all. I'm letting you know I'm here for you."

Carter let out an audible sigh, and Reed watched the internal struggle play across his face.

"Everything I did from the time I left home I did on my own. I wanted a clean start and no possible connection with my mother. To be brutally honest, I'd never wanted to see her again. But when I changed my name, I discovered I needed her one last time."

"Did she make it difficult for you?"

Carter's mirthless smile sent chills down Reed's spine. "In order to change my name, I needed to know in what state my birth certificate was issued so I could get a copy. Ugliness ensued."

Almost afraid to ask, Reed couldn't help himself. "What happened?"

An unpleasant laugh escaped Carter. "True to form, she made it a business arrangement. I'd pay her and tell her my new name; only then would she give me the information I needed for my paperwork. I had no choice, so she ended up knowing my new name and address." That haunted look Reed now recognized darkened Carter's eyes. "I thought I managed to put those days and my real name behind me, but I guess that's never really possible, is it?"

Thinking of himself, Reed had to agree. "No matter how much we try, no. I don't believe we can ever fully escape our past. Take us for example. We couldn't seem to."

"I guess I have my answer." Carter drained his glass. "You speak of us in the past tense. I guess that means we're done."

How quickly Carter shut down and presumed the worst; that defense mechanism of his—pretending the hurt didn't matter—so achingly familiar to Reed. He'd used it himself for almost half his life. But no longer. He wouldn't let Carter go without a fight.

"Is that what you assume? I thought you were smarter than that."

Carter glanced up at him sharply, but Reed pushed on and sat down next to him on the sofa. There'd be time enough in the future for Carter to tell him everything about his past; it didn't matter at this point. He knew what he needed to know. Reed would make damn sure his future included Carter. Most important now was for him to reassure Carter that he had no intention of leaving. That sometimes things worked out in the end.

"You think I'm going to walk away from you for good without looking back? Tell me," said Reed, plucking the glass out of Carter's hands and setting it on the coffee table. Yes, he'd made the promise not to get physical, but that was before Carter unburdened himself, sitting broken and strangely hesitant. Reed discovered he hated seeing Carter as anything but the slightly arrogant, cocky, self-made man, and right now Carter needed to hear how much Reed wanted him. "Would you leave me if I'd done what you had to do? It's made you who you are, and so far I haven't had a problem with that."

"Who I am." Carter's laugh was anything but humorous. "I have no idea who the fuck I am. Son of a woman who didn't give a shit about me and a nameless father I'll never know. A liar, thief…"

"All things you had little or no control over. I see someone who made me feel safe when no one ever bothered to find out why I was afraid. A man who gives money to children's charities but doesn't blow his own horn." Reed took Carter's face between his hands and brushed their lips together, almost reeling from the waves of pleasure and sweetness crashing through him. *This man.* This man was his, and he had no plans to let him go. "I also see the man I've come to love and want to be with."

Carter slid his hands over Reed's, his palms damp with sweat. His voice shook. "That's crazy. You don't love me—you can't."

"Says the man who never lets anyone tell him what to do or say. If you don't believe my words, then feel them." Reed kissed him again, his tongue pressing against the seam of Carter's lips and finding little resistance. "Feel what you mean to me. It's you. *You* are everything to me. How could I not love you?"

All pretense of sweetness ended; they ate at each other's mouths, their kisses greedy and urgent. Their tongues met and battled; then Reed found himself flipped underneath Carter, who with a wicked glint in his eyes popped open Reed's jeans and drew the zipper down. "Lift up."

Reed complied and allowed Carter to yank his pants down.

"Tell me again." Carter traced the outline of Reed's dick with his tongue, the heat of his breath drifting against his thighs. "Say it." He mouthed Reed's cock through the thin fabric, wetting it, then reached inside his boxers to fondle his balls.

"What, that you never let anyone tell you things?"

He hissed and threw his head back against the cushions, unfathomable, delicious thrills sparking through his body.

"No, you bastard. Tell me again. Please." From his place between Reed's legs Carter gazed up at him, and his honesty almost took Reed's breath away.

"I love you."

Carter smiled, his silvery eyes glinting in the light, and he freed Reed's dick from his boxers, then engulfed the head, his firm lips sucking first at the tip before sliding down the rest of his shaft. Reed reached down and grasped the nape of Carter's neck to steady him while he flexed his hips, urging Carter to take him deeper.

He undulated his hips faster and faster, but Carter took it all in his mouth, creating a sucking friction Reed felt down in his toes.

"Fuuuck." Reed groaned.

Carter responded by slowing down, tracing the thick veins down the side of his cock while hefting his balls, squeezing them slightly. His teeth grazed the underside of the flared crown. Through half-lidded eyes, Reed watched the flushed, reddened head of his dick, wet with precome and saliva, disappear into Carter's mouth. Carter hummed deep in his throat.

Reed began to fuck Carter's mouth in earnest, emotions mixed up with the bone-melting pleasure battering him until all sensation centered upon his groin and his cock and he couldn't hold back if he tried. His orgasm tore through him, and he caught his breath, unable to speak or even cry out. Carter made little self-satisfied noises as he drank him down, not letting go of his cock even after Reed had softened in his mouth.

Reed lay spent, flattened like the tread of a cheap, used tire. He doubted his ability to stand as he couldn't feel his legs. Carter, on the other hand, looked supremely pleased with himself, his lips curled in a crooked grin. He wiped at his mouth with the heel of his hand, and a rush of happiness poured over Reed.

"Will you stay with me tonight?" Carter slid in beside him on the sofa and took his face in between his hands, his touch tender and loving. "I have the room anyway; I wasn't taking it for granted that you would." Their kisses turned sweet in contrast to their earlier desperation.

They lay snuggled together; Carter's head rested on his shoulder, their fingers entwined, softly playing with each other. Reed, drained from the highs and lows of the day, felt strangely content and at peace. While he'd neither asked for nor expected a response, he could tell Carter cared for him. It might take him time to understand his feelings and say it, but their talk tonight had opened the door.

"Yeah, I'll stay." He struggled to remain awake, but the pull to sleep proved hard to resist and he succumbed, only dimly aware of Carter taking off his sneakers and jeans; then he drew Reed into his arms, his lips brushing the top of his head.

Chapter Fourteen

A BUZZING AND ringing startled Carter into immediate wakefulness.

"What the fuck?" He untangled himself from Reed's arms and jumped up from the sofa where they'd fallen asleep. His phone kept buzzing, and good thing it lit up when it rang so he could find it in the pitch black of the room. When he saw Michelle's name flash on the screen and the time was 3:30 a.m., dread whited out his vision.

"What's wrong?" Carter didn't wait for niceties. He knew Jacks must be in trouble. All along he knew it was a bad idea to let him go on a sleepover and yet he let himself be talked into it. "Is it Jacks? Is he okay?"

"Carter, calm down. He had a bad nightmare and was calling out for you. We got him up, and he's here in the kitchen having hot cocoa, but he says he doesn't want to go home."

Carter alternated between wanting to throw up and pass out; he vaguely felt a hand on his back, but Reed's touch barely registered. "I'm coming over right now."

"I don't know—"

"But I do. I'll hop in a cab and be there in half an hour. At this time there'll hardly be any traffic. See you soon." Before Michelle could voice a protest, he ended the call.

On his way to the desk he banged his knee on the coffee table. "Fuck, ow." He bent over and cradled his knee, and in the interim Reed turned on the light. They squinted at each other in the glare, and Carter reached out to grab his jeans, which lay in a heap on the floor where he'd kicked them off only a few hours earlier.

"What's going on?" Reed stood in his T-shirt and boxers, rubbing his eyes, and Carter hesitated. If he left now without telling Reed about Jacks, no matter what Reed had said earlier, he'd never want to see Carter again. The execution was terrifying, but the payoff—having Reed in his life with Jacks—was huge.

"I have to go. The sibling I mentioned earlier—the child you've asked me about before? He's my brother, my little half-brother. I've been taking care of him for three years. He-he has some issues, and I don't have time to explain everything now, but he's at his first sleepover tonight, and he woke up from a nightmare, and I have to see him and make sure he's all right."

"Carter." Reed walked over and put his arms around him. For a moment Carter allowed himself to sink into Reed's embrace. It felt so good to be held for once. To allow someone to carry the weight with him and tell him maybe it would be all right.

"Take a breath. Slow down. It's okay." Reed's fingers tangled in the hair curling at the nape of his neck, and Carter breathed against Reed's shoulder, feeling Reed's strength in the tenderness of his touch and the play of muscles underneath his skin. "Stop talking; let's get dressed, and we'll go. Okay?" Carter allowed himself a smile against Reed's shoulder.

"You're getting kind of bossy. I like it."

"I had a good teacher. He taught me to go after what I wanted and never take no for an answer."

Carter cupped Reed's chin. "I don't think I could say no to you anymore."

"Good." Reed kissed his palm. "I'll be ready in a second."

They dressed and left the hotel, catching a cab idling near the hotel entrance. Carter automatically gave Michelle's address, then leaned back in the seat, his heart pounding from a combination of worry and tension. Was Jacks scared waking up in a strange place in the dark, thinking Carter had finally abandoned him? He'd never forgive himself if that proved to be true.

Probably understanding his need to be inside his head, Reed said nothing on the way to Brooklyn. Instead he held Carter's hand until the cab pulled up in front of the wood-framed house.

"Go on inside; I'll take care of it."

Carter squeezed his hand and ran out of the cab, taking the front steps two at a time. Not wanting to wake up the other children, Carter tapped lightly on the glass front of the wooden door, hoping Michelle would hear him. Within a few seconds the door opened and he faced a man in his mid-thirties, his sandy-blond hair looking like he'd spent the better part of his night running his hands through it. But his eyes behind his tortoiseshell glasses were kind, and Carter instantly warmed to him as a man he could trust.

"Carter? Hi, I'm Evan, Michelle's husband. Come on in."

He heard steps behind him and paused a moment, waiting for Reed to catch up.

"Hi. This is Reed."

Evan walked down the long center hall, beckoning them to follow. From his last time there, Carter remembered the big modern kitchen took up the whole back of the house. He hurried after Evan, with Reed falling into step right behind him.

The sight greeting him when he entered the kitchen hurt his heart. Sitting at the table, huddled under a Superman comforter, Jacks held on to a big mug, his face pale and sad. When Carter walked in, he set the mug on the table and ran to him, flinging himself in Carter's arms.

"I'm sorry. I didn't mean it. I'm really sorry." His voice came out muffled, buried in the thick of Carter's jacket, but Carter heard his words. He always heard Jacks.

Carter held on to his slight, trembling frame, clad only in a T-shirt and sleep pants. Michelle wordlessly handed him the comforter, and Carter tucked it around

Jacks's narrow shoulders. From the beginning when Jacks first came to live with him, he'd reminded Carter of a wounded baby bird; fragile yet desperate for survival.

"Shhh. You didn't do anything wrong. Everyone has bad dreams sometimes. Even me."

"You do?" Jacks gazed up at him. "But you're old. What are you scared of?"

Everything, Carter wanted to say. *Failing you, failing in my business.* Thinking back on earlier in the evening and the talk he had with Reed, Carter swallowed hard at the thought of how close he'd come to failing Reed and losing him for good. Of course he didn't yet know Reed's reaction to Jacks, and how or even if he'd fit into the family dynamic where Jacks and his needs would have to come first.

"I worry about you."

Jacks pulled away from him and straightened his shoulders in an attempt to act grown up. Carter's heart squeezed watching his little brother's struggle for independence.

"You don't have to. I'm almost eleven." In a smaller voice he said, "And I'm getting better, right? The doctor said I was."

Oh, God, if he fucked this all up, he'd never forgive himself. Where did he come off thinking he could be responsible for another human being when he'd made such a mess of his own life? But he was, and Jacks needed him.

"You are, buddy. You're doing great, and I'm so proud of you. But no matter what, I love you, you know that, right?" He smoothed Jacks's hair off his face. "Nothing will ever change that."

"Okay, but..." he bit his lip and rubbed his eyes, stifling a yawn.

"You need to get back to sleep, buddy. It's way too late for you to be up."

"Please, can I stay? I know you came all the way here, but I don't want to go home."

Carter hesitated, his urge to circle around Jacks and protect him warring with the knowledge that Jacks needed this independence.

"Are you sure?"

"I don't want them to make fun of me for going home." Jacks dragged his feet back to the table and sat down, the picture of exhausted dejection. "What if they call me a baby and don't want to be my friend?"

Michelle piped in. "Don't you worry about that. It's not gonna happen, I promise."

"But I wanna go back upstairs. We were gonna play more Minecraft in the morning and then go to the park." His little face crumpled. "Can't I stay, please?"

"Of course you can." Carter knelt at the side of Jacks's chair. "If that's what you want, then you go back upstairs with Henry's mom and go back to sleep. I bet in the morning no one will even remember what happened."

Casting him a doubtful look, Jacks hugged him, the

comforter sliding off his shoulders and onto the floor. Carter picked it up and handed it to Michelle. "You call me in the morning and let me know how you feel."

"Who's that?" Jacks pointed to Reed, who'd remained standing in the half shadows of the kitchen, pale moonlight laying stripes across his solemn face.

"That's a friend of mine. His name is Reed."

"Is he your best friend?" Jacks yawned through his question.

A sweet smile curved Reed's lips, but he said nothing.

He shot Reed a quick glance. "Something like that. Right now you need to go back to bed, but maybe you can meet him tomorrow."

Carter kissed Jacks's cheek and watched as Michelle tucked her arm protectively around him. Jacks lolled against her, half-asleep, and together they walked carefully up the stairs, leaving him alone with Reed and Evan.

"I'm really sorry for all this."

Evan waved him off. "No big deal. It wouldn't be a sleepover without one of the kids waking up." He yawned. "Can I get you guys anything?"

"Not a thing. I'll wait until Michelle comes back, and then we'll be on our way."

"Here I am." Michelle reentered the kitchen from the back staircase, so prevalent in these old homes. She slipped her arms around Evan's waist and rested her head against his shoulder. "Jacks was out even before I pulled the covers over him."

"Thanks." The weight of fear lifted from his chest, and Carter found it easier to take a deep breath. Reed put an arm around his shoulders and gave him a quick hug, and Carter flashed him a grateful smile. "We should get going."

"Is this the man you told me about? I'm Michelle, by the way, nice to meet you. I tried to fix your boyfriend up with my brother a few months ago, but Carter was quick to inform me that he wasn't interested."

Remaining very still, Carter cursed inwardly. Michelle was nice and all, but damn she was nosy.

He needn't have worried, as Reed understood his need for privacy and remained quiet. Or perhaps it was because he had no idea what they were to each other.

"Nice to meet you. I think Carter's right and we need to let you guys get some sleep."

Carter zipped his jacket. "I'm sorry we all caused you such a rough night. Thanks so much for everything, and I'll call you in the morning."

Before Michelle could say anything further, Carter gave her a kiss on the cheek, thanked Evan, and took Reed's hand. They walked out to the front where Evan unlocked the door for them.

"Nice job. Many have tried but few have succeeded in shutting Michelle down."

Carter laughed aloud for the first time since receiving the phone call and, still holding on to Reed, walked down the steps of the porch to the street. The night air blew cool, and only the faintest sounds of traffic could be heard from the avenue in the distance. It was getting on toward dawn, and perhaps he was giddy from lack of sleep, but Carter wasn't tired any longer. He wanted to bring Reed home with him. He'd already seen him at his worst and hadn't run.

"Should we go back to the hotel?" Reed nervously played with the zipper on his jacket, pulling it up and down, over and over. "I left my bag there."

"Would you mind if we stopped somewhere first? I want to show you something."

"Okay, but I'll need to get my bag sometime this morning."

Wondering what Reed had back at the hotel room that caused him such concern, Carter held out his hand. "We can walk. It's only a few blocks."

They walked in silence, Carter finding he liked Reed's company because the man didn't fill his ear with incessant chatter or try to make small talk over nothing. Reed also didn't bombard him with questions about Jacks, showing respect and understanding that Carter would tell him everything.

After about ten minutes they reached his house. Pride rose within him that this pretty limestone with a small garden and glossy black wrought-iron fencing in the front belonged to him. Instead of going up the steps, he stopped and faced Reed, who slouched against the fence, a tired but quizzical expression in his eyes.

"This is my home. Mine and Jacks's. I've never brought anyone here before, but I'd like you to come inside and see how we live. If you want to, of course," he added hastily, suddenly cognizant that he'd dragged Reed here without any idea what the hell he was getting into. "I mean, I understand if you're overwhelmed by all this, but I wanted to explain Jacks's situation to you, and if you still want to be involved with me after that,"—he scrubbed his face with his hands, then smiled tiredly—"I'd like to try."

In wooing new clients to sign with his firm or in negotiations over contracts Carter prided himself on possessing a natural instinct to pick up positive signals and move in to finalize the deal, or cut his losses when the transaction went sour. But that was business, something he was familiar with. In treading the waters of personal entanglements, Carter was a novice and more scared to hear Reed's answer than if he was diving off a high board, fifty feet in the air.

Reed closed the distance between them, and wrapped Carter in his arms. A quiet peace descended over them in the hushed pre-dawn on this narrow little street. A wonderful languor stole through Carter as they stood, clutching each other.

"Don't worry about me leaving, Carter. I've been running for forever, and I'm ready to be caught. After you tell me your story, I'll tell you my own. But I promise I won't be going anywhere unless you're with me."

Chapter Fifteen

HAVING NO IDEA what to expect from Carter any longer, Reed certainly didn't imagine him living in a house where, when he entered and followed Carter down the side hall, almost all the free space on the walls was filled with pictures drawn by a young child. Or where a big box of Legos sat side by side with a state-of-the-art computer system Carter needed for his publicity campaigns at work.

The kitchen stopped him in his tracks. Comfortable and country-like, glass-fronted light maple cabinets ran the length of the wall painted a mellow lemon-yellow color. A huge center island took up residence on the working side of the room, its wide, white expanse the setting for a large bowl of citrus fruits as well as the art supplies he assumed Jacks was using to create his pictures. The other side of the room had a cozy eating nook, complete with a homey, round wooden table and deep-cushioned chairs. Two bay windows flanked either side of a tiled fireplace, its mantel crowded with pictures of Carter, Jacks, and an older woman.

This home was the antithesis of the style Reed imagined Carter living in. On the weekends when he and Carter didn't see each other, Reed had pictured Carter entertaining in a trendy loft apartment with views of the city skyline, the furniture polished and sleek, befitting a high-powered, single Manhattan executive.

Instead he found a home that exuded the essence of family, warmth, and love, and his admiration for Carter grew exponentially, recognizing he'd done all this for his little brother.

He pulled out one of the barstools and sat, patting the seat next to him. "Come on, let's talk."

Rather than choosing to sit by his side, Carter circled around to the opposite side of the island to face him. Reed recognized that as a defense mechanism, putting space between them in case Reed bolted.

"Jacks, if you didn't notice, isn't your average ten-year-old. Most likely he was born prematurely and he's had to deal with a whole host of problems. Our mother,"—Carter pursed his lips in distaste—"dropped him off here one day, claiming she was tired of dealing with his issues and didn't want to be weighed down by him anymore. He's only recently begun verbalizing, and we have no clear idea what he went through when he lived with her, and maybe we never will. But it doesn't matter." Carter's voice wobbled, and Reed's heart lurched.

"Of course not. He's your little brother. You love him."

"It's more than that—he was neglected. He wasn't like me; he didn't have the capability to be independent and take care of himself. He suffers from anxiety and is slightly learning delayed although he's recently begun catching up so quickly even the doctors are amazed. I've gotten him occupational therapy that dealt with some physical problems, but he still sees a psychiatrist for his other issues."

Carter braced his elbows on the top of the island and avoided Reed's gaze, as if he didn't want to see his expression. "So, if you want to be with me, you also take on the responsibility of Jacks. He's my brother, and I want him to have the life I never had—family, stability, and love. He's the reason I only go away once a month; every other weekend I spend with him."

Watching Carter discreetly wipe at his eyes, Reed blinked away his own tears. How foolish and tragic it would have been for him to walk away from Carter, thinking he was nothing more than a vain and selfish player. What he'd created all on his own paled in comparison to the trials he'd lived through as a child and the selfless dedication he'd shown to his little brother. If Reed had thought he might be in love with Carter before hearing this final piece of his life story, now that love was cemented forever. But the time had arrived for Reed's own midnight confession. Or, actually five a.m., if one wished to be technical.

"Carter, there's something—"

"Can we table this for the night, though?" Carter

came around from the other side of the island and slipped his arms around Reed, nuzzling into the curve of his shoulder. "I'm beat, and you look half dead as well. I think we ought to get some sleep."

Thwarted, Reed considered Carter's suggestion and thought it might be a wise one. He was hardly in the best mindset, and maybe a night's rest would make it easier to talk. Carter might be worried about Reed's reaction, but Reed had no problem thinking Carter wouldn't want the extra burden of a lover with a mental illness.

"Sure, that's a good idea."

He allowed himself to be led up the stairs, where they passed a bedroom Reed immediately identified as Jacks's, with comic book superheroes hanging on the wall. It was the picture perfect boy's room, and imagining Carter in a children's store, picking out all the decorations, desperate to give his brother a happy, normal childhood, Reed's heart squeezed with love for Carter.

They headed to the third level. "Here's my room." Carter opened the door to a surprisingly large and airy master bedroom and flicked a switch, turning on a small lamp on the nightstand next to the large king-size bed that dominated the room. The polished oak floors gleamed here as they did in the rest of the house, and small Turkish rugs lay by the side of the bed. In a corner Reed spotted a door leading, he presumed, to an attached bathroom.

Carter closed the door behind him and toed off his sneakers, leaving them to the side of the doorway. "You know, you're the first man I've ever wanted to bring to this house and into my bedroom." They stripped in silence leaving their clothes on the floor and climbed into the most comfortable bed Reed had ever slept in. Carter rolled toward him and held him close for comfort. "Let's try and get a little sleep, shall we?"

If Reed had his way, he'd be the last. But he wondered, as he drifted off to sleep with Carter's arms still around him, if Carter would still want him in the morning.

WAKING UP, REED stretched and found himself flush up against Carter's very warm naked chest.

"Good morning, beautiful."

Sliding his leg over Carter's hip, Reed nestled his groin against Carter's, and they rocked, their stiff cocks rubbing and thrusting against one another. Reed reached between their bodies and grasped both their cocks, running his hand up their rigid erections. The coating of their sticky precome helped him stroke faster and harder over the heated silken skin. Carter arched his back, groaning deep in his chest, his dick thickening in Reed's hand. Liquid seeped steadily from the slit in the wide crown, and Reed knew now, from the increased cadence of Carter's breath to the tautness and twitching of his muscles, Carter was close to blowing.

Working him hard, concentrating all his efforts on taking care of Carter's needs, Reed nipped at Carter's neck, then sucked at the smooth skin. "God, you're so fucking sexy." He blew his heated breath over Carter's sweat-slicked skin. "Come all over me; go on, cover me with it."

Carter grabbed him by the back of the neck and crushed his mouth over his, sucking at Reed's lips until his torso stiffened, then shook, his cock shooting out stream after ropy stream of semen all over Reed's hand and chest. Reed continued to pump Carter through his orgasm until Carter weakly batted his hand away.

"Too sensitive." But he smiled as he whispered it and held Reed's hand as they both finished Reed off to his own bone-melting climax. Reed shuddered and spilled hot and hard between their fingers.

Held within the circle of Carter's arms, Reed waited to speak until his heart stopped pounding and his vision cleared.

"Before anything, I need to tell you some things. Things about myself that might change how you feel about continuing this relationship."

Carter rolled over and picked up his T-shirt from the floor and cleaned their hands off. After wiping each of their fingers, he tossed it down and held Reed close again "Highly unlikely." Carter kissed his jaw, then his lips. "But continue."

Here goes nothing.

"Remember the time I said I didn't feel well, that I

was coming down with a cold?"

"Yeah, the night we went dancing." Despite the sticky mess between them, Carter drew him closer. "I'd like to do that again."

Reed sensed Carter's smile against his skin, but it brought him little solace. "I lied. I wasn't coming down with a cold. I was having an anxiety attack. I forgot my medication, and that, coupled with the stress of not knowing if you really wanted to be with me or that guy who came up to us, triggered a bad reaction in me."

"A bad reaction?" Carter drew back to gaze into Reed's eyes. "What do you mean?"

"Uh." Reed gulped down his panic and barreled through. "I have severe anxiety and ADHD. Sometimes it's so bad I get these panic attacks where it feels like everything, the world, is closing in on me." Letting out a whoosh of breath, Reed squirmed in Carter's arms, wanting to run, hide, do anything possible not to have to look into Carter's pitying eyes.

"Don't." Carter tightened his hold, arms like steel around Reed. "It's fine."

Struggling in earnest, Reed pushed against Carter's chest. "No. Let me go. Please."

Carter loosened his hold and held his hands up. "Okay."

Breathing hard, his face hot with shame, Reed flung back the covers and scrambled off the bed. "I need to take a shower."

"Reed, wait. Please." Carter swung his legs over the

side of the bed and sat up but made no move to grab at him again. "I understand, really."

"You think you do?" That he sincerely doubted. And even if he did... "So what? You understand. Now you can make excuses for why you can't see me anymore, and even though you'll be nice about it, in the end, you'll leave because you won't want to be tied down to someone who's so nervous sometimes it feels like my insides are about to explode. Or you'll get tired of being with a man you think is listening to you, but in reality, a thousand different thoughts and sounds are vying for attention inside my head. You deserve better than damaged goods." Blinding panic ballooned inside him. Reed wondered what would happen if he burst apart from the tension of holding himself together.

The words Mason had flung at him echoed in his head. Reed choked up for a moment, then drew in a shuddering breath and continued. "You need to concentrate on your brother—he's still young and from what I see is a wonderful child. You have enough to handle without my mental illness adding to your problems."

A dark flush rose over Carter's face. By now Reed knew the signs of his anger, but he was angry as well. Angry that he'd let himself fall for someone he knew was so wrong for him right from the beginning. He turned and walked into the bathroom.

Reed heard rather than saw Carter come after him and tried to step aside, but Carter grabbed his arm and pushed him up against the wall. Those silvery eyes glittered like moonlight on the water, and his normally soft, full lips pressed together in a tight, white line. A muscle twitched in his jaw, and a shiver of fear trickled through Reed. His heartbeat sped up.

"Do you think I'd let you say those things about yourself and walk away? Is that what you think about yourself…and me? Because if you do, that way of thinking, not your anxiety, is what's wrong between us."

"It's true," said Reed. "I've tried to stop my medicine or play with my dosages to see if there was some way I could eventually stop taking them. But the worry and the anxiety always come back." He dropped his gaze to the floor. "Even now, I have to take my medicine but I forgot it at the hotel. I have to go get it sometime this morning. I hate it. I hate that I need it."

Carter tipped up his chin and their eyes met. The harsh planes of his face had softened, the flush of anger fading from his neck and chest. Rather than let go of his arm, Carter slid his hand up his shoulder and around his neck in a move so tender Reed bit his lip to keep from sighing his pleasure out loud. "There's no need to stop taking the medicines if they're working. You can't risk your health. I want you exactly as you are." He leaned forward until their foreheads touched and their lips were a breath apart. "I love you, every part of you—broken pieces and all."

For a second Reed thought his heart stopped beating. The enormity of Carter's words had blocked out everything else in his world—all sounds and incoherent thoughts—so that for the first time in his life, Reed's complete and total focus was on one thing only.

"You said you love me."

"I did, didn't I?" Carter brushed his lips over Reed's. "Is that a problem?"

"Not unless you think I'm a project. You're not going to be able to fix me. Who I am is always going to be a man with ADHD and an anxiety disorder."

Carter caged him in between his arms. "Why do you think I'll want to change you? You are who you are. I'm not looking to change you."

"You say that now, but how about when we spend more time together and you get sick of my panicking in new situations, or you think I'm not paying attention to you because I'm distracted, and it's beyond my control?" Even now, Reed could sense the apprehension building within him, flowing through his bloodstream. He needed his medicine.

"How about it? If I've learned anything from Jacks, it's that perfection is a myth, most likely spun by fairy tales. And even in fairy tales everyone struggles through shit until they reach the happy ending. Reality sucks; life is hard and kicks us in the ass. It's whether we choose to fight for what we want that makes us winners."

Reed smiled in spite of himself. "An interesting take."

"Do you think I'm lying? Or saying this to make you feel better? I'm not, you know. I'm not looking for perfect; perfection is boring and bland. I like the struggle; the hard climb up the mountain. The reward, in my opinion, is much sweeter."

He sobered up, and Carter cupped his jaw.

"What made you sad now? Your whole face changed from light to dark, and I hate seeing it."

"My mother left because she couldn't handle having a child with disabilities. Rather than fight for me, she left everything to my dad. It reminds me of the way your mom treated you and Jacks. As afterthoughts."

The storm clouds returned to Carter's face. "Some people don't deserve to have children. Especially wonderful kids like Jacks." He trailed his thumb over Reed's chin. "Or you. I've learned so much from him—he's taught me not to judge people by looks alone and how to be a better person. Having him with me changed my life. I wouldn't trade him for anyone." Carter kissed him lightly. "And I wouldn't change you either. You're perfect for me."

Who could've known when they made this arrangement last year they'd end up sharing lives that on the surface appeared so different but in peeling back the layers proved shockingly similar? The last vestiges of fear and self-loathing still clung to Reed.

"My only serious relationship ended when my boyfriend told me he was tired of my problems—my mental illness as he called it. He wanted perfection; he was into his clothes and appearance. Once we got beyond that, he had zero interest in me or my life." Unwilling to see the pity in Carter's eyes, Reed looked away and drew his toe along the grouting of the floor tiles. "When we broke up, he called me damaged goods."

He jumped as Carter's fist banged against the wall by the side of his head. "That fucker. That piece of shit. Who the hell is he or anyone to call someone that? Was he so perfect?" His ragged breath reverberated loudly against the walls. "I'll bet he wasn't. Did he make you feel like I do?" Once again, Carter pinned him against the wall. A thick, muscular thigh slid in between Reed's legs, putting delicious pressure on his balls and cock.

"No," said Reed, sliding his hands up Carter's arms. "No one has. I never cared about perfection. All I wanted was for someone to care about me notwithstanding my imperfections. I've spent my whole life worrying about what other people think of me."

"Fuck that, Reed." Carter skimmed his fingertips over Reed's face. "Everyone has problems. No one and nothing can define you unless you allow it. Own it, control it, then smash it to pieces if you want to change. But I think you've already conquered it. You have a job where people care about you, you go to school, and most importantly, you're kind, loving, and caring."

"That's the nicest thing anyone's ever said to me."

Carter traced Reed's lips with the pad of his thumb, his eyes darkening again, but this time with rising passion, not anger. "Then you've been horribly neglected. I'll have to think about ways to make it all up to you."

"This might help you think." Reed pressed his lips to Carter's, their addictive softness as necessary to him now as breathing. His home; his forever.

At the first swipe of Reed's tongue, Carter trembled. Reed loved unnerving this strong, self-confident man.

He smoothed his hands over Carter's ass. "I can think of a few suggestions."

Reed peppered small kisses along Carter's jaw, the hitch of Carter's breath music to his ears. More self-assured than ever, Reed sucked at Carter's neck, tiny ripples beneath Carter's skin quivering beneath his lips, loving how his touch made Carter come undone.

"Don't start something you can't finish, Reed. We have to go to the hotel to pick up your medicine, then come back to get Jacks." With one last kiss and regret shining in his eyes, Carter stepped back. "Rain check on the shared shower?"

"Yeah," Reed said with a smile. "Definitely."

Chapter Sixteen

AFTER SPEAKING TO Michelle and receiving her reassurance that yes, Jacks was fine, and no, he couldn't come to the phone because he was outside in the back yard playing, he and Reed headed back into the city to the hotel. Neither had spoken much since their mutual confessions of last night and this morning, but their shared smiles and simple touches brought Carter a comfort and peace he hadn't known existed.

He checked out of the hotel, and after paying the bill Carter wondered if this would be the last time they'd need to do this. He'd have to discuss it with Reed, but once he and Jacks met, there was no reason to only see each other once a month. Perhaps, eventually, Reed might even move in with the two of them.

Odd that it took thirty-two years for him to feel intimate with someone despite all the men he'd slept with. Perhaps all those love songs weren't so wrong after all, and there really was one person to make everything all right. Carter wasn't certain of much, but after he told Reed he loved him this morning, if he didn't have Reed by his side, nothing in his world would ever be right again.

Immediately upon entering their hotel room Reed had taken his medication, and Carter could tell his anxiety levels had visibly decreased; he rested against the seat of the cab and was unusually still. Having lived with Jacks for over three years, Carter was amazed he hadn't picked up on the little cues from Reed, such as his distraction, constant need to be in motion, and his frequent, misplaced panic.

These were the pieces of Reed he'd missed, which wasn't surprising since most of the time they spent together was in bed…or in the shower…or against the wall. With a self-satisfied smirk, Carter glanced over at Reed, imagining spending every night with him.

"I know you're staring at me. I can tell." A grin tugged at the corner of Reed's lips though his eyes remained closed.

"What are you, a magician?" Carter teased and found that he liked being in a relationship. Being in love. The words still sounded strange, but it didn't make them any less important or real.

"No," said Reed, opening his eyes. "It was a feeling."

"Oh yeah?" Carter leaned over and gave him a quick kiss. "I get feelings about you too, but they aren't the kind I can show you in the back seat of a cab. Or anywhere in public for that matter."

"Oh, brother. Who knew you were so cheesy?" Reed rolled his eyes, but Carter caught his smile.

"I'll remember that the next time we go out dancing." Carter folded his arms and watched a fiery red blush stain Reed's cheeks and his breathing quicken.

"I thought so." He quirked a brow, and Reed shifted in his seat. Carter saw the heavy outline of Reed's cock in his jeans, and giving him no warning, leaned over and gave him an open-mouthed kiss while squeezing his erection.

"Jesus, Carter." Reed gasped out loud against his mouth but made no move to get away.

"Hope you didn't think that was too *cheesy* either."

"Idiot." But Reed grasped him by the nape of his neck and kissed him back, their lips clinging together until the cab turned the corner to Michelle and Evan's block. They broke apart, but each remained smiling as they got out of the cab and walked up the front steps.

By now it was midday, and Carter suspected Michelle would appreciate the kids being picked up even though she'd waved her hand in the air and answered him, "Anytime, don't worry," when he'd dropped Jacks off Saturday afternoon. One ten-year-old boy was hard enough; Carter couldn't imagine having four at once.

That's why he was surprised when Michelle answered the door and said the boys weren't home yet, that Evan had taken them out for burgers, but he and Reed could come in and wait.

"They shouldn't be too much longer. The others are coming around one. We can have some coffee and sit and chat for a while."

Great. Trapped with the Question Queen of Brooklyn for who knows how long. Carter gave her a wary smile and braced himself for Michelle's inevitable nosiness.

"So Reed, how long have you two been dating?"

Carter groaned inwardly. He should've known she'd start in on Reed; he radiated goodness. Maybe that's what attracted Carter to him from the start.

"We've known each other over six months now."

"And what do you do? Are you in public relations like Carter, is that how you met?"

Reed stretched his legs out in front of him, and Carter caught a glimpse of a smile on Reed's lips and relaxed, knowing Reed had Michelle figured out.

"I work in a bar and go to grad school for hotel management."

Idly, Carter wondered if he could help Reed with all his contacts and made a mental note to talk to Jerry Paulson, one of his clients who owned a boutique hotel in Tribeca. Much as Reed loved working at the bar, Carter suspected he did so out of familiarity. Knowing now about his anxiety issues and his ADHD, it made sense. Stay in your comfort zone, do what you know works. But Carter, trusting his instincts, could see Reed needed to challenge himself and shouldn't be afraid to step outside his boundaries—color outside the lines like he told Jacks to do.

"You must meet a lot of interesting characters," said

Michelle with a smile, handing Reed a cup of coffee.

"You don't know the half of it." Reed's lips curved around his coffee mug as he took a sip, and Carter bit back his own grin. He still had memories of their first kiss in the bar. From that moment on he'd unknowingly become hooked on Reed.

Leave it to Michelle, obviously experienced enough in ferreting out unspoken signals between people; her eyes lit up and a delighted grin broke across her face.

"Oh, is that how you two met? That's so cute. It's like a real New York City love story."

"You make us sound like high-school kids. Cute." Carter scowled into his own mug. He hated having his personal life discussed; this was the reason he kept away from most people. They annoyed the hell out of him.

"I meant it as a compliment. You two look sweet together."

Reed set his mug down on the table by his side. "Well, we're grown men; I hardly consider us cute. People think because we're gay that our relationships aren't as serious as straight peoples are or that we're only about looking perfect. That we aren't interested in commitment or building lives together that may face bumps in the road."

Carter couldn't believe Reed was saying this. It was everything he'd wanted to say and more. He sat quiet and listened, his admiration and love for Reed intensifying.

"We've fought so long and hard for basic rights that

mostly everyone takes for granted, and it's frustrating to think people judge us and our relationships simply by outward appearances."

"I wasn't doing that, Reed. I'm sorry if you thought I was being flippant. And I understand your frustration. My brother feels the same way."

Reed's face fell. "I didn't mean to snap your head off. That was rude. I'm sorry."

"Don't be. You have every right to speak your mind."

They sat in silence for a while, sipping their coffee, and Carter began to feel bad for Michelle. She didn't mean any harm.

"What does your brother do?"

"He's an accountant, a CPA."

Good God, that sounds dull as dirt, but Carter managed to muster up some enthusiasm.

"That sounds interesting."

Michelle snorted into her coffee cup. "Are you kidding? It's boring as hell; even Blake, my brother, says so. But the pay is pretty good, and he has a nice apartment; all he needs is the right guy."

"I'm sure he'll find someone."

They were interrupted by the front door opening and the sound of running feet. Actually it sounded more like a herd of buffalo tramping about. Four boys practically tumbled into the room, and Carter's eyes lit up at the sight of Jacks, his face bright and alive with laughter. He showed no ill effects from his middle-of-the-night escapade, and the other boys obviously couldn't have cared less.

Though physically less developed than the others, it hardly seemed to be holding Jacks back socially. Carter realized he owed Michelle a hell of a lot for being the type of person who wouldn't shy away from having her child play with a boy whom everyone knew had learning issues as well as other problems. So much of Jacks's recent emotional growth was due to his friendship with her son, Henry, and these other kids. It was a testament to her decency as a person and to her parenting, and Carter vowed to treat her with more respect and kindness.

"Hey, buddy, how's it going?" Carter stood and waited for Jacks to come over and give him his usual hug. This time though, Jacks held back, staying within the circle of his friends. Reed remained sitting in the chair as a spectator.

"Do I hafta go home? We're still having fun."

" 'Fraid so, kiddo. It's Sunday, and Henry's mom has stuff to do and so do we. Why don't you get your things from upstairs and we'll go home?"

"But I don't wanna go. Why do *I* have to be the first one to leave?"

Stymied, not used to resistance, Carter turned to Michelle, beseeching her for assistance. It was one thing to be firm in your own home when it was only the two of them. Carter couldn't and wouldn't treat Jacks like a little kid in front of his friends, but as this was his first time in this situation, he didn't know the boundaries of after-sleepover parent pick-ups.

Luck was on his side as the front doorbell rang. From the sound of the voices, one of the parents had showed up to pick up their child as well. Carter pasted a smile on his face, prepared to meet and answer questions about himself and Jacks.

A huge man, his head covered with a green Jets cap, entered the room. He had to be at least 6'4" and 230 pounds, and though the room was spacious, his presence made itself known. His smile beamed wide, and he waved.

"Hey, Michelle. How's it going? They didn't drive you crazy yet?"

"Hi, Vinnie. Nah. I'm used to it."

Vinnie scanned the room, and his eyes lit up when they settled on one of the boys who, Carter assumed, was his son. The boy towered over the others in the group and had the same big smile as his father.

"Joey, you ready? I got your mom and sister waiting in the car. Let's go. Chop, chop."

Without a word, Joey ran upstairs and came flying back down in a matter of minutes with a backpack.

"Say goodbye to Henry's mom and dad."

"I know, Dad. Jeez, I'm not a baby."

Carter bit back a smile.

"Hey, how're you doing? I'm Vinnie Esposito, Joey's dad."

The big man stuck out his hand, and Carter took it,

liking his firm grip and no-nonsense attitude.

"I'm Carter Haywood, Jackson's brother."

"Oh yeah, Jacks. I met him last week. He's a real sweet kid."

Joey tugged at Vinnie's sleeve. "I'm ready."

"Okay. I'll be right out; go to the car."

Joey flashed him a shy smile, and after exchanging goodbyes with the other boys, walked outside with Evan. Jacks, Henry and David ran into kitchen, leaving the grown-ups alone.

"Nice boy. He looks like he'll be a big guy like you."

Vinnie chuckled, rubbing his chest. The obvious pride in his son sent a pang of longing through Carter, but whether it was for Jacks or for himself, he had no idea.

"He's already eating us out of the fridge every week."

"I'll bet. Jacks is finally starting to come into his appetite, but it's been slow in getting to this point."

"Was he born premature?"

His protective hackles raised, Carter observed Vinnie; there was nothing but genuine warmth and interest in the man's dark eyes.

Carter hedged, a bit reluctant to open up. "I didn't start taking care of him until about three years ago, and our mother didn't leave me with much in the way of information. Are you a doctor?"

"Me?" Vinnie laughed again, pulling off his cap and smoothing his hand over the top of his bald head. "Nah,

I'm a service technician for one of the cable companies. But my wife is a labor and delivery nurse, so she's seen it all."

"Got it. Well, I got him therapy, and it's only been recently that Jacks has come out of his shell and begun to verbalize and make friends. He's a little delayed in speech and other milestones, but I'm excited to see what he's got in store. He's progressing by leaps and bounds recently, and I think having good friends really helped."

Fitting the cap back securely on his head, Vinnie eyed Jacks who'd come back into the living room with the other two boys. "Looks like you're doing fine. My wife says they've done amazing things in the last few years. If you ever want to talk to her, give me a call." A horn beeped. "Oops, gotta go. Nice to meetcha."

Surprisingly light on his feet for a man his size, Vinnie ran to the door. "Thanks, you two. Terry said she'll call you, Michelle." Carter wondered if he played football.

The house seemed eerily quiet without Vinnie's larger-than-life presence, and Carter became aware that the day was getting away from him. He needed to get Jacks home where he could sit down and introduce him to Reed.

"Okay, Jacks, now you're not the first to leave. Go get your stuff, okay?"

With a shrug, Jacks ran up the steps and returned a few minutes later with his own backpack slung over his shoulder. He took his jacket from Michelle, and Carter listened with pride as he said his thank-yous without prompting.

"Thank you for having me. I had a lot of fun."

Her face soft, Michelle gave Jacks a hug. "You're welcome, honey. You can visit anytime."

Jacks zipped himself up, and after saying goodbye to the other boys, spoke over his shoulder to Carter, "I'm ready. Are we gonna have pizza like always?"

Reed had remained silent throughout, and after thanking Michelle and Evan, followed him and Jacks out of the house. Only then did Jacks notice Reed and pointed.

"Who's that?"

Did he not remember Reed from last night?

"Reed was with me last night when I came over. Remember? He's my friend."

"Hi, Jacks. It was so late I figured I'd wait until the morning to introduce myself. I'm Reed, a friend of your brother." Reed gave Jacks his easy, wide-open smile, but it seemed Jacks was having none of it.

"Oh." No return hello or smile.

They continued to walk down the block, the light wind stirring up scents of fresh earth and green grass. Spring was firmly entrenched, and Carter couldn't be happier.

"Is he coming home with us?" Jacks moved closer to Carter and sneaked a peek at Reed as they turned the corner to their house. "I though you said we had stuff to do. I did all my homework already." He shuffled along, his steps growing slower.

The one thing Carter hadn't anticipated was Jacks's resistance to Reed; who wouldn't love Reed? Maybe Jacks needed to get back to the familiarity of his own house, where he felt more comfortable. They could sit and talk, and Jacks would warm up to Reed.

"Yes, he is. I figured we could all hang out, and you could get to know each other better. Then maybe Reed could stay for pizza night."

Sunday had always been pizza night, and Carter knew how much Jacks liked routine and loved pizza night. Including Reed in on their evening would show Jacks how special Reed had become in his life.

"Why?" They mounted the steps to the limestone, and Carter unlocked the front door. When they entered, Jacks dropped his backpack on the little chair sitting off to the side. "It's always only been me and you."

The complaining surprised Carter, and he found himself for the first time getting not so much annoyed with Jacks but frustrated at his unwillingness to be friendly to Reed. Jacks didn't seem to even want to give Reed a chance. Right from the start he wanted him gone. And from the sad expression in Reed's eyes, he saw it as well.

But Carter wasn't about to give in to a sulky ten-year-old. "Because I want you two to get to know each other better. Reed is going to be around a lot more, and I hope you can be friends."

Carter had never thought to explain his sexuality to

Jacks. Up to now it hadn't been necessary or important; working on Jacks's socialization skills and getting him to feel safe remained paramount. Perhaps, Carter thought as he hung his and Reed's jackets on the newel post of the winding wooden bannister that led to the second floor, it was time to introduce, carefully of course, the idea of Reed as his partner. He couldn't even begin to think about sleeping arrangements or Reed staying the night. Carter groaned at all the obstacles, yet recalling their time last night and this morning, giving Reed up was no longer an option.

They walked into the living room, and Carter flopped down on the sofa while Reed remained standing. Carter pointed to the club chair, but Reed gave an almost indiscernible shake of his head. Frowning, Carter made room for Jacks, who scrambled up next to him.

"Why is he gonna be over more?" Jacks's prodding cemented Carter's decision to tell him the whole truth. Jacks was going to be eleven, and Carter had no concerns he wouldn't understand.

"I gotta pee first." Jacks raced out of the room, and Carter ran his hands through his hair in frustration.

"I'm sorry." He held out his hand. "He'll get used to you, don't worry. It'll just take some time. Come sit next to me for support, please."

To his surprise, Reed shook his head. "I'm thinking maybe I shouldn't be here and you need to do this alone. I'm too much of a distraction for him, and it's making me nervous as well."

Fuck. This wasn't how he'd thought it would be. He got up from the sofa and walked over to Reed who looked as though he was ready to bolt. "Please stay." He took Reed into his arms. At first Reed stiffened and tried to pull away, but Carter wouldn't let go. This was his home, and if he wanted to hug Reed, he would. He held on until Reed relented and returned the hug. "I need you with me to do this."

"What if he hates me?" Reed pulled back and chewed at his lip. "He might think I'm taking you away from him."

"He might," said Carter, admitting Reed's concern was totally valid. "But all the more reason for you to stay and show him that isn't the case. That he's not losing me but gaining you."

"Why are you hugging him?"

They sprang apart at Jacks's question, and even Carter needed a moment to catch his breath and wait for his heart to stop pounding. Jacks stood at the entranceway, his eyes wide, a frown tugging his lips downward.

"Come sit next to me." Carter sat on the sofa and patted the space next to him. "We can talk."

Shooting suspicious looks at Reed, who'd retreated to a club chair opposite the sofa, Jacks sat next to him. "Talk about what? I want a snack."

"Wait until we finish talking 'cause this is important. Reed is a friend of mine, a very good friend."

"Like me and Henry and David?" Jacks scuffed his sneakered toe on the wooden floor.

"Sort of, but more." Carter's heart began to pound, and he searched for Reed, who gave him a brief nod and an encouraging smile. "You know how Henry's mom and dad love each other and are married?"

"Yeah, so?"

"Sometimes two men or two women fall in love like that."

Jacks's foot stopped swinging. His eyes widened, and his mouth made a perfect O. "Like boyfriend and girlfriend? You and him are boyfriends?"

The dryness in his mouth prevented him from speaking at first. He pulled at his shirt collar, which suddenly felt two sizes too small, and finally managed to answer. "Yeah, we are. How do you feel about it?"

It might have been his imagination or a trick of the light, but Carter swore he saw something flicker in Jacks's eyes before he shrugged. "I'm hungry." Without another word to either of them, he ran from the room and within moments Carter heard the refrigerator door open.

He faced Reed. "Well, that went pretty easy, don't you think?"

To Carter's surprise, Reed stood and instead of joining him on the sofa, went to the hallway and picked up his jacket from the bannister. "I think you're fooling yourself if you believe Jacks is okay with this. Before we jump into this relationship, you need to take a step back." He slipped on the jacket, then picked up his overnight bag. "Call me after you talk to him without me around and find out how he really feels."

Before he could open his mouth to answer, Reed walked out the front door, leaving him standing all alone, wondering what the hell just happened.

Chapter Seventeen

"To what do I owe this dinner invitation? Aren't you working tonight?"

Reed and his father sat at a table, away from the noise of the bar area. He'd brought them out a plate of sliders and fries, along with a green salad for a pretense of healthy eating. His father took a healthy swallow of his beer, but Reed sipped on plain ice water. With his thoughts jumbled more than ever, and more anxious than even during finals, the last thing he needed was his mind clouded with alcohol.

"No, I mean, kind of. Yeah I did. A half shift until 6:30. I was supposed to work a full, but I asked Vernon if I could go home early. It's Wednesday and slow, so..." Realizing he was babbling, Reed set the water down and forced a smile. "Can't I see you for dinner without an ulterior motive? We haven't spent much time together lately, and I wanted to catch up. That's all."

Grabbing a slider, he took a huge bite. Since leaving Carter's house three days ago, he'd gone to his classes but done little else except mope about. There'd been no contact from Carter, and Reed assumed he'd spoken to Jacks who obviously had no desire to share his brother's time with a boyfriend. And Reed could understand the little boy completely. The love between Jacks and his brother was obvious, and after all those years with it being only the two of them, Reed knew he'd be seen as nothing more than an interloper.

His father raised a brow. "Hmph," he said and chewed on some fries. "You know, you've always been the worst liar."

"I have?" Amused, Reed dipped a fry in some ketchup. "And you can tell how?"

"Aside from the fact you can't look me straight in the eyes, your breathing is quicker than normal, you're tapping your feet under the table, and I bet you're eating without even tasting the food."

Damn. That was the problem with having a close relationship with your parent. They really did know you better than you knew yourself sometimes. "I'm not lying. I was supposed to work a full shift and—"

"I'm not talking about that, and you know it, Reed. What I don't understand is why you won't talk to me about it. You're still my child, and I'll always worry about your happiness, yet for the last few months you've pulled away from me, and I don't know why."

"You have your own life to lead, Dad. And now you have Ariel, the person you should be thinking about, not your adult, twenty-seven-year-old son. I'll be fine; I mean, I'm fine."

Shit.

His father's eyes lit up with victory. "Huh. I knew it. Now spill; tell me what happened. I'm here to help. I can be a friend as well as a father, you know."

Reed considered his father's words as he aimlessly stuffed a few fries in his mouth and chewed. Anything to give himself time to think and consider. Over the years he'd tried to become more independent, if for no other reason than to prove to himself he could make it without having someone there to hold his hand to quell his fear. Bad enough he had to still see his psychiatrist; he didn't need to lay his burdens on his father. The ever-present anxiety made him second-guess himself on so many aspects of his life there'd been times he couldn't decide what to order from a menu.

But one thing had never wavered; the love he had for his father. The close relationship he'd seen between Carter and his little brother as well as the other families he'd met that afternoon with Carter had unleashed a flood of emotions inside Reed. He didn't want something to happen to his father without him knowing how much he was loved.

"The guy you met briefly at the bar, Carter? You were right about it being serious."

"That's good, then. But I'm confused. I thought you weren't seeing him anymore."

Apparently he was a better liar than his father thought. For while it may have taken Reed breaking up with him for Carter to realize he loved Reed, Reed's heart knew he was in love long before.

"It wasn't supposed to be serious. I thought I could forget about him, but you can't control how you feel, right?"

"No, you can't. But are you telling me he doesn't feel the same way? That's surprising, considering I remember how he looked at you that night. Like he knew how special a man you are."

A mirthless laugh escaped Reed. "Oh no, he told me he loves me, and I believe him; he's no liar. Carter is like no other man I've ever met in my life. He's guarded and protective. His incredibly hard life shaped him into a man who appears confident and ruthless, but it's all for show. I've seen otherwise. He's sweet and loving without even knowing it. It's all in there but buried so deep I'm not sure it can be unearthed."

A ball game was on the television, and the Mets must've scored since the men at the bar roared their approval and got busy high-fiving each other. It reminded Reed how Carter had mentioned he'd wanted the three of them, him, Reed, and Jacks to go to a game that summer. At the time, Reed could think of nothing that would make him happier; now he wondered if it would ever come to pass.

"Then what's the problem?" Forgetting about the food and putting his glass of beer off to the side, his father braced his elbows on the table, cradling his chin in his hands. "Am I missing something? All relationships take work."

"This past weekend I found out Carter has a little brother, a half-brother he didn't know existed until his mother dumped him and disappeared. The little boy has some physical and emotional problems as could only be expected with such trauma. Carter has basically given up his own life to make sure he gives Jacks a life of safety and security."

"And now Jacks feels threatened by you."

Dumbfounded, Reed stared at his father, who leaned back in the booth. "Um, how did you figure that out so quickly?"

Crossing his arms, his father gave him a tender smile. "After your mother left, my sole focus was making sure your life continued on as normally as possible. My sole focus had to be you. A parent's job is to protect their child and I did whatever I could to the best of my ability. Carter is Jacks's surrogate parent and worries about him as a father would about his child."

With the vagueness of passing years, Reed now struggled to remember his mother. All he could conjure up was her yelling at him for not paying attention to her at home or to the teacher when he was in school. She didn't want to hear how the slightest sound easily distracted him, or how he'd rarely finish a quiz without running out of time because he couldn't focus and needed to read and reread the questions four, five, sometimes six times to get the information to sink into his head.

"She hardly was a normal mother."

His father's lips tightened. "My biggest regret is not seeing her behavior sooner and intervening. I'd give anything so that you didn't have to live like that."

"Don't," Reed broke in, unwilling to let his father berate himself one minute more for his mother's abandonment. "Don't you dare blame yourself. It all worked out; *we* worked out fine. I was hoping I'd be able to get close enough with Carter and Jacks to help somehow, but it doesn't seem likely."

"Because?" his father prodded. "Did Carter tell you he couldn't see you any longer because of his brother?"

"No, Reed did."

Startled, Reed spun around so quickly he almost spilled his water glass and stared at Carter. It must've started raining while they were inside as droplets of water ran down Carter's face and his leather jacket glistened from the damp.

"Carter? What are you doing here?"

Carter's lips twisted in an attempt to smile but failed. "No offense to your boss, but it isn't for the food."

Reed drank in Carter's appearance, taking in his mussed hair and day-old growth covering his face. His eyes held no life, their normal sparkle dimmed to a flat and lifeless gray. He looked the picture of absolute dejection.

"Would you like to join us?"

"I don't want to intrude…" Carter searched Reed's

face, a hesitant smile touching his lips. "I was hoping we could talk."

"Well, we were talking about you anyway, so you might as well sit down and set the record straight." His father chuckled, lightening the mood a bit.

This time Carter managed a full-blown grin. "Nice to know." He slid into the booth next to Reed, their thighs touching under the table.

"Reed told me about your little brother. Sounds like you have managed to turn around a bad situation and make it work. That couldn't have been easy."

Carter placed his hands flat on the rough wooden table. "I did what anyone would do. He's a helpless child—my only relative."

"You're not in touch with your mother, then?"

Carter's hands curled into fists. "Not for years. The last time was two years ago, a year after she left Jacks with me. She tried to hit me up for money and threatened to take Jacks away. So I made a deal with the devil: I paid her what she wanted, and she gave up all legal rights to Jacks. Thank God."

In Reed's mind, what Carter had done for Jacks was nothing short of a miracle, but Carter didn't seek praise.

"Before that?" Carter's lips curled in a sneer. "Aside from what we talked about last night, I hadn't seen nor heard from her in almost twelve years. As far as I'm concerned my past is wiped clean."

Reed nodded in agreement, and his father sighed, his expression grave. "You're very young, Carter. You've been on your own all that time?"

"Yes. And better off for it. She was no mother."

When it became apparent Carter wasn't going to give any more information—that the painful story of Carter's early years had been told to him in confidence—Reed thought for a moment and then spoke.

"I can relate to that in a way. We haven't heard from my own mother in over fifteen years as well. She walked out on us when I was twelve. Said she couldn't handle me or my problems."

Carter turned to face him, his dark brows twisted in obvious confusion. "You mentioned that before but I don't even know what that means. What problems?"

Anxiety meds could only do so much; they didn't stop his heart from pounding or his breath from catching short. "I told you, my anxiety, my ADHD."

"Yeah, I know that. But so what? That's what parents do. They take care of their kids and get them help." With a flip of his hand, Carter gestured to Walter. "Am I missing something?"

"No," said his father. "That's it exactly. But even after all these years, Reed still for some reason blames himself. Am I right?"

Reed hated the question. It put a spotlight on everything he tried to hide from people: his insecurity, inferiority, and feeling that no matter how hard he tried, he'd never measure up to the person he wanted to be.

"I—I wanted to be like everyone else; I didn't need to be the smartest or the best at anything. But she made me feel dumb. Like if I had problems, it was all my fault because I didn't try hard enough, even though I tried so damn hard."

Carter laced their fingers together, and Reed could feel the strength flowing between their connected hands. "No matter what I did it was never good enough. If I did well in one class, she'd point out how I failed in other ways. But when we went to my psychiatrist, she'd tell him how much time she gave me, that she tried working with me, but I wouldn't pay attention. She lied to protect herself instead of helping me."

"Reed," said his father. "Why didn't you tell me?"

"She was my mom, and you were together. I didn't want to be bad. She told me not to say anything, or you'd leave us."

His father interrupted. "I'd never—"

"I know that now, but not when I was a kid. I loved you. I didn't want to be the cause of you leaving."

It hurt him so much to see his father's eyes shining bright with tears and lines of sorrow etched in his face. Perhaps this day had been a long time coming.

"So when she left, even though I kind of missed her, I hate to say it, but I was happy. No more criticism and making me feel stupid. And it was she who left and not you. I don't know what would've happened to me if you'd left."

Everything around them faded away, leaving only the bare, ugly truth between them.

"The truth can be freeing, right?" Carter squeezed

his hand, a knowing smile curving his lips.

"In a way, yeah. My dad, he's like no one else." He reached across the table with his free hand to grasp his father's. And like he had been all his life, his father was right there for him.

"This man stepped in and took over. He became my champion and best friend and got me to a psychiatrist I could relate to."

"I love you, Reed. Never doubt it."

"I never have. I may not have loved myself, but I knew I always had you."

To his surprise, his father let go of his hand and stood. A smile tugged at the corners of his mouth. "You guys have a lot to talk about. Make sure you don't leave until you work it all out. I have a feeling Carter has some important things you need to hear."

Carter saluted Walter with two fingers. "On the money, Walter. Right on the money."

Baffled, Reed waited until his father disappeared through the front doors to turn back to Carter. "What is it? Where is Jacks, by the way?"

"He's with our neighbor, Helen. She's a retired special ed teacher and has been with us since the beginning. But you know I wouldn't leave him alone, so don't deflect. I came here to talk to you."

"About what?"

"About us. You, me, and Jacks. And why you think it wouldn't work. And why didn't you tell me about your mother?"

"It doesn't matter; she doesn't matter in my life anymore."

Grim-faced, Carter stared at him. "How can you say that? Of course she does. Your childhood was shaped by how she treated you. You're the man you are partly because of her. And I have to say, you came out the winner, not her."

No winner if he lost the ultimate prize of having Carter. Exhaustion rolled through Reed. "I can't do this. Certainly not here, in a crowded bar."

"Then let's go." In one swift move, Carter extricated himself from the booth and stood. "Come with me."

"Where to?" Reed watched Carter's reaction with trepidation. "I'm not going to the hotel."

For the first time that evening, Carter flashed a full-blown smile. "We don't need that any longer. Besides, it's a working day tomorrow. I have an idea to make this night special."

Still wary, Reed gave in to his curiosity and followed Carter out of the bar and into a taxi they found disgorging its passengers right outside.

"A HORSE-DRAWN CARRIAGE ride? Are you serious?"

They walked along the outskirts of Central Park and surveyed the line of carriages. Some horses had roses woven in their manes and others had bells. Carter ignored the waves of the carriage men and came upon a beautiful jet-black horse with a white star and dainty white fetlocks. The freshly painted red carriage gleamed, and there were red and white roses in the back seat.

"How are you this fine evening? I'm Patrick, and would you be likin' a ride tonight?"

Reed couldn't help but smile back at the man's strong brogue and engaging grin.

"Yes. We'd like a ride, please."

"Sure you would. Hop on, and Tommy and I will be givin' you a perfect evening ride through the park."

Carter extended his hand. "After you."

Resistance proved futile against Carter, so Reed stepped up, and a moment later Carter joined him.

"Feel free to partake of any of the items in the back seat; the water and blankets are complimentary."

"Thank you, Patrick." Carter shook out the blanket and tucked it over them, then leaned back on the bench and draped his arm across Reed's shoulders. Patrick clucked his tongue, and Tommy the horse took off at a slow clop into Central Park.

The wind blew softly, and the trees rustled. "What is this? Why are we here?"

"It's a beautiful night. Why not?"

Exasperated, Reed threw back his part of the blanket. "Come on. We're here to talk about us. And Jacks. I know you'd like us all to get along, but the fact remains that you have a responsibility that's never going to change. And I couldn't and wouldn't ever want to be the one to come between you."

"Why do you think you'd have to? You walked out

so quickly you never gave it a chance." Moving closer, Carter pulled the blanket over them both again and pressed up against him. "I had a talk with Jacks's psychiatrist today, and he said it would be beneficial for Jacks to start learning he can't always be number one; that I shouldn't make myself a doormat and never put my feelings first. I've devoted three years exclusively to his care. The doctor said it could actually be helpful to show Jacks I can have a loving and solid connection with another adult. That it will give him even more stability." Carter kissed him with soft, tender touches of his lips. "Are you giving up on us so easily when we can finally have it all?"

Would there ever come a time when having Carter near wouldn't cause his blood to race or his heart to pound in slow, almost painful beats?

"I don't want to hurt Jacks and the relationship you have."

Carter slid his hand down Reed's thigh, brushing close to his half-hard cock. "First of all, you couldn't. It's not a matter of either/or with you and him. He's my little brother, and by default he'll always have my protection and my love. That doesn't mean I can't love you too; I'm not choosing you over him. I think I have a right to be happy now, and you need to create a separate, special relationship with him. Don't piggyback on mine. Give it a chance to grow and for him to know and love you."

Reed opened his mouth to speak, but Carter's lips

covered his while his hand became busy under the blanket, unbuttoning his soft cotton pants and drawing them down out from under his ass to release his fully erect cock. His mind spun hazily, wondering how Carter once again maneuvered him into having semi-public sex, but with Carter stroking his dick and his tongue probing his mouth, Reed cared about nothing else except the incredible pressure building up inside him.

The horse's hooves beat a steady pace along the path, and Patrick called back to them. "How're you gentlemen doing? The night treating you well?"

Carter broke free of the kiss. "Just fine, thanks," he said, wet lips hovering over Reed's mouth. They stared at each other, both breathing heavily. "Have some important business to get down to." Even in the dim light, Reed caught the glint of Carter's wicked grin.

"I understand." The undertone of laughter in Patrick's voice left little doubt he knew exactly what was going down in the back seat of his carriage. "I'll leave you two to your privacy."

"Carter, what are you doing?" Reed kept his voice down.

"I thought it was obvious. I'm trying to love you." Carter nuzzled Reed's neck and stroked his cock from tip to root. Carter had barely touched him, yet Reed was dangerously close to coming. What did it say about him that having sex in a public place was such a fucking turn-on? The ache in his groin had him not caring at all.

"If you can't figure it out, I'll need to do a whole lot better than this." He grasped Reed's cock and slid his hand down the rigid length to his balls, rolling and squeezing them.

"Better?" Reed managed to choke out, before he fell back against the seat and squeezed his eyes shut, his tense body vibrating. Any better and he might fly to pieces from the pleasure.

"I love your balls; they fit perfectly in my hands. I love how I can tell when you're going to shoot 'cause they get all tight and springy." Carter sucked, then bit his earlobe.

Nothing existed for Reed outside of the carriage. The velvety darkness of the evening hid them well. Carter kissed a path down Reed's neck to the top of his chest, forcing Reed to bite the inside of his cheek to keep from crying out. With deft fingers, Carter unbuttoned his shirt, and swirled his tongue around Reed's nipples, sucking the pointy nubs into his mouth. Reed groaned and arched his back; a jolt traveling straight to his cock, sending out a spurt of precome against Carter's hand.

Chuckling deep in his chest, Carter slid his sticky hand down Reed's throbbing cock, reaching farther between his legs to slide the tip of a wet finger past the rim of his hole.

At that precise moment they hit a rut in the path and the carriage bounced, forcing Carter's finger farther inside Reed. Without warning Reed yelped and came hard, spurting across his stomach.

"All right back there? Sorry about the rough ride. The damn city never keeps up with the roads these days."

"It's fine; no problem at all." Carter smothered his laughter, then leaned over and brushed their lips together. He rested his lips on the corner of Reed's mouth and whispered to him. "Come home with me tomorrow, please. Be with me and Jacks. You never gave us a chance; you walked out and didn't look back."

In his sleepy, blissed out state, Reed struggled to remain strong, then wondered what he was fighting and why. If Carter proved correct, he could have everything he'd always wanted; a man who knew the real him and not only didn't run away spitting hurtful words but embraced his differences, understood him, and loved him anyway. Unconditional love, something he thought he'd only have from his father, now within his reach. A forever. A home.

He'd have to be crazy not to grab on, hold tight, and never let him go.

"Reed?"

Even in the dark Carter's face stood out to him like a beacon of hope and love. It always would.

"Yeah, okay. Tomorrow."

Chapter Eighteen

"CARTER, RELAX. IF Reed is as special as I'm guessing, everything will work out fine."

Unable to control his pacing, Carter continued to walk up and down the hallway, waiting for Reed to show. Luckily Jacks didn't have school tomorrow because it was some administrative day, so Carter had planned a surprise for when Reed came over. Knowing how much Jacks loved art and that his doctors and aides used it as therapy over the years, Carter signed them all up for a pottery painting class tonight. They served pizza and juice to the kids and wine to the adults if they wanted.

"Yeah? I hope so." He stopped for a moment and scrubbed his hands over his face. "You think I'm doing the right thing, don't you? What's best for him, I mean."

Among the myriad of other reasons why Helen had become almost like a surrogate mother to both him and Jacks was her unshakable honesty. If she thought he wasn't proceeding on a course that best worked for

Jacks, she told him so.

"Absolutely. And it's not only Jacks I'm thinking of." She crossed the room to put a hand on his shoulder. "You've become like the son I never had. You think I'm helping you, but you have no idea how much you've helped me these years. After Marty died so suddenly, I was lost; I had no clue what to do with myself. We were never able to have children, but it almost didn't matter; being a teacher gave me a new family to love every year. All that was lost to me when I retired. Finding you and Jackson gave me a purpose and a reason to get up every morning once again."

Life could be so fucking unfair. Here was Helen, the best person he'd ever known who, though she lost her husband young and wasn't able to have children of her own, never held a grudge or became bitter. Instead she focused on the positive and helping others. Unlike his own mother who considered her children burdens and couldn't wait to dump her responsibility for them on someone else.

"Neither one of us would be at this point without you. Jacks and I owe you more than we can ever hope to repay. And I know I haven't said it enough, because I'm a thoughtless bastard, so thank you."

Her blue eyes shone with good humor. "Not completely, at least not anymore. I noticed the change about three or four months ago."

When he began to fall for Reed. Had he known back then how much Reed would come to mean to him,

Carter might never have continued with the relationship; he'd have done what he did best and shut it down by running away. Running away before he allowed himself to feel and care. Running away from the best thing he'd ever found.

The bell rang.

"Is that Reed? Go on, let him in." Helen wiped her eyes, smoothed her hair and straightened her blouse. Carter watched, amused and touched by her caring.

Surprising both Helen and himself, Carter leaned down and kissed her cheek. "Oh, he's going to love you, don't worry."

"Let your boyfriend in." She snapped a dishtowel at him, grazing his ass.

Boyfriend. He shook his head. Who the hell would have ever thought that? Chuckling, he walked down the hallway and opened the door. Reed stood on the stoop, his backpack over his shoulder. He gave Carter a slightly tense smile.

"Hi."

"Hi yourself." He leaned against the doorframe, wanting a few moments alone together before Helen and Jacks joined them. "How was your day?"

"Uh, good, thanks. Listen." Reed's gaze darted over his shoulder, then focused back on Carter. "Are you sure this is the right thing? I don't want to push Jacks."

Carter moved close enough to feel Reed's breath upon his cheek. "Last night you thought it was. What changed your mind?"

Golden heat rose in Reed's eyes. "Last night you could've gotten me to agree to almost anything. In case you haven't noticed, you're very persuasive."

"I like persuading you." Carter slid his hand around Reed's neck, enjoying the hitch in Reed's breathing. His fingers skimmed light and teasing along his shoulder, drawing him close. "It's one of my favorite things to do. Now be quiet while I persuade you some more."

He kissed Reed, their lips softening against one another, and immediately Carter felt the beginning of that familiar buildup of want and need that always occurred whenever he touched Reed. He pushed his tongue into Reed's mouth, tangling with Reed's, fighting the urge to crush their mouths together. The small, distinct sounds of desire from Reed didn't make it any easier for Carter to slow down and taste Reed, drinking in his sweetness and passion.

They stayed that way on his stoop, holding each other, Carter's kisses replacing the words he sometimes felt too overwhelmed to speak out loud. Several moments passed until his muddled brain began to work, and he realized it might be time to bring the public display inside. With regret, Carter pulled away from Reed, who stood, lips dark and swollen and gasping for breath. The naked hunger in his eyes had Carter reaching for him again until a voice behind him called out.

"Carter? Where are you?"

He stiffened and pulled back from Reed at the

sound of Jacks's voice. He'd had a little resistance this morning convincing Jacks that having Reed join them would be fun; the last thing he wanted was to push his relationship with Reed in Jacks's face. Slow and easy was the right way to go. Carter knew it would take some time for Jacks to warm up to Reed. It had taken him almost a year before that one special night when he gave Carter a hug and told him he loved him, and they were brothers. Jacks's reticence, and holding back wasn't disapproval. For throwaway kids like them, it was called survival. If he didn't get close to people, he couldn't miss them when they eventually left. Because before Reed, the one thing Carter knew, was everyone left in the end. They only pretended to care.

"Come on in. And yes, I'm sure. It will work out." He opened the door wide, and Reed, tense once again, walked past him into the house. He set his backpack on the stairs' landing and followed him down the hall.

Jacks stood at the kitchen entrance at the end of the hallway with Helen. Her hands rested on his shoulders, and Carter wondered if she did it deliberately for comfort and to keep him centered. Jacks's gaze honed in on Reed behind him, and if his face didn't register outright hostility, neither did it radiate friendliness.

"Helen, this is Reed. Reed, Helen saves my life every day."

"Don't be silly." She held out her hand to Reed. They exchanged smiles. "It's lovely to finally meet you."

"Jacks, remember Reed from the weekend?" At his

nod, Carter continued. "I invited him to come to pizza and painting with us."

"Okay." Jacks shrugged, and Helen whispered something to him. "Thanks for coming."

"Oh, wait." Reed ran back to the stairs where he'd left his backpack and came back with a bag in his hand. "I got you a present, Jacks. I hope you like it."

They all watched as Jacks opened the bag and pulled out a set of colored pencils, a sketchpad, and several coloring books. His eyes grew huge, and a smile broke across his face. The hopeful smile on Reed's face made Carter want to hug him. How thoughtful of Reed to remember him mentioning that Jacks loved drawing; he might have noticed all the drawings on the walls from the other day as well. He squeezed Reed's arm.

"When I was your age I drew a lot. Especially after my mom left. My dad got me into art therapy, and somewhere I still have those pictures. They weren't happy, but I could express everything I couldn't say out loud sometimes."

Something stirred deep within Carter, rolling through him with such strength he almost felt dizzy. This right here, these people were now his world—the family he'd always craved yet never imagined possible. A shiver rippled through him, and Carter blinked against the stinging wetness in his eyes.

"I like to draw too." Jacks traced the edge of the box of pencils with a finger. Carter strained to hear his soft voice. "I go to art therapy in school, and my teacher says my pictures are really good."

"I bet they are. And it helps." Reed leaned against the wall, his concentration solely on Jacks. "Sometimes you can't say what you think, but you can draw it, right?"

Carter held his breath, and he felt Helen move closer and hold his arm.

He might not be looking at Reed, yet Carter knew Jacks spoke directly to him. "Yeah. My mom left me 'cause she said she couldn't deal with me and my problems." Jacks slanted a look up at Reed, and the hurt and confusion in his eyes almost broke Carter's heart. "She'd call me stupid and told me to shut up so I did. I guess because I stopped speaking she thought I stopped listening when she complained about me. But I heard everything she said to her boyfriends. It made me feel bad."

"I get it. My mom was the same, except she said it to my face. When she left, even though I loved her, I thought I hated her too. I was glad she was gone and it was just me and my dad." Reed pointed to the coloring books. "I used to draw mean pictures until I stopped being angry."

"Reed's wonderful with him," Helen whispered in his ear. "Why was he so worried?"

Carter had no answer but knew it had to do with Reed's anxiety. The way Reed explained it, the more he tried to reason with himself that he had no cause to be anxious, the more anxious he became. Watching the two of them interact, seeing Reed draw out confessions from Jacks even he hadn't heard, Carter knew everything would be all right, not only between himself and Reed but with Jacks and Reed as well.

Without another word, Jacks took the pencils and coloring books, walked into the kitchen, and put them on the big island, then returned to them. Carter couldn't take his eyes off of his little brother, the love for him so deep and strong it was impossible to imagine life without him now.

"Can we go? I want to go paint."

"Sure, buddy. Let's go. We'll walk Helen home too."

They all put their jackets on, and Carter locked the door behind when they left. Walking in the early spring evening air, Reed stayed behind with Jacks while Carter accompanied Helen to her door.

"I got the chills watching Reed with Jacks. He's a special man, and you better hold on tight to him."

He gave her a kiss on the cheek.

"Not a problem. Holding Reed happens to be one of my favorite things to do."

Impulsively, Helen kissed him back. "I never thought I'd see you this happy. I can't tell you how thrilled I am. You deserve it, so very much."

Unable to wipe the smile from his face, Carter waited until Helen went inside, turned on the lights, and locked the door behind her.

Upon rejoining Reed and Jacks, they continued to

walk to the painting studio, and Carter listened to their conversation, which had returned to their discussion of their respective mothers. Carter allowed the two of them to walk ahead of him, and he wondered if Reed even understood how monumental it was for Jacks to be opening up so freely to him. Kindred spirits recognized each other, and Jacks naturally gravitated toward Reed, whose confession about his mother's abandonment sounded uncannily close to Jacks's own.

"It took me years before I could understand why my mom left. I don't hate her anymore; you know why?"

"Uh-uh." Jacks stuffed his hands in his pockets. "Why?"

"I feel sorry for her instead 'cause I know I'm a nice person. And smart. So she missed out on having me as a kid. It was her loss, not mine. Same for you."

"Me?"

"Yeah. Definitely. Your mom lost out on having both you and Carter. I think you're both pretty special, and I'm guessing she doesn't have anyone who could ever replace you guys."

Carter refused to cry, so it must be those damn allergies that made him sniffle and rub at his eyes. He couldn't have been a complete shit if someone like Reed said he loved him.

They reached the studio and entered. Long wooden tables with benches took up the rear of the space, and Carter spotted groups of paint pots and brushes at each one. The front of the studio had unpainted pots and figurines, and Carter watched as Jacks allowed Reed to take his coat; then he joined the other kids in picking out what he wanted to paint. Glowing, Reed joined him at the opposite side of the studio.

"I think he's warming up to me."

Giving Reed a smirk, Carter skimmed his hand over Reed's jaw, rubbing the pad of his thumb over Reed's lips. "I'm always hot for you. I promise to show you later just how much."

"Idiot." But Reed smiled as he said it.

"I told you he'd love you once you gave him the chance and didn't run away from it." Carter slipped his hand around Reed's neck, forcing him to look straight into his eyes. "I don't care if you have anxiety or ADHD or any other initial in the alphabet. I'm not going anywhere. Understand?"

Reed's smile dimmed. "Your concentration needs to be solely on Jacks and his recovery. Not me."

"And it has been for three years. But he's grown so much this past year, perhaps he's ready to take a new step and allow other people into his life." Carter brushed their lips together. "Like I did. You know I never intended to fall in love with you, but,"—he shrugged—"I guess it's true when they say you can't control your heart forever. I'd stuffed it away for so long that I thought I had it all under control."

"You were tough," said Reed, humor making his eyes shine with golden light. "But I saw your soft side almost from the first. You couldn't hide it even if you tried."

Fascinated by Reed's insight, Carter smiled and waved at Jacks who sat at a table with the rest of the kids. Six months ago, a night like this would have been impossible.

"And here I thought I was such a tough bastard." Not really, though. At least not with Reed. "Let's sit where we can talk and watch Jacks."

They walked to the space set up for the parents, but Carter made no move to join any of them. Reed pulled out a chair at a table for two, and Carter joined him. A bottle of wine and two glasses sat in the center next to a glass jar filled with spring flowers. Reed poured them each a glass of red wine.

Cradling the glass between his palms, Reed stared into its smooth ruby depths. "You *were* a complete bastard at times, but then you'd do something sweet and thoughtful. I didn't know what to make of you."

"I had no idea either." Carter sipped the wine, savoring the sweet, rich taste bursting in his mouth. "I had no experience dating or being in a relationship. I only knew I couldn't see you be with anyone but me."

Reed set his wineglass down untouched. "And I never intended to fall in love either. My relationship with Mason ruined me for a while, but I think it actually made me stronger, giving me the impetus to regroup and get to know who I am. I've learned to live my joy, not waste time in trying to define it or figure it out."

"I can tell you who you are. You're a part of us now, part of Jacks and me—our family. It took almost losing you to finally open my eyes and see that this isolated bubble I'd secluded myself in with Jacks and me on the inside and everyone else on the outside couldn't work anymore."

"I'm your family?"

"How can you doubt it? When I had no ability to love myself, you loved me."

Joy, like the morning, returned fresh and new with hope at its side. It was time he learned to live his own joy, with Reed by his side.

At that moment Jacks ran over, his normally pale cheeks flushed, eyes sparkling with a light and life Carter for years had yearned to see and never thought would happen.

"Look what I made."

He gingerly set a large wet plate down in front of Carter. A painting of a house, depicting their limestone, dominated the center of the plate. On one side were two figures waving goodbye to a smaller figure on the other.

"That's great, Jacks. I like how you drew Helen, you, and me."

"That's not Helen." He bit his lip and gave Reed a shy smile while delight burst like fireworks through Carter. "It's Reed. Since you said you liked him I wanted to like him too and thought it might make him feel good."

Watching Reed give Jacks a careful hug, this time

Carter could make no excuse for the tears streaking his cheeks.

"I think it does; what do you say, Reed?"

Reed swiped at his own tears, his smile rivaling any Carter had seen before.

"I've never felt better."

"Is Reed gonna stay for breakfast tomorrow?" Jacks's hopeful gaze flitted between him and Reed, who sat frozen in his chair. "Helen showed me how to make French toast."

"Um…Reed?"

His smile and nod were all the answer Jacks needed.

"Can I paint a mug for Helen to drink her tea in?" To Carter's shock, Jacks kissed him on the cheek. "I promised to make her something."

"Of course."

Jacks hugged him around the neck, and then Carter watched as he tore off back to his seat. The dizzying ups and downs in their life could have gone so terribly wrong at so many junctures, but after years of disappointment, fear, and solitude, Carter had what he never thought he would. A home and a family.

"Hey."

He shook himself out of his internal musing to see Reed smiling at him from across the table.

"Hey yourself."

"That was pretty special."

"You're pretty special. And now Jacks sees it as well." He picked up his glass. "So do you really like

French toast?"

Reed clinked his glass to his. "I do now. I can't believe he asked me to stay."

If Carter had his way, he'd never let Reed go.

Epilogue

One year later

"WALTER, HOW'RE THOSE burgers coming?" Carter pushed open the sliding door to the back yard and handed Reed's father a beer.

"All done. I was just getting ready to plate them and bring everything to the table."

Jacks came running from inside the house. "I can help." He took the plate and brought it to the redwood table where Helen, Ariel, Dr. Childs, (who insisted they call her Elizabeth) and Vernon sat, enjoying the late May sunshine.

Today was Reed's graduation party; he'd graduated with honors and had accepted a job as manager with one of Carter's clients who'd recently opened a boutique hotel in SoHo. It wasn't your usual job for a graduate, but Carter had called in a favor. He didn't want Reed to work nights and spend less time with him and Jacks.

"You've raised a great boy there, Carter. You should be proud of yourself."

"I only got him the help he needed." He took a long

drink from his bottle of beer and watched Jacks throw a ball for the puppy they'd adopted last week. The two, boy and puppy, then ran into the house, and Carter could only shake his head and laugh. Since they'd brought the dog home, he and Jacks had been inseparable, and Carter discovered the puppy had set up his sleeping residence at the foot of Jacks's bed.

"Don't be ridiculous. I know what you did; Reed told me everything. Many parents don't do for their children what you did for your brother. I know it's been a long, hard road."

It had been. And Carter knew he was lucky as hell to have the resources needed for Jacks's continuing care. There was no magic wand to be waved which could make his problems disappear. He continued to see the psychiatrist for his anxiety and his physician remained concerned about his growth. But Carter didn't care how tall or short Jack was as long as he remained happy. Seeing him video chatting with his friends on the computer, his face alive with laughter, or snuggled in bed with his puppy gave Carter the peace he never thought he'd have. He planned to set up a foundation to help parents with expenses for children with learning disabilities and mental health issues. Every child should have the chance Jacks had to grow and thrive.

"Carter."

He spun around to see Reed motioning to him from inside the house.

"Can you come inside? I need to ask you something."

He set his bottle down on the deck railing and walked inside.

"What's up?"

To Carter's surprise, Reed backed him up against the wall and kissed him, lightly at first, then with a deepening hunger. Carter slid his arms around Reed's neck, his hands sliding into the silk of Reed's hair. He molded his body to fit Reed's, and his tongue swept lazily through Reed's mouth, then took control to nibble along Reed's jawline and lick a path down the straining cords of his throat. The friction of Reed's erection pressing against Carter's through their jeans drove him wild, his nerve ends sparking a fire through his blood. Carter twisted them around so that he now pinned Reed to the wall.

Reed's head fell back. "Fuck, Carter. Don't start what you can't finish."

With a groan of annoyance, Carter continued to kiss Reed for several more minutes before pulling away, but only far enough to lean his forehead against Reed's. Even in their bedroom, he found himself unabashedly spooning against Reed. On one of the occasions he joined Reed at his sessions with Elizabeth, he'd jokingly mentioned it, but she took it seriously and explained it could be his fear of abandonment that made him want to hold on to Reed. Maybe. It made sense to him. All Carter knew was that for the first time in his life he slept through the night, and if holding on to Reed was the cause, so be it.

The day after Reed officially moved in, he and Elizabeth sat Reed down and lectured him about the seriousness of him taking his medication properly. With Elizabeth's approval, he used a secret weapon against Reed—Jacks.

"How would you feel if you had a bad reaction from not taking the meds and now that you're living with us, Jacks found out? What's stopping him from following your lead and refusing to take his meds, using you as an example? Would you want that?"

Reed paled and Carter knew he'd made his point. Several moments passed and Carter empathized with Reed's internal struggle, but knew if he didn't conquer his demons now, the road ahead would be almost impossible to travel.

"I—you're right," Reed said, chewing his lip and gazing down at his lap. "I'd rather be an example of how to live with my anxiety and ADHD than wind up hospitalized from taking too many chances. After hearing Jacks's story I realize he needs to see a positive role model with mental illness." Sounding more determined than Carter had ever heard, Reed looked directly at him with a fiery glint in his eyes. "I'm ready to take on that position."

Carter had never been prouder of anyone, watching Reed finally come to terms with his issues and put his fears to rest.

Jacks suffered no ill effects from Reed living with them either. Before Reed officially moved in, Carter made sure they met with Jacks's psychiatrist and teachers at school. Helen, of course, loved Reed to death. Reed had come home with him that first night after the painting class and never left. The plate Jacks had painted sat with pride in the center of the dining room table, a memento of that special night and their new family.

"You started it. We can run upstairs for a quickie. No one would know." He grinned, and Reed rolled his eyes, sidestepping his grasp.

"No, wait, come on. I said I wanted to ask you something."

"What?"

"Well, we've been living together for almost a year now, right?"

Reed sounded nervous, and Carter couldn't understand why.

"Yeah, why? You're bored already? Want your own place back?" Carter laughed, but when Reed didn't join him and began instead to play with his hair and twist the hanging strings of his leather bracelet, it was Carter's turn to feel anxious. "Reed, what is it? You look sick."

Jacks ran into the room, the dog yapping at his heels.

"Did you?"

At Reed's shake of his head, Jacks spun around and sped out.

"Did you what?" He grabbed Reed by the arm and yanked him close. "What's going on? Jacks knows and I don't?"

Pale and sweating, Reed placed a slightly trembling hand on his shoulder and forced a smile. "I don't want my own place back. I'm in love with you. More than I thought I could ever be. More than I ever thought I'd deserve."

"That's—"

Reed interrupted him. "Let me finish. I'm hoping that you want this to be forever. Because I do. I know I've found my forever with you, and I want to make it official."

"Offi…" His voice trailed off when Reed took out a ring and laid it flat on his palm. Carter began to shake, and from the way the ring shifted in Reed's palm, he knew Reed's nerves hovered at the breaking point.

"Will you marry me, Carter? I've been thinking about this for weeks, and I wanted to plan something more elaborate, but then I assumed—"

"Shh." Carter placed his fingers over Reed's mouth, and Reed stopped talking but not shaking. "This arrangement of ours has certainly come full circle from what we intended, hasn't it? What started out as something fun and light turned into a lifelong commitment. One neither one of us could walk away from."

"So you're saying yes?"

Carter laughed. "Of course I will."

"Yay." Jacks ran into the kitchen again. "I told him you'd say yes."

Carter took Jacks in his arms and held him close. "Would you like that? Is that what you want?"

Suddenly still and solemn, Jacks nodded. "Then everyone will stay. And no one has to ever go away again."

He'd never cried so much as he had since he met Reed. But then again, he'd never had anything worth crying over.

"When I walked into the bar that night, I never expected to find my life. But that's what taking a chance with you did for me. You gave me a life I'd dreamed about as a child, then dismissed as impossible. Because of you, I became a better man and a better brother. Now you give me the chance to be a husband."

"My husband." Reed smiled.

"Yours."

Reed slipped the ring on his finger, and the heavy weight surprised yet comforted him. It felt completely normal…right. Like something he'd been waiting all his life to bear.

He held out his hands, one to Jacks and the other to Reed.

"Let's go tell the others. They'll want to know don't you think?"

Reed leaned over and kissed him soundly, the taste of his love and longing lingering on Carter's lips.

"They've been waiting a long time."

They all had. Holding Reed's hand, Carter let Jacks lead the way outside. From the smile on his face, their news wouldn't be a secret much longer.

It was time to make this a permanent arrangement.

The End

About the Author

Felice Stevens has always been a romantic at heart. She believes that while life is tough, there is always a happy ending just around the corner. She started reading traditional historical romances when she was a teenager, then life and law school got in the way. It wasn't until she picked up a copy of Bertrice Small and became swept away to Queen Elizabeth's court that her interest in romance novels became renewed.

But somewhere along the way, her tastes shifted. While she still enjoys a juicy Historical romance, she began experimenting with newer, more cutting edge genres and discovered the world of Male/Male romance. And once she picked up her first, she became so enamored of the authors, the character-driven stories and the overwhelming emotion of the books, she knew she wanted to write her own.

Felice lives in New York City with her husband and two children and hopefully soon a cat of her own. Her day begins with a lot of caffeine and ends with a glass or two of red wine. She practices law but daydreams of a time when she can sit by a beach somewhere and write beautiful stories of men falling in love. Although there is bound to be angst along the way, a Happily Ever After is always guaranteed.

Newsletter:
bit.ly/FeliceNewsletter

Amazon Author Page:
bit.ly/felicebooks

Website:
www.felicestevens.com

Facebook:
facebook.com/felice.stevens.1

Twitter:
twitter.com/FeliceStevens1

Instagram:
www.instagram.com/felicestevens

Other titles by Felice Stevens

Through Hell and Back Series:
A Walk Through Fire
After the Fire
Embrace the Fire

The Memories Series:
Memories of the Heart
One Step Further
The Greatest Gift

The Breakfast Club Series:
Beyond the Surface
Betting on Forever
Second to None
What Lies Between Us

Other:
Rescued
Learning to Love